This Too Is Love

Twelve Stories
By J. H.

This book is a work of fiction. Any resemblance to actual events, locales or persons, living or dead, is entirely coincidental.

ISBN 1-59196-549-7

e-mail: jh@writeme.com

To BCBH

And fashionable madmen raise
Their pedantic boring cry:
Every farthing of the cost,
All the dreaded cards foretell,
Shall be paid, but from this night
Not a whisper, not a thought,
Not a kiss nor look be lost.

W.H. Auden
From "Lullaby"

Table of Contents

Two Afternoons

I like swimming lessons. But I've got to poop. We are sitting on the bench. I can see goose bumps on the tops of my legs. That happens when I am cold and shivery. We are all naked. We're all boys so that's OK. If there was girls we'd be embarrassed. Girls aren't supposed to see boys naked.

I like being naked. I used to run around in the house naked until mom said I couldn't. When I did it anyhow after my bath one day she took the yard stick to me. So I stopped doing it. Mr. Khan is showing us how to move our arms when we swim. He's from India. But he never saw any snake charmers. I asked him that once. He said there aren't really a lot of them around. He has Ted helping him. Ted is my best friend. I'm going to ask Mom if I can sleep over at his house tonight.

I don't want to bother Mr. Kahn. Sometimes when you have got to poop you can make it stop. Then after a while you don't have to poop any more. Sometimes I do that when I'm out playing because I don't want to come in. When you have to pee it doesn't go away like that. It just gets worse and worse every time. But you don't have to stop playing and come home to pee. You can just hide behind a bush and do it. But if you pooped outside people might see it. Then they would know what you did. They wouldn't like it.

*****

All those beautiful boys. I see them in my mind sitting naked in a row at the edge of the pool. I hate myself for how I treated Alex. What a lovely boy he is. Intelligent and gentle. And those brown eyes – big and full of curiosity. It's as though he'd like to swallow the whole world through those eyes. I could fall in love with such a boy. He's only seven. So young. So much time we could have known each other. At that age accidents can still happen. I know that, and yet I was impatient with him, allowed him to be humiliated. I could have made it up to him, and he would have forgiven me. But that turned out to be the last swimming lesson I'll ever teach. I'll not be able to see him again to make it okay. So my clumsiness will remain as a smudge on my memories. I will miss him. And all the others.

Why did Mr. Ray have to walk in on Michael and me? And why did he have to report it Mr. Niles? I suppose that Mr. Ray – obnoxious bastard that he is – never did anything wrong himself. So now I'm finished at the Y. And somehow Mr. Niles felt honor-bound to tell my boss here at the insurance agency who in turn felt it necessary to tell the board. The whole board for Christ sake! It will be all over town now. Mr. Nadir Khan – the child molester. The monster from India. They all think people from India are weird enough to start with. And a Muslim to boot, though I can't ever remember having been inside a mosque. I did try to pass as a regular guy here in this country. God how I tried. Went to church even. I found some company there – people I could be with – not Community, spelled with a capital C, of course, but one must make do. How could I ever face the people there not knowing for sure who knows? So much for the little bit of acceptance I managed to gain in this town.

Why are they taking so long in there? I hate the way Mrs. Green keeps staring into my office at me. She looks like an owl in those ugly bifocals she wears. I hate these big windows that let anybody see in. It's my own office. I ought to be able to have some privacy here. She knows something is up. Nosy bitch. I'm reading my newspaper, Mrs. Nosy-Bitch Green, and I don't even see you. **GANDHI ASSASSINATED**. God. How horrible. Every gentle thing gets destroyed in this world. I've read this headline about six times now and can't get any further. I guess all hell will break loose over there now. Muslims and Hindus killing each other on account of religion. Imagine that. In the name of religion! It makes me ashamed. What is keeping them? Those board members are a bunch of pompous asses. It's hard to care about those people in India, even my relatives, when my own life is coming apart. I hardly know them anyhow. How old was I when I was last there? Seven, I think. Where will I go if this thing gets really nasty here. Not back to India – I wouldn't be welcome there.

And I'm certainly not going to Pakistan. "The Pure Country." God, what a repressive place that's going to be.

*****

Down by the diving board bigger boys are diving and playing. Mostly they are sharks or whales. You begin as a minnow, then you become a bass, and then a tuna. After that you can be a shark. If you swim real good, almost as good as Mr. Khan, you can be a whale. I'm still a minnow but if I can pass my beginner's test next week I'll be a bass. Michael is down there with the big boys. He sees me and waves. I smile and wave back. Michael is already a shark. He's 13. He doesn't ignore me like a lot of the other big kids, or push me away. He plays with me – throws me around in the water and stuff like that. Some day I'd like to be a shark or even a whale. Some of the big boys have hair around their things. It looks kind of funny. But they don't have as much hair as my father. He has lots of hair around his thing. I saw it when we took a shower together. He has hair on his face and his back too, and all over. Even on the backs of his fingers. When I sit in his lap, sometimes I play with the hair on the backs of his fingers. It's black. Mr. Khan probably has hair too, like my dad, but I can't tell. He wears his swimming trunks. I don't know why he wears them. He's the only one who does. It's because he's grown up I guess. There are different rules for kids and grown ups. I can see my thing. Sometimes it sticks up when I look at it or play with it. Right now it's small and all scrunched up. It gets that way when I'm cold. When I'm warm my balls hang down in my sack more and my thing gets bigger. But it's not as big as the big kids who have hair. I have some hair on my body. You can't tell right away when you look at me. That's because the hair on my body is short and blond. You have to look real close. I can see it on the backs of my arms. I only have long hair on my head. Dad cuts my hair himself because it doesn't cost so much that way. I like it when he cuts my hair now because he has new electric clippers. They don't pull my hair like the old ones did.

*****

Being a claims adjuster isn't necessarily what I would have chosen for myself but I had no special talent for music or poetry or any of the kinds of things that I really like. Its hard to make a living at that sort of thing anyhow, so I'm just a dabbler and an appreciator with the things I love. It is nice to have a pay check that enables me to help my mother out. She has needed that ever since Dad died. I don't know how she would have managed if I hadn't been there. I still remember Mr. Van Dine telling me about all the opportunities that are available in the insurance business for smart and ambitious men. One could become a supervisor, and then a department head in a branch office, and from there one might have a chance at heading up a local office somewhere, which is usually what they want before they move anyone into a higher administrative position in the central offices. That was 12 years ago. God, how time gets away. And I'm still a claims adjuster. I think my foreign background works against me. On the other hand maybe they sense my lack of enthusiasm. Climbing that ladder of success doesn't excite me that much. Not that it wouldn't be nice to have the extra money. They have been grooming me this last year to take a step up. It would require moving but that's not a big issue. I have no family to worry about except my mother, and no deep attachments here, except maybe to Michael, and Timmy, and some of the other boys at swimming lessons. I hadn't been aware until recently how intense my feelings were for Alex. He's the youngest boy I ever felt this strongly about. When I held him to teach him how to coordinate his arm and leg motions I got so aroused I was afraid it would be evident even though I was wearing my trunks. I hate having to wear trunks but if anyone ever saw me getting an erection it would be all over. I guess it is anyhow. And I don't suppose they will keep on grooming me for a move up the ladder of success in the insurance business now. I'll do well to keep the job that I have.

*****

I really have to poop. You call that "number two." That's the right way to say it to grown-ups. I have to do number two, you say, and they know what you mean. I have to do number two now. It's not going away. I have to raise my hand even if Mr. Khan doesn't want me to bother him. I feel shivery. When you get wet in the shower and then just sit around you get shivery. Mr. Khan is holding Timmy and telling Timmy to show how you move your arms. Timmy is the best swimmer in the beginning class. But I can do almost everything he can do. Except float on my back. I keep getting water up my nose when I try to do that. It stings when you get water up your nose. I wish he would call on me. My hand is up. It gets tired if you have to hold your hand up too long. Sometimes Mr. Khan holds me when he teaches me something new. I like it when he holds me. I like it when he uses me to show the other kids something new. But today he chose Timmy. He sees my hand up.

"Just wait until I finish showing you this before you ask questions." he says.

My bottom is beginning to hurt. It does that when you have to poop and you try to hold it in. I begin to wave my hand in the air. My teacher told my that you should just hold you hand up quietly. Waving it is not polite. I want to be polite but my bottom hurts too much. I think he saw me but he pretended not to. I almost stand up and I wave my hand real much because I have to do number two so bad. Mr. Khan calls on me finally.

"Yes, Alex?" he says.

His voice has that bad sound like he's mad at me. He doesn't want me to interrupt him but I can't help it.

"I've got to do number two," I say.

"Just wait a couple of minutes," he says. "It's almost time for free swim."

I try to wait but I can't pay attention to what he is showing us. The poop is beginning to come out no matter how hard I try to wait. I wave my hand real hard this time.

"What is it Alex?" he says.

"I can't wait," I say.

"Just five minutes," he says.

"Not even one second," I say.

"OK," he says. "Only you should go before you take a shower and come in for swimming."

I stand up. I'm afraid it will fall out on the floor. I look back. A little bit of poop is on the bench. It's not very much but the other kids will see it.

*****

Michael, my love, I saw you waving at little Alex. A nice cozy friendship that is. Would we have been competitors in a year or two? Or maybe we already were. Well, no more. It was my idea that from time to time we stay for a while after lessons were done so that I could help you with your diving, and your mother was grateful to have someone drive you home. Of course I wanted time alone with you. You're the one who got us into this, not that I am complaining, but in spite of all my desires I would never have dared, had you not come and put your arms around me while we were showering and hugged me until we were both aroused and looked at ourselves and each other, and we were a little embarrassed but also proud, not just of our members standing erect, but proud that we could arouse in each other such excitement, and you made sure that I noticed that little bit of fuzz that was just beginning to encircle the base of your penis, and we laughed, and neither of us knew what to do with all this preparation so we just dried off and put our clothes on and drove home in happiness that I have never known before, nor will ever know again, and little by little after that we fumbled our way into new discoveries not being quite sure what we should do with all this enormity of feeling, and we progressed with you as much the teacher as the student until we relearned the ancient arts of pedagogical love between men and boys, and I told you about the literature that I had over the years found in libraries while leafing furtively through books by Walt Whitman and Andre Gide and Thomas Mann and the Greeks, as a young boy might sneak a look at a Playboy magazine, and thus I could show you how we were not alone, and how only recently in terms of world history has our kind of love been so cruelly condemned, and on that final day which I mark on my calendar now as the end of my life we were, as we had done many times before, showering and laughing together, and we talked about Alex and how I was ashamed of how I handled it when he shat on the bench, and how I now saw it as an almost endearing little carry-over from infancy into boyhood, and how I wanted to make it up for him, and you did not confess your attraction to him though by your intense interest and a slight flushing as we talked about him I could tell you too had been taken in by his brown eyes, but I was only a little jealous, and our common interest in him served perhaps as another bond that enhanced our love, and after washing each other all over I was just bringing you to the moment of climax when the door was flung open and Mr. Ray saw us.

Damn him.

Damn his short, squat, hairy, dull-witted self.

He later claimed he was just late with his cleaning responsibilities, but I am certain he suspected something and that he ambushed us on purpose.

And of course he had to tell Mr. Niles.

Ah, Michael, how I will miss you.

I am always thinking about you and Timmy and Alex, and Paul.

Paul was my first boy-friend, Michael, as you were my last. I was about your age and he was perhaps a year or two older than Alex. We met during summer camp in the craft building where the older and younger boys were able to mingle, and each day we held hands as we walked together from the craft building to the mess hall. Nothing more than that ever happened or likely would have happened that summer. I loved his red hair and the freckled face that looked up at me with such rapture in his blue eyes while we giggled about the dirty jokes he was just beginning to understand. It was the boys from my cabin who ambushed us and called us those names and pushed me down in the dust. From that I learned that my way of loving is a matter of shame and must be hidden, and indeed, I was never discovered again until Mr. Ray walked in on us.

*****

I walk as fast as I can to the dressing room. I walk sort of funny because I am trying to hold it in. I get to a toilet and I poop just as I sit down. That feels good. But now I still have a problem. The other boys will see the poop on the bench. They'll think I'm a baby. Mr. Khan won't like me any more. I think maybe I will just clean myself real good and go get my clothes and go home. I wipe myself real good and go to my locker. Mr. Khan comes into the dressing room. "Did you have an accident, Alex?" he asks.

I try to look away so he won't see my face. "Yes." I say. "I couldn't wait."

"Why didn't you tell me you couldn't wait?" he asks.

"I did," I tell him.

He looks at me and shakes his head. It's just as I thought. He doesn't like me. "Why did you wait to the last minute?" he asks.

"I raised my hand," I said. "But you didn't call on me."

He sighs and kind of rolls his eyes. He tells me to go take a shower and to wash my but real careful. "Then," he says, get some toilet paper and clean the bench off."

I nod. He goes out to be with the rest of the class. He isn't being fair. I did try to get his attention. And he looked at me so mean. I'll bet he did worse things than this when he was a kid. I hope he poops in his swimming trunks and everybody can tell.

*****

Mrs. Green is still trying to get an eyeful. She stares so hard that I almost imagine she can see what's in my head. Maybe she would enjoy it. My mind keeps going over all those events on my last day in the Y. Maybe she would like to see that. Who knows. Maybe she would find naked boys as exciting as I do. Maybe she would even like to see me naked in the shower. Who knows what goes on in other people's minds? They probably hide as much as I do. Why don't you type a letter Mrs. Green? Or dwell on your own memories? Or if you don't have any memories worth thinking about, make up your own fantasy. You said you would call me when Mr. Van Dine was ready for me. I guess the plan is for the board to discuss my situation, and come to some sort of decision regarding it, and then have me talk with Mr. Van Dine individually. I suppose that's better than having to sit before the whole board. Of course one should have an opportunity to defend himself, but I don't know what I would say to them. My coffee's cold. I should have drunk it when I first brought it in. I guess I was too anxious to eat anything then. That's why my mouth was so dry. It still is dry. But I think I'll try eating one donut just for Mrs. Green's sake. I'll eat with my mouth open and maybe that will cause her to turn away in disgust. Oh God. They are beginning to come out of the board room now.

This is worse than dealing with Mr. Nile's at the Y. Niles didn't even ask me to sit down, that big blond musclebound shit head. All those photos of the swim teams on the wall behind him, and the individual shots of boys who won this or that competition – I don't suppose he ever noticed that any of those boys were beautiful. The only love he ever feels is the approved Christian kind. Like St, Peter judging my soul he sat there behind his desk and said "Well Mr. Khan, I'm sure you can understand that after this we will not be able to use your services here anymore."

"Yes, sir," I said. "I can see that."

During the silence that followed his lip turned into a sneer. I think he was trying to figure out whether I was a Negro. He never was very clear about where somewhat dark people from India fit into the scheme of things. God forbid that he might have let a Negro swim in his pool, and even teach the children. Bad enough that a white man might have touched one of the boys in a loving way. Finally he said, "We have decided not to inform the police."

"Thank you sir, I said." So long as he promised that, I would kiss his ass as many times as he wished.

"But we have notified Mr. Van Dine at the insurance office."

"I see, sir," I said, "And why did you do that?"

He smiled. What did that smile mean? An attempt to show compassion? A sad smile perhaps? Or just a mask for the contempt he feels. "We felt it was only fair to them," he said.

"I see," I said. I didn't, but I wasn't going to argue about anything if the police were not going to be notified.

"You can pick up your things in the locker room before you leave." he said. "We will send you the balance that we owe you, so you need not come back in here."

And that was it. The end of everything.

There's the telephone. "Hello... hello? Oh, yes. Mrs. Green."

I can see her talking to me on her phone. Why the hell didn't she just come to the door.

"Yes, of course, Mrs. Green. I'll be right out."

He'll see me now. That's kind of him. Jesus I've spilled powered sugar all down the front of me. My shirt, pants, everything. I can't get the smudge out of my black pants by just brushing them. I'll just stop here in front of the door for a minute and get my bearings. Try to get some of that powdered sugar out. Shit. It's just smudging in worse now. There are so many of them out there and Mr. Van Dine's office is clear across the reception room and down the hall. So many people out there. I don't want to talk to any of them. Don't want them to see me. Maybe if I just keep my head down as I walk past them.

*****

I get the water just warm enough and take a shower like Mr. Kahn told me to. I even use soap on my butt. Then I come out. I go get my towel and dry off so I won't get so shivery. Then I get some toilet paper and go to the door to the pool. Just before the door there is the foot bath. Mr. Khan says never to try to jump over it. We must always put both feet in the foot bath so we don't track bad things into the pool. I stand in the foot bath. It's nice and warm on my feet. I look at the door. I don't want to go out. All the boys will laugh at me. I want to go back and get dressed and go home. But I would be in trouble then. Mr. Khan would call my mom. So I just stand there in the foot bath for a long time. Then Mr. Khan comes and opens the door.

"What are you doing?" he asks.

"I'm using the foot bath," I say. He sees that I have the toilet paper.

*****

I can't bring myself to go through this door. A few of the board members have left. But most are still in there milling around. What will they see when they look at me? A foreigner. A disgusting pervert. A creep. I wonder how much the others in the office know. Clearly they know something is up. This isn't the board's regular meeting time. And they know I'm hiding out in my office – not being my regular friendly self. I don't know who has said what to whom. Maybe they all know. "Now we know why he is 38 years old and still not married," they will think. They will believe that they know who I am, but they will know nothing. They will think I am one of those grotesque cartoon figures they carry around in their heads. Maybe I'll just make a dash for the front door and leave. But where would I go? If I leave without notice how will I ever get another job? Here comes Mrs. Green. She is knocking. I don't want to open it. She opens the door herself, and sees me standing here just behind the door with powered sugar still visible on my pants.

*****

"Come on out and clean up the mess," he says. He holds the door open for me. I don't have any choice now. I go out. I see all the boys lined up on the bench. They all stare at me. I was sitting on the part of the bench farthest away from the door. That means I have to walk past lots of boys. I don't look at them as I go by. When I get to my place I wipe up the poop that is on the bench.

Melvin, who was sitting next to me, says "eeeew."

"I couldn't help it," I say.

I start back and I hear Mark say, "gross."

"Remember what I said about making fun of him," Mr. Khan says. And Mark doesn't say anything more. I throw the toilet paper in the toilet and go back out. I go to my place and sit down. No one is laughing or making fun of me or going "eeeew." But I think they will later when Mr. Khan isn't there. Mr. Khan is done with the demonstration.

"It's free time, now," he says. All the boys yell and go jump in the water and start to play. But I don't want to. I don't think I like swimming lessons so much. Maybe I won't come back anymore.

*****

"Mr. Van Dine called again to say he is waiting for you, Mr. Kahn."

"Yes. Yes. Of course. I was just coming. Tell him I need to stop in the rest room for just a moment first if you will, please."

I slip past her and with my head down stride across the reception room and duck into the men's room. The sugar comes off with water but leaves a wet spot on the front of my pants. Still, that isn't quite as conspicuous as the powered sugar . Mrs. Green will probably come and pry me out of this room too if I don't hurry. Her passion for control knows no bounds. I open the door and without looking to either side go directly to Mr. Van Dine's door.

"Come in." he says in response to my knock. He invites me to sit down and swivels around in his big leather chair to face me. His eyes, cold and gray, latch onto me. His hair and suit are also gray. They are set off by a tasteful maroon striped tie. All at once I am aware that my tie and sports coat don't match. And I think he has noticed the wet spot on my pants. "I'll come right to the point, Mr. Kahn," he says. "The board members were quite distressed at the report we received from the Y."

"Yes sir, I can imagine they were," I say. I avoid his eyes by staring at the glass paper weight on his shiny desk top – the one with the picture of Mt. Rushmore embedded in it.

"On the other hand you have been a reliable employee here for 12 years." His fingers form themselves into the rafters of a church and he peers at me over them.

"Yes, it has been a long time, hasn't it," I say.

He nods. "So in lieu of that we will be keeping you on."

He seems to be waiting for something from me. "Thank you, sir," I say. Finally I glance up at him. "And please say thank you to the board."

"I will," he says. A thick folder sits on the table in front of him. I think it is my personnel folder. He opens it and leafs through some of the pages. "We will be setting aside the plans for training you to become a supervisor for the moment," he says.

"I understand, sir."

He smiles, sadly. Just like Mr. Niles. Why do they all smile?

"I trust we won't ever hear about anything else like this again," he says. "

"No, sir, you won't." I say.

"Good," he says. He closes a folder on his desk and pivots slightly to one side. "Do you have any questions?"

"Would you object if I were to take the rest of the day off?" I ask.

He shakes his head, "No that would be fine."

I shake the hand he offers me and back out of his office as quickly as I am able. I slide past the remaining board members milling around the office and hurry out the front door. Shoppers and workers of various kinds are going about their business all around me. It's just another day for them. They will go into their offices, or shops or houses and have ordinary conversations with each other about the weather, or their jobs, or the kids, or the latest news. Most of them will feel they belong in their little niches. I never will. I wish I did not have to live here.

Night Shift

A pink band about four feet off the floor transects the room. Above the band the wall is yellow. Below, it is gray. That doesn't really tell you much about where I am. Can you tell me where you are? Can we talk together? Obviously not. But listen. I will try.

I am alone.

On three of the walls around me there are windows made of glass bricks. One of the windows looks out into the TV room (or the living room as it is sometimes called), one looks out into the play room, and one into the hall – not "the" hall, but one of the halls. There are several halls. And the windows don't "look out" of course. They are just there. Sometimes words pick up hitchhikers and arrive at their destinations with all sorts of baggage you never intended to send. I am trying to be careful, so that you will understand.

Sometimes I look out – that is out of the window I just told you about. (You see how difficult this is.) The glass in some of the glass bricks is wavy. Through it everything looks distorted. Right now there isn't much to see out there. It's one o'clock in the morning and all the boys are in bed.

I lied. Already I lied. I tried not to but there are so many things to tell that I can't help lying. Actually there are windows on all four walls. On the wall I didn't mention there is also a door. That's in case I not only want to look out but want to go out as well. With there being both a door and a window on that wall and with both of them leading out onto the hall, it seemed too complicated to tell about. I lied because I didn't want to confuse you. I just want to tell you where I am.

Now I am out in the hall of Maple Cottage. Maybe I should

say the long hall so that you won't confuse it with the short halls. But you don't even know about the short halls so I suppose it doesn't make any difference. Perhaps I can at least make you understand about the long hall. It is the backbone of the entire double unit. At each end there are identical clusters of rooms which operate as separate units during the day. At night, one counselor must serve both cottages. This is why I moved out into the hall. I can see down into the other end while I sit in this one. Actually, of course, both ends are not the same. Even from here I can see that the wall above the tiles at the other end (which is called Oak Cottage) is pink. There are a lot of differences like that but I told you that both cottages were identical, as if one mirrors the other, to give you a general idea of how it is. It is very hard to tell the truth.

As I look down the hall I can see lots of doorways coming off the right side of the long hall. Also there is a doorway separating the units. It's open. That's because it's night. If I ignore the differences of the various sections of the hall, it is as though I were looking into an image of my own hall reflected back in a mirror at the central doorway, except I am not reflected in the mirror. But never mind. That's only the way it seems, not the way it really is.

Perhaps you would understand better about this hall where I am if I told you about the pattern of broken tiles that I can see on the corner which leads into the vestibule for the side door. But you don't know what that pattern is and it's far too difficult to tell about. There is no other pattern quite like it. Would it help then to tell you that the doors are all gray? Not really. You may get a picture of gray in your mind but that doesn't help very much. The fact is there is no way for you to reach through these words to see and touch the things that I am telling you about. The words bounce back into you own head and gather their meanings there. Like that mirror between the halls that isn't really there, if you see what I mean. How then are you ever to know where I am?

I am in an institution for juvenile delinquents. The institution is in the woods. It is 1:27 in the morning. I'm sitting in the long hall acting as the night counselor. There are 22 boys in the dorm at this end of the cottage. Most of them are between eleven and thirteen years old. Twenty of them are asleep and two are masturbating. That's as it should be. There are five boys on the honor hall, which makes a total of 27 boys in the unit. On the honor hall the boys have private rooms. One of them is locked up. That's not as it should be, but he gives his butt to all the other boys and he wants to be a girl. So we put him there.

The other end of the cottage is very similar to this one. There are a total of 28 boys down there, with five in private rooms. Again one of those boys is locked up for giving too much butt. Those are statistics.

The bed chart down in the office of Oak cottage is also of statistical interest. It shows that they have nineteen Protestants (indicated by "p"), 9 Catholics (indicated by "c"), and 7 enuretics (indicated by "*"). By the "P*" after Leroy Hicky's name, for example, we can see that he is a Protestant enuretic. Down at this end they don't keep such accurate records. All that can be discerned from the bed chart here is where the boys sleep. Probably if we had more complete records here they would reveal a very similar situation to what they have in Oak. Say 18 Protestants, 9 Catholics, and 10 enuretics. I am guessing that there might be more enuretics in Grant because the boys here are younger. I'm just speculating of course. They might have a higher or lower proportion of Catholics and that might, in turn, effect the number of enuretics. There are so many variables in something like this that it is hard to make an estimate with any real confidence. At any rate those are the statistics. As for the boys, individually, there are simply too many of them to tell about. Besides, I don't know them very well – at least not the ones down in Oak. In Maple Cottage where I work on the afternoon shift, I know them better.

I can hear groaning noises coming out of the dorm here in Maple cottage. I believe it's Farnsworth. He has an asthma condition. That may have something to do with it. Even though it's not on the bed chart, I also happen to know that he's a Catholic enuretic. That also may have something to do with it. It's hard to say. Someone has also been crying out down in the Oak dorm. I have been down there several times to investigate but I still don't know who it is. If I let my imagination run wild, I think of it as a disembodied cry in the wilderness. That, of course, is silly. It's probably just another catholic enuretic.

One must be careful when working here at night. It is so easy for the imagination to run wild. I was telling you about where I am. I don't want imagination to get in the way. I'm on the long hall now, as I already said. I repeat it so that you won't forget. From here I can see a bulletin board on the wall to my left. It is a calendar of May. On a yellow background there are black numbers cut out of paper. Mr. Rush fixed it up earlier this evening with the help of some of the boys. It is already the 23rd of May at 2:26 in the morning. Time has slipped by. Sometimes I stop writing a bit and then start again. I might even doze. Even though the display on the bulletin board is only a few hours old, it already shows over 22 useless days. Had he put up a calendar of June he would have been ahead. But of course I didn't say anything. It's best not to interfere too much with what other people do. Still, it does bother me to see all those obsolete days – days that were marked off in a block as though nobody had used them.

As a rule I work the afternoon shift – from 2:30 to 11:00 – in Maple, as I may already have said. But for the last two evenings the regular night counselor didn't come, so I'm working his shift for overtime. That's why I'm here now.

During the afternoon it is very different than at night. There is a lot of confusion. Take this afternoon for example. I was taking the 28 boys from Maple cottage up to the dining hall for supper. They were all walking in two lines. It's true the lines were wobbly and confused but still, they were lines. I don't really believe in lines and the boys know it. What I believe in doesn't have much to do with my job. I thought I was doing pretty well because anybody could see that the boys were in two lines rather than just a bunch, whether they believed in lines or not. Then all at once the front of the line sort of exploded. Boys started running around and ducking. "Get back in line," I said. "What are you doing?"

"They're throwing rocks at us," said one of the boys. He pointed to a group of boys from Elm Cottage in the doorway of the dining hall. I didn't know those boys because I have never worked in Elm Cottage. Palmer came up to me to point out the boys who did it. I went up to one of the boys that was pointed out and asked him his name.

"I ain't got no name," he said. Just then Mr. Springer came out to see what was going on. He was working Elm Cottage. He is very big and, as one of the other counselors put it, "always mean as shit."

"You wouldn't talk to me that way if I asked you your name," Mr. Springer said. "Tell the man your name."

"Mike Judkins," said the boy.

"Were you throwing rocks at my boys?" I asked.

"I didn't throw no rocks," he said. Then to Palmer, he said, "I'm going to beat your ass."

When he was done threatening Palmer he cocked his head to one side and looked at me with an insolent grin.

"So you're cool," I said.

"Yeah, I'm cool," he said, and he swung his shoulders a couple of times and snapped his fingers to prove it. Then Mr. Springer called them into the dining room.

While I was trying to eat supper I was furious. "I should have beat the shit out of him," I kept thinking. And my stomach got all tied up knots.

Fortunately I had some Rolaids with me so that I was able to get over my indigestion about an hour after finishing supper. One of the boys in the cottage, however, did get sick. That was Thurlow. He must have had his reasons but I don't know what they were. Maybe it was something he ate. I gave him two of my Rolaids and sent him into the dormitory to sleep. About an hour later he threw up all over the floor. I had a boy I was mad at clean it up, and I sent Thurlow to the Center Hospital. Then I thought about how I'm not really fair.

I didn't feel quite right all evening and that made it hard. When two boys came in hollering and fighting about whose turn it was on the pool table I didn't really care, so I put them both on the hall for making too much noise. After they calmed down I let them go. It's always like that. Every day the boys fight with each other, with teachers, and with counselors from the time they get up to the time they go to bed. Pretty often it gets me down and I think I can hear a boy inside of me screaming and wanting to stick a pen in somebody's eye. But I'm an adult so I don't attack anyone with my pen. Instead I write reports and passes with it. Actually I carry out my adult counselor role pretty well most of the time. After all, I have a certain reputation to keep up.

Earlier this evening McNally laid his head on my lap while we were watching TV. He generally doesn't respect authority and is mean to the to the kids in the cottage. I'm very fond of him and I wanted to caress his forehead and cheeks and chest. But of course I couldn't. That would have been sodomy or something akin to it, and I do have a reputation to keep up. He does too, so he wouldn't have allowed it anyhow. So I pretended that he was just trying to be comfortable while watching TV and that it was a matter of indifference to me. That's the only way we could have even that much. Then we had to go to a program at the school, and the confusion began again. Stewart didn't want to go and wouldn't put his shoes on.

It's very quiet now, about three-ten in the morning. I am in the long hall, listening. I can hear the motor to the water fountain, boys snoring in the dorm, and faint creaks and snaps here and there throughout the cottage. In the quiet, it seems clear to me now. I can never touch McNally. But that's because he isn't the one I want to touch – the one that I love, and fear and who shames me. That boy is inside of me – in my darkness – in my past. Sometimes I see him in a field running free and happy. Then I see him on a beach exploding out of the water, grinning, glistening and salty. I want to caress all his parts with my eyes, my hands. I love his shoulder blades and knees and belly and buttocks. I want to hold him, to take his penis in my mouth and let him explode and be happy. I want to be him. That's what I want – sometimes.

It is easy to let your imagination run wild here at night. Really it is. I'm not sure if that's what I want or not. I mean what

I was just talking about. Maybe I do just want to touch McNally.
I thought it was clear there for a minute but, as I tell about it, it
doesn't turn out that way. Its hard to tell the truth. It's like that
mirror in the hallway – the one I told you about that really isn't
there. Only this time I don't know whether I'm looking into a
mirror or not. It seems that if it were only me I wanted to touch,
and not McNally, that would be lonely. At any rate I can't touch
McNally. That much is clear.

I'm sitting at this chair at a table in the hall – the main hall.
Yes, now I remember. I was trying to tell you where I am. This is
Maple Cottage. It's about 3:45 in the morning. The dorm is pretty
quiet now but it isn't always that way. I try to get the boys to leave
the noise outside when they go in the dorm to sleep, but sometimes
it doesn't work that way. It seems terrible to me when the noise is
where the quiet should be. Take last night. After everybody should
have been asleep I went in and found the dorm in chaos. I had the
boys who were causing all this noise and confusion write about it
today as a punishment. So I'll let them tell you about it. I wasn't
there:

*It all started when we all were in bed talking about
things we did on the street. Then all of a sudden someone
leaped over the wall laughing very loud, with a spread
wrapped around him, and ran over to my bed looking at
me. Someone said, "get the fuck on your own side." Then
a voice said, "Fuck you man," and then he threw the
pillow and hit McNally with it. McNally said "Ima kick
your ass. Just keep that shit up." So he went back over
the wall. A sponge came and hit Preble, and Kingston
said, "I think I know who it was. It was Ezzy." So
everybody got excited and started talking loud and Ezzy
said "wanna have a pillow-fight?" So Lovett said "Ya."
So McNally said "You better not get out of bed."
Everybody got up and started playing and the one who
said don't get up got up too. So we Saw Mr. Foster In the
locker room and I said "Che-che." Engston came and hit
me with a pillow and I said "Che-che, man. Stop*

playing." So Mr. Foster left and Linscott said "you guys almost got busted." So I said "che-che for us, Linscott" By that time everybody except Hicks got up and started playing again. Well, after a little while Mr. Foster walked in and said "someone is busted bad." Then he asked Markus who it was. So Markus told who it was and Mr. Foster left and before he left he said "I hope you start it again." So after a while we made a little too much noise and Mr. Foster returned and said "all right, who was it." The people who got busted said it was Engston. Mr. Foster said who else was it besides Engston. McNally said "it was Dagle." So Mr. Foster called us in the office and beat our butts with his belt. Nothing else happened so we all went to sleep. That is my version of the pillow fight.

Conrad Dagle

So that's how Dagle saw it. He writes a lot better than most of the kids in the cottage, so I am sharing his version with you. I did sort of beat their butts, but not very hard. I had to do something to calm it all down.

McNally also saw it but he didn't feel like writing so much.

I was laying in the bed and Kingsbury snatched a pillow. Lovett started throwing pillows. They started making noise. I looked up and someone knocked the hell out of me. Someone started shooting spit balls. Pillows started flying in the air. Boys started jumping up. I'm lying about all this.

James McNally

So that's how it is sometimes. But tonight it's quiet. When it's like this my imagination can get carried away. But right now I'm trying to tell you about where I am and how it is here.

One sees a lot of cockroaches when working here at night.

They are obviously breeding very fast because I can make out at least three generations. The standing joke around here is that if you want to get around the cottage easily and quietly you just put your feet on the cockroaches and they carry you where you want to go. I have had to laugh at that several times. But I don't mind. I even found myself saying it once.

The exterminator should come soon because... because why? Oh yes, the cockroaches. The cockroaches are dirty. Something funny is happening in my head. Should I let it? It is very quiet here. Cockroaches. No, I should stop it. I am in Maple cottage. Cockroaches are with me. I mean in the hall here. In the long hall. In other places too. McNally came out because a cockroach crawled on his face. I remember that. That happened one time. Not tonight, but one time in Maple cottage. McNally is black and brown. In the dorm with the cockroaches. But that was then. Black and brown and golden boy on the beach is or isn't he McNally? On the beach running. Drowning. Dying. Dying into nothing. No. How shall I say about no? Words – so many words. Hand won't write. Why? Allow it. Let it. Quiet now and snoring in black and brown in the dorm. Cockroach. Cock. Roach. Roach, no, in the sand. Falling apart. Into the lake. It goes. Sand. Words. Apart. Falling apart. Into words. Testicle. Sand. Roach. Cock. Shit. Words. What? Words. Loving. Sex. Possessed. Words. The flow. Where to? To touch. Hold. To where? The McNally Christ Child, black and brown and running and is he the Christ Child? Could we ever touch? Touch. Hold. Run. McNally my Doom. But where is the Christ child? Who? The Lice Child. No, my Death. How shall we touch? How should I, could I, can I, will I? Allow. A roach on your face. Something more to allow in my sickness? The Christ child, yes. Him. Lying in the vomit and vermin, lice in his hair. Sickness, yes, but there is the Christ with testicles and with his cock... there he is coming, emerging, destroying, falling apart in the vomit, the sickness, the bile, the lice the roaches creeping him all over and Christ the Child lying in vomit, golden. Wash him Pick him up. Clean him with yes. Wash him. All over his golden smelly body reeking in vomit. The knees and the belly and his small private places, and his golden, and his eyes brown and black in the vomit. Wash him. Words. So many words. Beer. Drink. Eat. Piss. Shit. Smell. Words. How shall I say? How shall? How shall they judge my McNally Christ Child with their words? And how shall they burn with words? Words letting, allowing and words killing. How is the darkness less by words? And the Burning? Yes my black and Golden Christ Child lying...

I was interrupted. Yes, confused. I don't know where I was exactly. How shall I tell you? Imagination runs wild you know. I think I told you that. Interrupted, yes. I was interrupted. I am in Maple Cottage. It is 4:15 in the morning. Almost light. Linscott just now came in. That's how I was interrupted. Linscott came to tell me that Lovett was playing around his butt. I went to Lovett's bed and told him that he knew better and that I might write him up for sex play.

I'm back in my office now. The one with the glass bricks. The band going around the room isn't really pink, exactly. It's hard to say what color it is. I have a pen in my hand and I'm looking at a form. Naturally I won't actually write Lovett up for what he did, unless Linscott raises a stink, but I had to say something firm. I am, after all, a counselor.

Wild Dogs

Charlie Montecheli was running down the tracks in my direction. He glanced over his shoulder at the boys behind him. "You'll be sorry!" he hollered. Taking his eyes off the railroad ties cost him his balance, and he fell into the cinders. His tormentors jeered and laughed. I remembered the warning from his cottage counselor when I agreed to take Charlie on the camping trip: "He'll be nothing but trouble – can't get along with the others."

Charlie picked himself up and walked the rest of the way to me. His curly brown hair was matted with sweat and dust. Tears streaked his face. Through a rip in his blue jeans, I could see that he had skinned his knee.

"What happened?" I asked.

"They threw rocks at me," he said.

"They hit you?"

"Yes."

"Where?"

"Here and here." He pointed to one place on his head and another on his back.

I examined his head and then pulled up his T-shirt to look at his back.

"I can't see anything."

"They weren't big rocks, but they hurt."

"Looks like you scraped your knee when you fell," I said.

He looked down. "Its bleeding," he said.

"I don't think it's cut deep," I said.

"Look at my hands." He held them out to me. They were imprinted with the cinders but were not bleeding.

I nodded. "You caught yourself when you fell."

"Hurts," he said.

"Who was throwing the rocks?" I asked.

"Rufus and Scar, and the twins and Pisser, and... everybody. They all did. But Rufus was the boss of them."

"Rufus Olsen!" I shouted. "Hold it up. And tell the others to wait also." I have a bellowing voice which is an asset when working with a group of boys.

"We didn't do nufin," Rufus hollered back.

"Never mind. Just wait."

I heard the expected grumbling but was confident they would follow my instructions.

"I wanna go back," Charlie said.

I frowned. "Maybe everybody will go back," I said.

"You mean we ain't going?" Saturn asked. He and Barbie had been lagging behind and had just now caught up.

"We'll have to see," I said.

Barbie lowered himself to his knees in front of Charlie. "Lemme see your scrape," he said.

"Careful!" Charlie pulled his leg back.

"I won't hurt you."

"OK," said Charlie. He let Barbie pull open the torn place in the knee of his jeans to examine the injury.

"Ain't too bad," said Barbie.

Barbie earned his nick-name when he chose to bring a Barbie doll to Forest Glen. The boys in his cottage, who were between eleven and thirteen years of age, would have accepted a teddy bear as sufficiently manly, but lugging around a Barbie Doll was another matter. Barbie was unabashed in his desire to be a girl, and he was not entirely unhappy with being named after his idol.

"I'll let you doctor him in a little bit," I told Barbie. "But let's go talk to the others first."

We walked down the tracks in silence. Charlie was limping, somewhat theatrically. Barbie had offered himself as a crutch.

The boys waited for us, most of them sitting on the tracks, sweating in the hot sun.

Tall and very dark, Rufus was the undisputed leader of Maple Cottage. He sat at the end of the row nearest to us. Next to him was his first lieutenant. "Scar," as he was known in honor of a large scar on his nose, was the strongest boy in the cottage, but he deferred to Rufus because Rufus was smarter, wilier. On the rails opposite Rufus and Scar, Paul and Roy Houston leaned against each other. Their red kinky hair disclosed their mixed racial background. They were twins, but were by no means identical. Paul was slightly overweight. From behind the thick lenses of his glasses, his soft eyes studied the world with unwavering attention. Roy was thin, dreamy and taciturn. James Jefferson, grossly obese and known as "Fats," had stripped off his shirt and was sprawled on his back between the tracks, his head propped up on his pack. He was sweating profusely. The rest of the boys were lined up on the tracks down the line.

"Wha'd little Mama's boy tell you?" Rufus asked, squinting and shielding his eyes from the sun as he looked up at me.

"Charlie told me you threw rocks at him," I said

Scar shook his head and groaned. "Aw, they was just little pebbles, man," he said.

"So why were you throwing any rocks at all?" I asked.

"Cause he such a baby," Rufus said. "We don't want 'im hangin with us."

"It's 'cause I'm white," Charlie said. "They call me `Honky.'"

I was in an awkward situation. Being white myself, I didn't want the problem defined as a racial one. Charlie and Saturn were the only two white boys in the group.

"Ain't cause he's white," said Paul. "Saturn's white. He's okay."

"Charlie cries too much." Roy said.

"And tattles," Paul added. "Nobody likes him."

"You'd cry too if everybody picked on you," Charlie said.

"We've got a problem here," I said. I scratched my head and looked around at the boys.

"That's the problem," Rufus said, jabbing his finger toward Charlie's face.

Charlie backed off a step.

"He's not my problem," I said.

"What's your problem?" Paul asked.

"Well, my problem is how am I going to take a group of boys on a trip if they can't go by the rules."

"So we'll stop messing up," Rufus said. "Can we go now?"

"You want to continue the trip? "I asked.

"'Course," Rufus said. The other boys nodded and said they did too.

"Well, I'm going to let the group decide," I said.

Rufus sat up. "Cool," he said. "We all wanna go, right, guys?"

There was almost unanimous consent. With a sigh of relief the boys started gathering up their things.

"Wait a minute," I said. "I didn't finish with the conditions."

"Conditions?" Rufus said.

"Yeah, I got some conditions."

"What's the conditions?" Paul asked.

"First condition is that you got to cut this shit with the rock throwing."

"Right," said Paul. "No more rock throwing."

"Second condition is that you don't have to like Charlie, but you got to stop tormenting him."

Scar looked up and frowned. "He deserve the shit he gets," he said.

Rufus elbowed him in his side. "Shut-up," he said.

"No tormenting Charlie," Paul said.

"Everybody hear that?" Rufus said. He looked around the group. Several boys nodded.

"The third condition..." I began.

"Jeez, man, how many conditions you got?" Rufus asked.

"This is the last one," I said.

"I hope so," said Rufus.

"Everybody's got to agree that they want to go on this hike."

Rufus glanced at Charlie. "Everybody?" he asked.

"Everybody," I said.

Rufus scratched the back of his neck and frowned.

Charlie sat down. All the eyes in the group fixed on the scrawny, dirty child sitting cross-legged in the gravel between the rails. "I wanna to go back to the cottage," he said.

The group sat baking in the sun, like a becalmed vessel. The cawing of a crow could be heard, and a locust chirping.

Finally Rufus Spoke. "Shit," he said.

"I'm a kick some ass, when we get back," Scar said. He glared at Charlie.

Several boys said "right on," and "Yeah."

"Shut up," Rufus said. "Threats is no good."

"You got that right," I said.

"Look here," Paul said, "It's no big problem. Just let Charlie go back. That's what he wants. Everybody else wants to go camping."

I shook my head.

"Roy and I'll take him back, and catch up with you later," Paul added, trying to make an offer I couldn't refuse.

Roy nodded.

"Nope," I said. "We're a group. It's all or none."

"He ain't no group wif me," Scar said.

"You're not helping, man," Paul said.

"You ask him," Roy said, looking at Rufus.

"Ask him what?"

"To come. He'll listen to you."

"I ain't goin to beg him," Rufus said. He picked up a rock and threw it at a tree.

Barbie walked over to Charlie and sat down beside him. "Come wif us," he said. "Everybody want you to."

"Nobody wants me," Charlie said.

"I do," Barbie said. He put his arm around Charlie's shoulder.

"You're the only one," Charlie said.

"I want you to go," Saturn said.

"I'll be your nurse," Barbie said.

"My nurse?"

"You're hurt." Barbie pointed to his knee.

"Maybe I'm too bad hurt to go." Charlie studied the skinned knee, and searched his body for other injuries. "I think one of those rocks sprained my arm." He rubbed it in an exploratory manner.

"Look, man, I ain't beggin you," Rufus said.

Charlie smiled at him. The missing two teeth — the left front one and the incisor beside it — gave his face a lopsided look. He understood that Rufus was about to beg him.

"I ain't beggin you," Rufus said. "But I'll see the boys don't pick on you no more."

"Well, now, there's a deal worth thinking about," I said.

Charlie frowned. He looked up at the sky and squinted. "I don't like being picked on," he said.

"Won't happen no more," Rufus said.

"You're sure?" Charlie asked.

"Sure I'm sure."

Charlie studied the gravel in front of him as he contemplated this offer.

"All right," he said finally.

"We go now, Mr.Foster?" Rufus asked. He jumped to his feet before I could answer.

"Just don't get so far ahead I can't see you."

"How come he gotta be wif us?" Scar asked. He stood up and took a step in Charlie's direction.

"Shut-up," said Rufus. He put his arm around Scar's shoulder.

"No tormentin, remember?" Paul said.

"Ain't tormentin him. Just talkin," said Scar.

"Don't need to do nothin' with him," Paul explained. "Don't be sayin' things."

"Talkin' ain't nufin'," said Scar.

"Paul's right," Rufus said. "Just act like he ain't here."

Scar allowed Rufus to steer him away from Charlie. He and Rufus started down the tracks.

When Saturn stood up and started to follow the other boys, his toothbrush, toothpaste and socks fell out of his torn gym bag. It was this kind of thing that led to his being called Saturn. It was as though he lived on another planet. Barbie pointed out to him that he was losing everything and helped him re-pack so that his belongings would stay together for the rest of the hike.

I went over to Charlie, who was still sitting in the cinders. "We better not fall too far behind," I said.

"They still don't like me," he said.

"Give it some time," I suggested. "You're still new here."

"Been here more 'n a month."

"That's not so long."

"I don't think I wanna go."

"You agreed to," I said.

"I can change my mind," he said.

After zipping Saturn's bag, Barbie joined us. "Come-on," he said to Charlie. "You, me 'n Saturn'll be our own club." Charlie allowed himself to be helped to his feet. We continued on down the tracks with Barbie and Saturn walking on either side of Charlie to support him, like soldiers helping a wounded comrade.

The other nine boys were a fair distance ahead of us, competing to see how long they could walk on one of the rails without falling off.

"Hey, you guys. Wait up," Saturn called.

"Let's try to catch up," I said, and I increased my pace.

Jerome LeChance, a dark and gentle twelve year old boy, dropped back and fell into step beside me. I felt his hand slip into mine.

"Paul and Roy say they saw dog tracks in the mud," he said.

"That worry you?" I asked.

He glanced up at me and wiped some sweat off his forehead with his free hand. "A little."

There was much talk among the boys at Forest Glen Correctional Facility about the wild dogs that inhabited the surrounding woods. A pack of eight or ten dogs, in fact, had been seen roaming the grounds the previous winter. During a spell of unusually cold weather they raided the garbage cans behind the mess hall. It was speculated that people abandoned their unwanted pets in the wooded area around Forest Glen, and that these dogs had formed a pack and survived by hunting and scavenging.

"The dogs won't bother us," I said.

"I heard they killed a hobo last spring," Jerome said.

"Really?"

"Yeah. Chewed his head clean off." I felt his hand grip more tightly.

"I think such a thing would have been in the newspaper had it really happened," I said.

"They cover it up."

"Who covers it up?"

"You know. The authorities."

"Why would they want to do that?"

"Cause they don't want people to know."

"Know what?"

"That Forest Glen ain't safe."

*****

Our "camp" was a clearing at the edge of a stream, with a circular fireplace in the middle and a "fort" at one end. The fort, nailed up between a beech and a pine, was about twelve feet wide and eight deep. It was the pride of our camping group. We had constructed it during previous trips from materials we floated downstream from the dump about a quarter of a mile away. On this trip we had come by way of the railroad tracks rather than the more direct route through the woods so we could check out the dump for materials for a roof. The current roof was constructed from a large piece of canvas scavenged from the dump earlier in the summer. The rotten canvass shielded us well enough from the sun, but it was full of holes, and we needed something more substantial for rain. On the way in we spotted some doors and a discarded piece of linoleum that looked perfect, and we made plans to retrieve them the next day.

When we arrived at the camp Barbie told Charlie to take off

his blue jeans, and took him down to the stream. Barbie washed his knee meticulously with soap, a process that Charlie tolerated bravely. Finally Barbie painted it with Mercurochrome and carefully bandaged it with materials I supplied him from the first aid kit.

It was already late in the afternoon, and we had time only to set up camp and fix ourselves some supper before it began getting dark. After the sun went down we huddled in the fort. A half moon, low on the horizon, provided some light, but neither it nor the fire dispelled the darkness that lay beyond the edge of the clearing. Jerome told the boys about seeing the dog tracks and about the hobo having his head chewed off.

A smaller boy they called Louie-Louie shook his head violently. "No," he said. "No."

"No, what?" asked Jerome.

"No, it ain't true."

"What's not true?" Jerome asked.

"That thing about his head being chewed off."

"Louie-Louie scared," said Rufus.

"I ain't," said Louis-Louie.

"You a sissy," said Scar.

"Ain't no dog what chewed a man's head off, is there, Mr. Foster?"

"Well, I don't know," I said. "Doesn't seem likely."

"See!" Louie-Louie said.

"He didn't say it didn't happen," Rufus said. "He said, 'don't seem likely.'"

"Unlikely things do happen," Paul said.

"They do," I said. "In fact I know something pretty creepy that has to with dogs and ... this place."

I allowed a silence to descend over the group.

"What's that?" Rufus asked finally.

"What's what?" I asked.

"What you said. The creepy thing."

"Oh that." I paused, staring out into the darkness surrounding our clearing. "Tonight's probably not a good time to talk about it."

"Why not?"

"It's too scary. I'm afraid nobody could get to sleep."

"We ain't babies," said Scar.

"Well, I know. But it really is creepy."

When the boys continued to protest my reluctance to tell them the creepy thing I raised my hands for attention. "All right," I said. "Only don't blame me if you can't sleep tonight." I frowned. The group became silent. "It concerns a murder," I said. I stared for a long time into the fire without speaking. "A murder that occurred right here in this clearing."

"A murder," Pisser said. "Cool." He pushed past the other boys, and settled himself in my lap. I put my arms around his wiry body and helped him settle into a comfortable position.

"Better not let 'im sit there," Fats said. "He ain't called Pisser for nufin."

"It ain't cause I piss the bed," the boy in my lap retorted.

"Why then?" asked Fats.

"Cause I won a pissin' contest last summer."

Several of the boys laughed at this. "Sure," Scar said.

"You weren't there," Pisser, said. "Tell 'em Rufus."

"It true," said Rufus. "He pissed further 'n anybody, even me." He turned toward me. "So get on with the story."

"Seems like there was this guy named Harry Hunckleburger..." I said.

Saturn guffawed.

"What you laughing about?" Scar asked. He threw a bit of bark at Saturn.

"It's a dumb name," Saturn said.

"What about Pooolinanskiski," Scar said. "What kinda name is that?"

"Poulanski," Saturn corrected.

"Hunckleburger *is* a dumb name," Paul said. He looked accusingly at me.

"Can I help that?" I asked.

"Just call him Harry," Roy suggested.

"Good idea," Paul said. He patted his brother on his back. "Just call him Harry. Then we can get on with this."

"OK. I'll call him Harry."

"And everybody shut up," Rufus said. "I want to hear 'bout this murder."

When I could hear the frogs croaking and the fire popping and crackling a bit as it settled, I continued.

> *Sometimes he might go out west and be a cowhand. Or he might work on a ship for a while. He might travel with some other drifter for a spell now and then but his only true friend was his dog, Buck. Buck was part German shepherd and part wolf. He was huge and gray. He was a killing machine — but he never threatened anybody so long as they left his master alone.*
>
> *"Now as he was coming through this area Harry was traveling with a man, name of Marvin Brockten. Marvin was a big bear of a man. He was wanted in lots of different states for all kinds of crimes, but Harry never read the newspapers, so he didn't know this.*
>
> *"One evening they went into town to live it up, and Harry got to gambling. He was in a lucky streak that night and made a bundle of money. He drank more than he should have, and when they got back to the camp here, Harry passed out almost at once. Marvin stayed awake thinking about all that money. Gradually greed got the*

best of him. So he found a big rock and crashed it down on Harry's skull, crushing it.

"He had forgotten about Buck, but heard him growl just in time to turn around and swing his rock a second time. He was lucky. It caught Buck right in the side of his head as he was midair.

"Marvin took all of Harry's money, and buried him at the edge of the clearing to keep any evidence out of sight. He didn't bother with Buck, as he figured nobody would pay any mind to a dead dog, and he took off.

"Where, exactly he bury this guy?" Paul asked.

"I don't know for sure," I said.

"Where you think?"

"Well, it might have been just about where we built that fort."

"You mean we be sleeping on top of this dead guy?" Scar asked.

"How come you never told us before we built the fort?" Paul asked.

"Well, I don't know for sure exactly where he's buried. It's just that one time I came out here and found a little rectangular place where the grass and weeds were growing real good, and I thought maybe Harry Hunckleburger was serving as fertilizer for all those green things."

"I seen that grass patch 'fore we built this fort," Louie Louie said.

"You makin' that up," Scar said.

"Am not," Louie Louie said. "I seen a patch, right under where this floor is." He slapped the floor of the fort for emphasis.

"But that little place where the grass grew real good doesn't prove anything," I said.

"Jeez," said Fats. I don't wanna to sleep on top a no dead man."

"See," I said. "I knew I shouldn't have told you guys about this."

"You all shut up," said Rufus. "I wanna hear the story."

"So what happened then?" asked Paul.

"Marvin decided he'd better clear out of this area before people came looking for Harry and got suspicious. So he gathered up his stuff and took off.

"Several hours later Buck woke up. Marvin had only knocked him unconscious. His head was bloody, and his left eye was missing. For two days he sat on his master's grave, whimpering. Then he started out after Marvin.

"He tracked him to a train station and then followed those train tracks more than a thousand miles out west until he found the place where Marvin got off. It took him two weeks.

"From there it was nothing for Buck to track him on out into the wilderness. He found Marvin sitting by himself at his campfire, poking the embers with a stick. Marvin heard a little growl behind him. When he turned his head to look, he was face to face with a one-eyed dog. Where the other eye should have been there was only a red smear. Marvin reached for his gun, but he wasn't fast enough. Buck was on him."

I stopped talking at this point and began scanning the edge of the clearing. Several of the boys followed my example.

"That the end?" Scar asked.

Probably it's all I should say tonight," I said.

Paul sat up. "Come on, Mr. Foster," he said. "What happened then."

"Sure you want to know?"

"We're sure," Rufus said.

"All right." I continued.

Buck didn't kill Marvin outright. Instead he chewed both his eyes out, and left him to fend for himself. Marvin was discovered by some local people a few days later. They took him into town where someone recognized him from a wanted poster, so they hung him for some murders he had committed.

Buck himself retraced all those thousand and some miles to return to this little clearing to be at the grave of his master. Every once in a while you still hear reports of a camper seeing a dog in the woods at night with a blood-red smear where one of his eyes should be — a smear that glows like a hot ember. Whether that is Buck himself, or his ghost, nobody can say. But some folks say he's still around guarding his master's grave.

"Cool," Pisser said.

"You made that up, didn't you, Mr. Foster?" Louie-Louie said.

I didn't answer.

"It just a story," said Paul. "Ain't it, Mr. Foster."

I shrugged my shoulders.

Maybe it's a story, 'n maybe not," Fats said. He looked from one member of the group to another, and nodded his head, knowingly. "But wild dogs *will* kill you if they gets the chance."

"Well, time to get to bed," I said.

We had brought only two tents along. One was mine, and Barbie brought the other. They were old and didn't have floors, but I hoped they would give us some protection against the mosquitoes. Barbie invited Saturn and Charlie to share his tent with him. Jerome and Louie-Louie wanted to sleep with me. The rest of the boys discussed whether Harry Hunckleburger really was buried underneath the fort, but finally convinced themselves they wanted to sleep there, whether or no.

After everyone was in his place, I gave back scratches to all the boys in the fort to help them settle down. Then I did the same for the boys in Barbie's tent. When I returned to my tent, Jerome and Louie-Louie were still awake, talking. Louie-Louie pulled his shirt off and spread out on his stomach. As I rubbed out some of the tension I said, "I'll tell you guys a secret if you promise to not tell the others."

"What?" Louie-Louie asked.

"I made that story up," I said.

I continued with the massage. I felt his whole body relax beneath my hands. "Good," he said. "Now I can sleep."

"Also," I said, "You don't need to call me Mr. Foster."

"They tell us to at Forest Glen," Jerome said. "It's respectful."

"That's all right for Forest Glen," I said. "But on this trip I'm just Alex, OK?"

"OK... Alex."

By the time I had finished giving Jerome his back scratch, Louie-Louie was almost asleep. I settled in between the two boys, and lay on my back. I could hear the murmur of a conversation over in the fort, but the voices were low and calm so I didn't worry about it. The fire popped occasionally. Louie-Louie snuggled in closer to me. The frogs were loud that night. I listened to them with a deep feeling of peace. Soon everybody was asleep.

I was wakened by someone calling. "Mr .Foster! Mr. Foster!"

"Yes?"

"I need you."

I looked up and saw Charlie crouched in the doorway.

"What is it?"

"I got to talk to you."

I dragged myself out of my sleeping bag and crawled through the door. Charlie, wearing only his underpants and a T-shirt, was shivering.

"Come closer to the fire," he said.

The last logs had finished burning, and the embers from the fire barely glowed. But they still gave off some warmth. The moon was low on the horizon.

"What is it?" I asked.

"It's Sniff."

"Sniff" was a big thirteen year old boy with dull eyes. His nickname came from his history of sniffing gasoline.

"What about Sniff?"

"He asked me for my butt."

"What do you mean?"

Charlie's mouth tightened in exasperation. "You know."

"Well, what exactly did he say?"

"He said `I'll give you a peanut butter and jelly sandwich for your butt.'"

"When did this happen?"

"Just now. He come to my tent."

I looked around but saw no sign of Sniff. "Where is he now?"

"I think he went back to the fort."

"What did you say when he asked you that?"

"I said no way. I said I'd tell."

Charlie held his hands out to the fire.

"So where'd he get a peanut butter and jelly sandwich?" I asked.

"Said he'd give me his next Saturday when we get them for lunch."

"OK," I said. I saw that he was shivering. "Go back to your

tent."

"Will he hurt me?"

"No. I'll talk to him."

Charlie returned to his tent, and I went over to the fort. I had noted where all the boys were sleeping when I was giving them back scratches. I went to the heap that was Sniff's sleeping bag and whispered his name. There was no answer. I reached down and shook him.

"What?" he said, pretending to be startled.

"Can it," I said. "You're not asleep."

"Was too."

"What were you doing over at Charlie's tent?"

"Nufin. "

"Don't lie to me," I said.

"I didn't do nufin," he said.

"Look, you like going on these trips, don't you?"

"Yeah .

"Well sit up and tell me the truth if you hope to go on another one."

He pulled himself up. For some time he sat, rocking gently back and forth.

"Well?" I said.

"I asked him somethin."

"What?"

"Can't say."

"Did it have to do with his butt?"

Sniff hung his head and said nothing. Finally he nodded.

"OK," I said. "You got a choice. You go apologize to him, or I take you home first thing in the morning."

I didn't rush him. When he was ready, he slowly got up and came with me over to Charlie's tent. I opened the flap.

"Sniff's got something to tell you," I said.

Sniff looked in. When he saw Charlie's face he said, "I'm sorry for what I done."

"You mad 'cause I told on you?" Charlie asked.

"No."

"Charlie wants to know whether you are going to try to get even with him for telling," I said.

"I won't hurt you," Sniff said. He shook his head. "You're... its...'cause..." He looked at the ground, paused, and frowned. "Cause you're nice," he said. Then he turned and trudged back to his sleeping bag.

"Sniff won't bother you," I said.

When I followed Sniff back to the fort, someone else called my name

"Who's that?"

"It's me." I saw Scar sit up.

"What is it?" I asked.

"Listen," he said.

I leaned my head out of the fort. "It's just a bull frog," I said.

"Not that. Listen."

Then I heard the howling. It was faint, but clear.

"It's the dogs," he said.

"It might be a dog," I said.

"Can I sleep in there wif you?" he asked.

I shrugged. "I guess there's room. Bring your sleeping bag.."

Soon there were four of us scrunched into the tent. He insisted on sleeping next to me and pushed Louie-Louie over to the side of the tent to make this possible. Louie-Louie woke briefly, said something incoherent, and fell back asleep.

The sun was rising before I woke again.

*****

After the breakfast dishes were washed, I told them we couldn't leave the fire burning unattended, and asked the twins to get some water from the stream to put it out.

"Why don't you get Pisser to pee on it?" Paul suggested. "That would do it."

Several of the boys laughed, and Pisser came over to offer his services.

"Hold it a second," I said. "I think its going to take more than one boy to do this, even if you are the famous Pisser."

"It's a lot of hot coals," Paul said.

"Might take everybody," Roy said.

The idea caught on, and soon all the boys were gathered around the fire.

"Cool idea," said Louie-Louie, and he unzipped his pants and prepared for action.

"All right. Everybody gotta go at once," Rufus shouted. "Get ready."

Following Louie-Louie's example, they all prepared themselves.

"Ready, aim, fire," Rufus continued, and under his able leadership thirteen golden arches of liquid descended in unison on the fire.

"Look at me, Alex!" said Pisser. " Scar, look at me!" Pisser's urine arched higher and went further than any other boy's. "Was I lying?" he said.

"You got it," Scar said, with real admiration.

Each jubilant parabola of urine joined in the common worship, and collectively we were a hymn to the newly risen sun.

This was joy.

For the moment, the dogs were forgotten.

We went to the dump where we gathered the doors, the linoleum, and miscellaneous other materials, and floated them down the stream to the campsite. After lunch and one more trip to the dump, we decided we had worked enough for one day. We would wait for tomorrow before actually constructing the roof.

I set some boundaries upstream and downstream to keep them from wandering, and told them they could skinny dip within the marked off area. Seven of the boys organized a game of team keep-away with a slightly deflated ball they had found at the dump. Barbie was washing Fats' hair. Sniff had decided not to go swimming because he wasn't feeling well, and was the only one in the group who remained dressed. He sat on the bank and watched Charlie and Saturn construct boats using bark and leaves.

"Hey, Saturn. Come and play keep-away," Paul called to him.

"I'm makin' a boat," he answered.

"Come on, man." Scar gestured for him to come. "We need you."

"Sides ain't even," Rufus said.

"OK." Saturn waded toward them.

Charlie jumped up. "Can I play?" he asked.

"We only need one," Rufus said.

"To make the sides even," Paul explained. "Its three against four."

Charlie called after Saturn. "Don't go," he said.

Saturn hesitated briefly, and then continued wading toward the boys. "Just for a little," he said.

"I got no one to play with," Charlie said.

After Jerome left, Charlie sat down in the shallow water near the shore and started piling mud and sand on his head. He watched Barbie and Fats for a brief period while he did this, and then climbed out of the stream and sat down in the dust on the bank. Sniff came over and sat down beside him. "What you doin?" he asked.

"Le'me alone," Charlie said.

"I wasn't 'bout to ask you for nufin," Sniff said.

Ignoring him, Charlie went back down to the stream where he washed off all the mud. Then he got dressed and disappeared into the tent he shared with Barbie and Jerome. I didn't see Charlie again until supper time. He roasted hot dogs with the others, but didn't talk with anyone.

After supper Sniff complained of a headache. When I went to look for aspirin, I realized that I had left the first aid kit at the dump that morning. I selected Jerome, Charlie and Rufus to retrieve it for me. They were pleased. This would be an adventure.

I gave them careful instructions about where I had left the first aid kit, supplied each one with a flashlight, and told them to follow the path on the other side of the stream. I calculated that dusk would be upon us by the time they returned, but was confident that if they followed my instructions there was no way for them to get lost. After they left, I sat against a tree and had Sniff lean back against me. I massaged his head, especially around his temples and his brow, and asked him about his life in the city.

When the boys had not yet returned by sunset I began to get nervous. I had almost decided to go look for them when I heard something splashing up the stream, and saw the beam from a flashlight searching the darkness. Everybody gathered at the bank to look.

"It's Rufus," Roy said.

"What happened to you?" Paul asked.

"Where's the others?" Louie-Louie asked.

Rufus looked up at the boys on the bank. "A wild dog!" he exclaimed.

His eyes were wide with alarm, and he gestured in the general direction of the dump. "He come after us."

Gasping for breath, Rufus clambered out of the stream and into the clearing.

"Jerome 'n Charlie ain't with you?" Roy asked.

Several boys began asking Rufus questions at once.

Rufus flopped down on the ground. "Wait," he said. "Got to get my bref."

"Just say what happen," Pisser said.

"It was huge," Rufus said. He patted his chest, still gasping for air.

"Where's Charlie?" Sniff asked.

Rufus shrugged. "We run different ways," he said. He breathed deeply a couple of times. "Don't know if it got the others."

"Must have," said Louie-Louie.

"Probably had a whole pack wif him," Pisser said.

"They's dead for sure," Fats said.

"You don't know that," Paul said.

The boys all started talking at once, arguing and pressing Rufus for more information. "Everybody shut-up." Rufus hollered. This created a lull. "Can't answer no questions if everybody talk at once," he said.

"How many dogs you see?" Saturn asked.

"Just one," Rufus said. "But I heard more."

"Was one eye red?" Pisser asked.

"Couldn't tell. I think so."

"We need weapons," Pisser shouted.

Arguing and speculating about the fate of the two lost members of the group, each boy found something to use for a weapon and they retreated to the fort. They began debating whether to go try to find the boys and kill the dogs, or remain in the safety of the clearing. No one listened to the opinions of the others, or waited for them to stop talking before giving his own opinion.

"Hold it," I said. "Everybody quiet!"

"Everybody Shut up," Rufus said. "Listen to Mr. Foster."

"Only one person can give orders here, and that's got to be

me," I said.

"So what do we do?" asked Paul.

"You guys need to stay here," I said, "while I go see if I can find Charlie and Jerome."

Nobody argued.

I gave them instructions that they were not to leave the camp site, and said that I'd be back soon. I went to my tent to find my hatchet and a flashlight. When I pulled my head out of the tent, I noticed that Sniff had followed me. "I go with you," he said. He held a heavy stick in his hand. I thought about his offer for a moment, and then said, "OK"

It was then I noticed that something was wading across the stream toward us. The boys heard it too, and raised their weapons in readiness.

A dark figure could be seen across the stream. We waited in complete silence.

"Ain't no dog," Fats said, finally.

"It's a boy," Paul said.

"Who there?" Rufus called out.

"It's me, Jerome."

"You alive!" Pisser exclaimed.

"'Course." I noticed a little swagger in Jerome's step as he climbed the bank and came into the clearing.

"Dogs didn't get you," Louie-Louie said.

"Didn't touch me."

"Where's Charlie?"

"He comin'."

"What happen?" asked Scar

"Well, we found the first aid kit just where Mr. Foster said to look."

"Then what?" asked Pisser.

"Then, we was coming down the path not far from the

dump, and this big dog jump out at us on the path. And barks."

"Jeezum," Louie Louie said.

"Rufus jump in the stream," Jerome said. " I run back toward the dump. But Charlie he just stand there."

Jerome paused.

"Wow," said Pisser.

"Go on, man." Scar said.

"At the dump I find a big stick, and I hide behind some junk. Then I wait... I don't hear nothin'... I creep out and sneak down the path. I'm thinking Charlie might be dead. I hope they haven't chewed his head off. I hold my club up...'ready. Every little noise jump me. Well I go on down the path, and there's Charlie. He scratching that dog behind its ears like they been friends for life."

"Cool," said Pisser.

At that moment we were all startled by a deep barking not twenty yards away. Then we heard splashing. Again the boys raised their weapons. Out of the darkness two figures emerged – a huge mongrel, and Charlie.

"Easy, Dog," Charlie was saying. "Ain't nobody here goin' to hurt you." He ran his fingers through the brown shaggy fur around the dog's shoulders.

"I think the dog's a little afraid of us," I said. "Maybe if we would just sit down and get quiet it would be better."

"Yeah," said Charlie as he came to the fort. "Don't move too quick. You scare him."

As the boys settled, Charlie managed to get the dog to sit down.

"Can I pet it?" asked Paul."

"Sure," said Charlie.

Slowly and with great caution Paul approached the dog.

"He won't hurt you," Charlie said.

With this encouragement Paul petted the dog. "He's nice,"

he said.

"I call him Dog," Charlie said.

"How'd you tame him?" Paul asked.

Charlie looked at me. "With hot dogs," he said.

"I wondered where those extra hot dogs went to," I said.

"I borrowed a couple. Put 'em in my pocket." He smiled. He knew I wouldn't get after him for stealing the hot dogs – not in his moment of glory.

"So you fed 'em to Dog?" Paul asked.

"Yeah."

"That took guts," Scar said.

"No," Charlie said. "Its jus' I wasn't afraid."

Scar looked at Charlie, his eyes wide with disbelief. "Why not?"

"Dog's the same as me," Charlie said.

"How?" asked Paul.

"He's just somebody what got dumped out here," Charlie explained.

*****

At about two in the morning I was wakened by thunder. Soon a wind whipped up, causing the ill-made tents and the roof of the fort to flap wildly. I opened a peephole in the door of the tent and peered out. In the bright lightning flashes I could see the trees bending in the wind, and sheets of water flinging themselves against the flimsy structures we had erected against the elements. The electrical display let up after a bit, and the wind subsided. I hoped that the storm would soon be over, but it settled into a drenching rain that continued relentlessly. I prayed that the tents and the fort would prove more waterproof than I thought them to be, and I fell into an uneasy sleep. When I woke again my feet were wet. I pulled them further up in the sleeping bag and wondered how the others were doing.

Paul was the first to arrive with unwelcome news.

"Everybody in the fort's wet," he said.

"I see," I said.

Huddled in his poncho, he waited patiently for instructions. I couldn't think of anything to say.

"Well?" he said.

"How bad is it?"

"Some's worse than others."

While I lay in my sleeping bag, trying to formulate a plan of action, Louie-Louie woke. "I'm wet," he said.

"What's hap'nin?" Jerome asked. He propped himself on one elbow and rubbed the sleep out of his eyes with his free hand.

"Wait just a second, Paul," I said. I crawled out of my sleeping bag, pulled on my pants and shirt, and located my poncho. I still didn't have much of a plan, but thought I would walk around and assess the damage.

Just then Barbie appeared at the door of the tent. "Charlie's cryin," he said.

"What's the matter?"

"He say he need you."

"I'll go back with you," I said.

"OK," said Barbie.

I turned to Paul. "Look," I said, "This rain isn't going to let up. Everybody's wet. We got to go back."

"I think so," he said.

"Go and tell the boys in the fort to get up, try to find something dry to wear, put on a Poncho, and get their stuff together."

"OK," he said.

"That's three things," I said. "Put on dry clothes, get a poncho, and get their things together."

"I got it," he said.

I followed Barbie back to his tent. When I opened the flaps

and shined my flashlight in, I saw Charlie sitting in the middle of the tent, crying. Saturn was still huddled in his bag. It was hopelessly wet. "Get up, Saturn," I said. And try to get into something dry."

"OK," he said.

I crawled into the tent, and Barbie followed me.

"What the matter, Charlie?" I asked.

He was shivering. "I'm cold," he said. "I'm too cold."

"Do you have anything that's dry?" I asked.

"I'm too cold," he repeated.

"You got to get into something dry," I said.

"His things is all wet," said Barbie.

"I'm too cold, " Charlie said. He hugged himself and rocked forward and back. His lips were blue.

"He needs something dry," I said.

"My things is dry," Barbie said. "I keep 'em in a garbage bag."

"Do you have a dry towel?" I asked.

Surprisingly he produced one. I pulled Charlie the rest of the way out of his drenched sleeping bag. Then I pulled his wet T-shirt and underpants off, and dried him, toweling his body vigorously to try to generate a bit of heat. He stopped crying. Like a dutiful nurse, Barbie supplied from his own things a dry pair of underpants which I helped Charlie get into. Then he gave me a dry T-shirt, a ragged, but dry flannel shirt, and a mostly dry pair of pants.

"You're a wonder, Barbie," I said.

He smiled, and handed me a pair of socks.

We found a poncho for Charlie and sent him over to wait in the fort, which provided some protection if you avoided the leaky places. After Saturn got himself into the driest things he could find, I helped him and Barbie dismantle their tent and get their things together. By the time I finished with this task, and made my way to the fort, Jerome had seen to it that the other tent was taken down and ready to go.

For a few minutes the thirteen of us stood in silence in tattered rain coats and ponchos under the leaking roof of the fort. Charlie clung to one of my hands. Jerome was at my other side.

"It's been a good trip," I said. "But I guess we got to go home."

Nobody argued.

"Rufus, you know the way back. You take the front. Scar, you go with him. I don't want anybody in front of Rufus or Scar. Jerome and I will bring up the rear."

"Dog's gone," Charlie said.

"Probably went to find someplace dry," I said. "But you couldn't take him back anyhow."

"Sniff helped me find him food," Charlie said. He pointed to a little mound of leftover lunch meat and some other odds and ends, and smiled at Sniff.

Sniff smiled back and nodded. Then he turned to me. "Didn't steal nufin," he said. "Got it from the garbage."

"That's cool," I said.

"What about the other dogs?" Scar said.

"You worried about them still?" I asked.

He nodded. "Charlie, he got a way with dogs."

I looked at Charlie. "I think they need you up in front in case we run into more dogs," I said.

"I want to be with you," he said, squeezing my hand more tightly.

"They need you," I said.

He looked at Rufus and Scar, and then at me. "OK," he said. "I know 'bout dogs." He went to the pile of food left for Dog, selected a couple of pieces of lunch meat, and put them in his pocket.

With Charlie between them, Rufus and Scar led the way out

of the clearing and started down the path back to Forest Glen.

Dipshit

In the fall of 1973, on a little ranch, just outside the grounds of Rivera State Hospital, God appeared to me in the form of a boy pissing in the dust. At least that's how it seemed to me. Something like that once happened to Meister Eckhart so I suppose it's possible. But you can judge for yourself.

As a second year student working toward my Masters of Social Work, I had been assigned to the hospital as my field placement. In order to gain some experience in group work I formed a little club with a group of boys who resided at the hospital. They were an energetic bunch whose ages ranged from ten to thirteen. I frequently took them on hikes or "picnics" to provide them some relief from the depressing institutional atmosphere in which they lived.

A small horse ranch was nestled in the rolling hills that surrounded the hospital. My vision of God happened while I was visiting this ranch on an outing with my boy's club. This ranch was within easy walking distance from the hospital, and was one of our favorite destinations for a hike.

My five charges were lined up on the fence of the corral. They were watching two men as they tried to capture a couple of skittish horses. One stalked a sorrel. Tall and muscular, he faced the horse squarely, with his feet slightly apart and his arms spread a little, as though preparing to attack the beast with some sort of wrestling hold. He held a halter in one of his hands. I remember thinking how afraid I would have felt had I been that horse. Whenever the man got too close, the horse backed off or trotted away to one side or the other. The man was trying to maneuver the horse into a corner.   When the horse trotted by close to the fence where the boys were lined up, Tyler and Craig jumped down and backed away. Tyler stood at what he considered a safe distance and stared at the animal. Craig started flapping his hands. "Too many people," he said. "Too many people. Go home." Sean put his arm protectively around Randy, the smallest boy in our group, and the two of them remained on the fence.

The second man courted a brown and white pinto. His approach was oblique. His manner seemed to suggest that he just happened to be out here where the pinto also just happened to be, and if he made a little eye contact now and then with the horse, it was nothing more that a bit of friendliness – a flirtation almost.

"Can we ride em?" Oscar shouted. He stood on the fence next to me. My hand rested on his shoulder. He addressed the man who was courting the pinto.

"I'm not sure *we* can ride 'em," the man answered. He smiled at Oscar. The pinto backed off and trotted over to the other side of the corral.

Maybe he scared of your beard," Oscar said.

"Aaaah, probably just my bad breath," the man said.

Oscar laughed. "What's your name?"

"Ted. What yours."

"Oscar."

"Well, Oscar, that's Dipshit there, making hisself hard to get. Dipshit, meet Oscar. Oscar meet Dipshit."

"Hello, Dipshit," Oscar said. He glanced at me to see whether I might chastise him for using the "bad" word. I smiled to reassure him that I didn't care.

I felt somewhat relieved at Ted's friendliness. He, at least, didn't mind our being there. The other one I couldn't tell about as he didn't seem to notice anything in his world except the horse he was intent on capturing.

"That his real name?" Oscar asked me.

I shrugged. "Ask Ted."

"Hey Ted," he called out. "That his real name?"

"It's what I call him," Ted answered.

At that moment a shirtless boy of about nine emerged from the stable and wandered toward us. He was wearing dirty tennis shoes with no socks, and ragged blue jeans that hung low on his hips. Brushing his sorrel hair out of his eyes, he stared at Randy's round and amiable face. "Hi," Randy said. The boy ignored Randy's greeting.

Tyler, who had returned to the fence, stared at the newcomer. When their eyes met briefly, Tyler waved in his girlish manner, but was no more successful than Randy in eliciting a response. Only Craig, bouncing on his toes several feet from the fence and mumbling to himself, showed no interest in this boy.

"What's your name?" Oscar asked. The boy gave no sign of having heard.

"Ain't you got a name?" Oscar asked.

"Don't seem to hear you," Sean said.

Oscar spat in the dust. "Ain't got no sense," he said.

"Maybe he deaf," Sean said.

"Hey boy, you deaf?"

Still ignoring him, the boy turned his attention to me. I smiled and waved at him, wiggling my fingers slightly. He smiled back. I felt oddly thrilled by this ordinary response. Whether this child was retarded, or autistic or deaf I couldn't tell. Clearly there was something different about him, but if his face revealed his character, he was neither dull nor crude. His mouth was delicate and his eyes wide set and clear. I discerned a faint little wrinkle of worry between his brows.

He half turned slightly to one side, unzipped his pants, and urinated in the dust.

Perhaps it was his smile. Or maybe it was the bright, hot sun beating down on my head, or the sound of the crickets. Perhaps it was something about the way the urine splattered in the dust. Whatever the cause, all at once time seemed to stop. The boy became a mythical being – a luminous epiphany – an entity from another world that had, for some obscure reason, crowded its way into the ordinary little events of my life. All the other events and people in my life, both those that came before and those that were to follow, receded into an gray and only vaguely differentiated ground.

The boy in the corral rezipped his pants, turned back to me, and smiled again. Then he turned and sauntered across the corral and finally disappeared behind the stable.

I became aware that Oscar had been pulling at my sleeve for some time.

"What is it?" I asked..

"That boy got no manners," Oscar said. He turned up his nose in disgust.

"Pee pee," Randy said.

"Shut up," Oscar said. "Don't talk baby talk."

I brushed Oscar's hand off my shirt. "Don't tug at me that way," I said, irritably.

He dropped his hand and turned away. I knew that I had hurt his feelings.

Ted had caught the Sorrel, and was leading him over to the fence where we stood.

"Horsy, horsy," Randy called. He had climbed onto the fence and was reaching out to greet him..

"Shut up," Oscar said.

"He can talk if he wants to," Sean said.

"Shouldn't use baby talk." Oscar said. "Mrs. Shepard says that."

"You ain't his boss," Sean said.

The two boys stared directly at each other for several seconds. Sean was bigger, and had once fought Oscar when Oscar had called him a "nigger." A staff member had pulled them apart before it became clear who was going to win. Oscar dropped his eyes. "Well, it sounds dumb," he said.

"Hey guys, you want to pet Dipshit?" Ted asked. He was at the fence with the pinto.

Oscar reached out toward the horse with a sudden movement. The horse raised up slightly with a whinny, and backed off. Ted patted him. "Easy boy." He turned to Oscar. "Move slow," he said. "Dipshit's the nervous type."

As he eased the horse back toward the fence, Randy climbed down and backed away. Craig stopped bouncing on his toes, and studied the horse out of the corner of his eyes.

"Hey, Dipshit," said Oscar. "I got an apple. You want an apple?" Oscar had collected some small, hard, green apples from a tree in the field. They were too sour to eat, but were good for throwing. He pulled one from his pocket and offered it to the pinto, holding it at arms length. The horse approached, sniffed the apple, and slobbered all over Oscar's hand as he tried to get it. Oscar pulled his hand back, allowing the apple to fall to the ground. The horse picked it up and ate it. Oscar wiped his hand on his pants. "Will he bite?" he asked.

"Not on purpose," Ted answered. "Hold your hand out flat with the apple on it, like so." He demonstrated with a small piece of carrot that he pulled from his pocket.

When Oscar tried what Ted showed him with another apple, Dipshit took it from his hand. Oscar reached out, slowly, and patted the horse on his forehead.

"We friends now ," he said to the horse. He turned to me. "See, I made friends with him."

"Cool," I said.

"Way to go," Ted said. He reached over the fence and ruffled Oscar's hair.

"Who's the boy?" I asked Ted.

"Who?"

"The boy who was just in the corral."

"Ah, you must of seen Jan," Ted said. "That's Mike's boy." He gestured toward the man with the sorrel. "Mike owns the place here."

Oscar was leaning over the fence petting Dipshit on the neck. "Can I ride him, Ted?" he asked.

"Can't let you," Ted said. "I got to take Dipshit back to the stable now. Mike needs me."

"How come?" Oscar asked.

"He's got Asskicker."

"Asskicker?"

"That other horse."

Oscar smiled. "That his real name?"

"It's what I call him."

Mike was leading he big sorrel around the corral on a halter. The horse would follow willingly for a few paces, and then balk. Mike would jerk his head back into line and pull him forward. The horse would follow him again for a while.

As Ted led Dipshit back to the stable, Mike called to him. "Bring a saddle and bridle."

Just as Ted disappeared into the stable with Dipshit, I saw Jan again. Keeping a safe distance between himself and Asskicker, he edged toward us. He carried a stick with a single green leaf on it. When he was about four yards away I called out. "Hello Jan."

He stopped without looking at me.

I could feel my heart beating within my chest. I was afraid that I had called too loudly. I waited.

Eventually he turned his head slightly, and allowed eye contact.

"Hi, Jan," I said, and smiled.

"Hey, they're going to do something with Asskicker," Oscar said, pulling at my sleeve. I pushed his hand away.

Jan smiled back. "Jan," he said.

"You live here, Jan?" I asked.

He didn't answer, but came over and stood directly in front

of me.

"It's a nice day, huh?" I said.

He stared at me, his head tilted slightly to one side. Then he reached out and handed me the stick.

"Thank you," I said, taking it. "It's nice." I looked around to find a pretty rock or a flower to give to him. Then I reached into my pocket thinking maybe I could give him a coin. I paused. I didn't want him to think I was paying for the stick, but I did want to give him a present in return. Then, buried in a corner of my pocket, I found a piece of hard candy. I unwrapped it and handed it to Jan. He popped it into his mouth.

Jan stared at me for some time, sucking on his candy. Then he mumbled something that I took to be "who you?" He didn't talk very clearly, and sucking on the candy at the same time didn't help. A bit of saliva dribbled out of the corner of his mouth, but he made no effort to wipe it away.

We're from Rivera," I said. He stared at me without giving any indication that he understood.

"Rivera State Hospital, dummy," Oscar said. "Over there." He pointed. A couple of the buildings were visible across some fields.

Jan looked where Oscar indicated. "Hospital." He repeated the word in a vague questioning manner.

Then he turned and walked away.

"Look," Oscar said. "They're going to ride him."

I allowed my attention to be drawn to the men with Asskicker.

"I ain't sure he's ready," I heard Ted say.

"I want to try," Mike said. "Hold him."

Ted held the horse firmly. He patted him and talked to him while Mike put the saddle on and fastened it in place. The horse shied and pulled this way and that. He was obviously not pleased with the process. It took several efforts, but Mike finally managed to cram the bit into the horse's mouth. Ted removed the halter and stood back. Mike held the reins firmly. The horse tried to rear up, but Mike pulled down hard on the reins and slapped him on the side of his head. "Bad horse," he said. He moved over to the horse's side and, when the animal was still for a moment, slipped his foot into the stirrup. He stabilized himself for a few seconds, and then, with surprising agility, he swung himself up onto the horse's back. True to the nickname given him by Ted, the horse's left back leg shot out in a kick. Ted, however, had made sure to keep himself a safe distance from the horse. The horse bucked a couple of times, but Mike remained in the saddle.

The children at the fence were wild with excitement.

"Wow," screamed Oscar. "Ridem Cowboy!"

Randy backed away from the fence, and Sean went with him, putting his arm around his shoulder for comfort. Tyler edged over to me and slipped his hand into mine. Craig paced back and forth along the fence, watching the events in the corral out of the corner of his eyes. "Too many people," he said. "Too many people. Go home. Too many people."

The horse stopped bucking and began running around the corral. He appeared uncontrollable to me. But the bit was a fulcrum by which Mike was able to get the leverage he needed to overpower the will of the much stronger animal beneath him. As they careened by the fence, even Oscar jumped off and backed away. I could see, as they went by, that the horse was bleeding around his mouth.

The ride did not last long. Very soon after he established control of the animal, Mike dismounted. He handed the reins to Ted. "Good," Mike said. "That was a beginning."

Ted nodded, and began walking Asskicker around the corral, talking gently to him.

"I'll have him doing tricks before cold weather comes," Mike bragged. He turned and strode toward the stable. Then, much to the boys delight, Asskicker shat. His back was to the boys, giving them a perfect view of the process.

"Awesome," Oscar said.

"Poo-poo," Randy said.

"Will you shut up?" Oscar said.

Watching Ted walk Asskicker around the ring soon became dull. Tyler returned to his search for dandelions and Oscar joined him. I was alone at the fence now. I listened to the insects humming and buzzing in the tall grass that surrounded the corral, and watched the lazy puffy clouds floating across the sky. Things moved around me, but I felt myself watching from a place of unexpected and perfect stillness. Then I saw Jan again. He was approaching me from a different part of the corral. This time he had a slightly tattered bit of goldenrod in his hand. He ambled slowly but purposefully, in my direction. I felt a growing excitement as he came nearer.

"Hello again, Jan," I said when he stood in front of me. He smiled and handed me the goldenrod.

"Is this your home, Jan?"

He mumbled something I could not understand.

"Do you have a horse?" I asked.

"Horses," he said. And he pointed to the stable.

Suddenly I felt something heavy land on my back. It was Oscar. He had a handful of dandelions. "For you," he said, and began stuffing them down the back of my shirt.

"Cut it out," I said.

He backed off, laughing wildly. I pulled the dandelions out of the back of my shirt. Most of them were badly mangled, but I found one that seemed to be in better condition than the rest and handed it to Jan.

"Hey, that's mine," Oscar yelled.

Jan took the dandelion and left. He walked more rapidly now and soon disappeared behind the stable.

I turned to Oscar. "Why are you such a pain?" I asked.

"I brought you some flowers," he said. He picked up the remains of his bouquet from the ground and threw them in my face, laughing.

I turned away from Oscar and walked up along the fence toward the other boys. Tyler, who had been sitting in a patch of dandelions, saw me coming. He stood up. "Look at me," he said. He had a necklace of dandelions hanging around his neck.

"That's pretty," I said.

"Tyler pretty," he said, dancing around in circles. "Look at me."

I was aware that Oscar had followed me, but I was deliberately ignoring him. When I felt him pulling at my shirt sleeve I turned and faced him. He had a green stick in his hand. It was a little thicker, perhaps, than a pencil. Without any warning he swung it in my direction and hit me across the front of my pants.

"Jesus, Oscar. That hurt," I said.

"Just playing," he said, with a silly grin on his face.

"Well, It's not the least Goddamn bit funny," I said.

"Just playing," he repeated, in a more subdued tone of voice.

I grabbed him by the shoulders and shook him. "Well, don't play any more. Just leave me alone. OK?"

With lowered head he wandered off a little ways from the group and sat down in the grass, with his back to me.

I was trying to gain some control over my feelings when I heard Randy scream.

"Christ, what now?" I said under my breath.

Sean was herding Randy in my direction. Although I could discern no obvious injury, Randy continued to scream as they approached.

"What is it?" I asked.

"A bee, Sean said. "A bee got him." He pulled Randy's arm up and showed it to me. A red bump was beginning to form, and in its center I could see the stinger. I pulled it out. "That will help," I said.

Ted called out from the corral where he was walking

Asskicker. "What happened," he asked.

"A bee got him," I said.

"Just a minute," Ted said.

While I tried to comfort Randy, Ted took Asskicker into the stable. He emerged a few moments later, Asskicker still in tow, and came our way. Randy looked up apprehensively as the man with the big horse approached, and he stopped crying.

"It's okay," I said, as he backed off. "the horse can't get over that fence."

Ted handed me a tube of ointment. "Put some of this on it," he said.

"What is it?" I asked.

"Stuff we use for horses when they get stung or hurt," he said.

I took it over to Randy. "Let me put some on your arm," I said. "Make the pain go away."

Randy held out his arm uncertainly, and allowed me to apply the ointment. I waved my hand over the area that was stung in order to add a bit of magic to the treatment. "When I count to three" I said, " the pain will go away."

When I finished counting Randy looked at me. "Hurts," he said.

"It takes a minute," I said.

Sean put his arm around Randy. "It be better soon," he said.

Oscar had returned to the group. "Randy's a cry baby," he said. "I don't cry when I get stung."

"Leave him alone," Sean said.

"Cry baby, cry baby," Oscar chanted.

"I said leave him alone." Sean glowered at Oscar.

When Oscar turned and walked off, I followed him. I saw him turn his head and I knew he saw me. He began walking faster. I had to practically run to catch up. I put my arm around his shoulder. "Hey, I'm sorry I talked so mean to you," I said. He shook my hand off his shoulder but he stopped walking.

"I don't know what else to say. I'm sorry."

He stood with his back to me, staring at the buildings of the hospital.

"Come on back, and lets get the group together, I said."

He didn't budge.

"Look Oscar. You were being a pest. You asked for some of what you got."

He started walking away from me. I watched, trying to decide what to do next. I couldn't just let him leave the group. "Please come back, Oscar." He kept walking. "OK," I hollered at the back of his head. "It was mostly my fault. I'm sorry." This didn't slow him down either. I watched helplessly.

Then, all at once, I knew what to do. I started galloping after him. I was a wild mustang. I cantered past him, whinnying and tossing my head. He stopped and stared. I swung back and circled around him, prancing and whinnying. He smiled just a little.

"I could be your horse," I said.

"Yeah?"

"Yeah," I said. I hunkered down in the grass, and offered him my back. "Get on."

He climbed on, piggyback style, and I stood up. Then I galloped back up to the corral to where the other boys waited for us. Sean was still comforting Randy. Tyler was trying to get a dandelion behind his ear so that it would stay. Craig was pacing back and forth on his toes. "Too many people," he was saying "Go home." But he was not quite so frantic now that Randy had calmed down.

"We got to go, " I said.

"I get to ride next," Sean said.

"OK," I said, "if I still have the energy."

With Oscar firmly in the saddle, I began leading the boys

toward the buildings that could be seen beyond the fields. When I looked back over my shoulder at the corral, I saw Jan standing near the fence, watching us leave. I wanted to go back to him. I wanted to hold him. I wanted to take him with me. I wanted at least to wave to him, but my hands were serving as stirrups for Oscar. I doubted that Jan would have waved back in any case.

"Giddy-up," Oscar hollered at me, bouncing up and down on my back in an effort to get me to move faster. "Giddy-up, Dipshit."

Running, leaping, prancing and twisting around dangerously this way and that, I followed his command. Soon we were both laughing.

The Whale Children

Wearing his newest blue jeans, and a dressy yellow shirt, Paul clearly had given some attention to his appearance in preparation for this appointment. He flopped down on the couch in my office, took a comb out of his hip pocket, and ran it through his blond hair.

"Are Alicia and Eugena coming?" he asked.

I sat down in the easy chair opposite him. "They should be here pretty soon," I said. "It's still a little early."

It was 10:40. The visit, in which he and his sisters were to say good-bye to their mother, was set for 11:00.

He nodded. "And Mom?"

"Far as I know, she's coming."

"She may not."

"Why do you say that?"

"She hates goodbyes."

"And you?"

"Me?"

"How are you on good-byes?"

"Not too good." He looked down at his shirt and brushed off a piece of lint that was too tiny for me to see.

"How are you feeling about the session?"

He shrugged. "I don't think it's really good-bye," he said.

"Your mother's agreement with the Department of Human Services is that this is the final visit," I said. "That would mean that she would not be a part of your life anymore – unless you should decide to change this when you reach eighteen."

"That's seven years from now," he said, rolling his eyes slightly.

"It's a long time," I said.

He nodded. "Too long." He put his hands in his pockets, slumped back on the couch, and peered at me through the slightly oversized glasses that gave him a bookish appearance. "No judge said this was final, did they?"

"Your mother agreed to it without taking it to court. The worker from DHS told me that when she asked me to supervise the good-bye visit."

"Why didn't she take it to court?"

"I don't know. What do you think?"

He sat up, leaned toward me, and shook his head. "I don't know either," he said. "Maybe she doesn't have money for a lawyer."

"The court could appoint her one."

He slumped back onto the couch and we were both silent for a while.

"I wish she'd hurry up and get here," he said.

"It won't be long."

He stood up, went over to the window, and pulled the curtain aside. "Here come Alicia and Eugena." He said.

"Good." I came over and looked out the window with him. I could see the girls coming across the parking lot. Their foster mother had sent them to the appointment by Med-Ride, a transportation service for people who can't afford the cost of getting to their medical and therapy appointments. As soon the driver saw me looking out the window, he waved and drove off.

"She'll come get me." Paul said this in a low voice, almost as if he were speaking only to himself.

"Sorry," I said. "I didn't catch that."

He looked over at me. "I said Mom will come get me.

Whatever DHS or the Court say, when she's ready she'll come and get me."

I didn't have a chance to respond. Alicia was already coming through the door into my office.

"Hello Paul," she said, giving him a hug. He returned her hug politely.

She pulled off her stocking hat, revealing a neatly trimmed afro, and let her coat fall on the floor behind her.

"Do I get a hug too?" I asked.

She nodded and I lowered myself to my knees, which brought me face to face with her. She threw her arms around my neck. "Is Mama here yet?" she asked, clinging a little more tightly than usual.

"Sure. I'm keeping her in the file drawer over there, until we are ready for her."

She smiled. "I mean really."

"Not yet. Are you... concerned." I didn't like the adult word, "concerned," but couldn't think of another one that was as indefinite as I wished it to be.

Alicia shrugged and sat down on the floor to take her boots off.

Eugena had arrived while I was talking to Alicia, and had greeted Paul without any show of enthusiasm. Being only a year and a half younger than Paul, she was not oblivious to his coolness. I was startled to see that her afro had been cut. Even with her new hair cut, though, she was still a strikingly beautiful child with her high cheek bones, her large soft eyes, and her smooth brown skin. She wore woolen stockings for warmth, as did her sister, and a long colorful dress. Both girls wore sweaters. Eugena's was pink with a picture of a cat on it.

"Is Mama really going to do it?" Alicia asked. I noticed the odd little wrinkle in her brow that made her look chronically astonished.

"It?" I said.

Tony threw one of her boots to the side of the room and began struggling with the other one. "You know. Leave?"

"I guess that's the plan," I said. "That's what we are here to talk about."

She threw the second boot in the general direction of the first. "Its dumb," she said.

"I guess this is pretty hard for you."

"Can I make a picture?" she asked, ignoring my comment, and crossing the room to the easel.

"I think we should probably all sit around in a circle when your mama comes, and not be playing or painting," I said.

"Just until she comes," Alicia pleaded.

"All right." I said. "But she may be here any minute now."

"OK." She took out a large sheet of newsprint, and fixed it to the easel, which was close to the wall, beside the window. Then she took out the magic markers. As she worked she tore off several sheets and threw them aside and began again.

Eugena and Paul, meanwhile, had claimed seats. Paul took the big easy chair that I usually use, and Eugena captured a place on the couch. I asked the children about how things were going for them at school, and got only one-word answers.

At five minutes after the hour Paul said, "She's always late. She'll probably be here any minute."

We sat, awkward and fidgeting, the only sound being the occasional squeak of Alicia's magic marker on the newsprint.

"I'm in basketball this year," Eugena said finally.

"That's nice," I said. How's your team doing?"

"We haven't had any games yet."

"I see."

The silence reasserted itself. At nine minutes after the hour Alicia whispered, "she's here." Both the other children hurried over to the window. Eugena waved.

Ginger Gagnon entered the office like a movie star. She

wore a fur coat, probably simulated, I thought, though I'm no judge of such things. Her blond hair was piled high. She handed me the coat to hang up. "Hello children," she said.

She was wearing tight-fitting black slacks, a frilly white blouse, and high heel shoes. Heavy make-up superimposed a second face over her real one. A black pearl necklace and dangling gold earrings completed her costume. "Isn't anybody going to give their mother a hug?" She asked.

"Sure Mom." Paul went over and wrapped his arms around her. He was almost as tall as his mother. Then Eugena took her turn. Alicia continued with her picture.

"And is that my other daughter hiding over there?"

Alicia peered out from behind the easel. Her face was dark and serious, the wrinkle in her forehead pronounced. "Hello Mama."

"Are you going to give me a hug, honey?"

Alicia slowly walked across the room to her mother, who removed the magic marker from her hand before allowing herself to be hugged. The hug completed, Alicia returned to the easel.

Ginger joined Eugena on the couch, looked at me, and smiled. She appeared to be waiting for me to give some structure to the situation.

"Alicia," do you want to join us?" I asked.

"No."

"We can't see you very well behind the easel."

"I want to finish my picture," she said.

I frowned. "Maybe you could finish it later," I said. "I think it's important for you to be a part of things."

"I'll turn the easel around so you can see me," she said. She pivoted the easel to where she could be seen but the picture she was working on could not.

"Well, okay, but you have to listen to what is going on."

She nodded. "I will."

Once again we were caught in an awkward silence, with everybody looking at me.

"I think all of you know that your mother and the department of Human Services have come to an agreement," I said finally.

"Is it true, Mom?" Paul asked.

"Yes, Dear."

"You're not going to see us anymore?"

"Not for a while."

"Until we are eighteen?"

She twisted her body around, as though she couldn't find a comfortable position on the couch. "I guess that would be it," she said.

"What about our agreement, Mom?"

"What agreement?"

Paul looked around the room at the other children, then at Ginger. "That you were going to come and get me out of foster care and we were going to live together – just you and me. And none of those stupid boy friends."

"Just the two of you?" Eugena asked. "What about me? And Alicia? You didn't tell Paul that, did you Mom?"

"Well, seeing as Paul is the biggest, and I needed someone strong... I may have said something like that. But I didn't mean that I wouldn't also come to get you and Alicia."

"When?" Eugena asked.

"Well, I don't know. It's not all that definite."

Ginger looked at me. "This isn't going very well," she said.

I shrugged, and looked around the room at the children. "I guess things like this never really go very well," I said.

"Are you going far away?" Eugena asked.

Ginger nodded. "Yes, very far."

"Where?"

"Mexico."

"How are you going to get to Mexico?" Paul asked.

"Well, there's this guy I've met..."

Paul rolled his eyes. "Another guy."

"This one's different. He's nice. He's got a good job in a fruit company down in Mexico."

"What about us?" Paul asked.

"And the twins," Eugena added. Before the three children in the room had come into foster care, Ginger had also given birth to a set of twins that had been taken by the state and had since been adopted.

Ginger glared at Eugena. "You guys are well taken care of," she said. "I couldn't look after you like these foster homes do."

"But it's not the same," Eugena said.

Ginger sighed. "You got more than I had when I was a kid," she said. She took a pack of cigarettes from her pocket book, began to tap one out, and then realized that she couldn't smoke in my office. With an impatient sigh she put the cigarettes back in the pocketbook. "I've never had a life," she said. "My mom was a whore, really. Never had no time for me. Soon as I got old enough to get out on my own, I had all you kids."

Her look at me was a plea to help her out. When I just nodded, non-committally, she turned her attention back to the children. "I'm not blaming you, understand. I mean you never asked to come into this world." She opened her pocket book to get a cigarette again, and then closed it. "But look at it from my side." she continued. She looked at me again. "I just wanted some nice things, and to have some fun, and maybe have a little freedom to do what I liked, and my whole life becomes just wiping asses and wiping noses and cooking and cleaning. I just couldn't take it."

For some time the only noise was the squeak of a magic marker on newsprint as Alicia continued methodically working on her picture. Finally Eugena spoke. "But now we could mostly look after ourselves," she said.

"Honey, it just won't work. There's too much water under the bridge."

"I guess we need to find a way to say good-bye," I said.

Eugena began to cry. "It's too long, Mama," she said. I handed her a box of tissues.

"Don't cry honey," Ginger said. "You got people to take care of you."

Paul came over and sat on the arm of the couch. From there he was able to put his arms around Ginger's neck. "It doesn't have to be until we're 18," he said.

"We'll see, Honey." Ginger extricated herself and stood up. "I don't see any point in dragging this thing out," she said. "Good bye is good-bye. There's not a lot more to be said."

I thought she was probably right, so I didn't intercede. Eugena stood up and hugged her mother tightly.

I went around behind the easel with Alicia and looked at her picture. In the middle of the page she had drawn a large zeppelin shaped form, with a fish tail on one end and an eye and mouth on the other. Inside this form there were little circles, and a couple of creatures that appeared to be baby fish. Outside the form, beginning near the tail, a progression of babies began, each one a little larger, as they swam away.

"It's a whale mother," she said.

"Maybe your mother would be interested in this," I said, loud enough to be heard by Ginger.

Ginger had just pulled herself away from Eugena's grip. "What you got honey?" Ginger came around to look at the picture.

"A whale."

"It looks like a cucumber," Ginger said.

"It's a mother whale," I said.

"Those are its babies," Alicia said, indicating the ones inside.

"And these," I asked, indicating the little circles. "What are they?"

"Those are eggs. They haven't hatched yet. First they hatch, and then they are babies, and then they come out of the mother."

"Looks like she's got a lot of babies," Ginger said.

"She does." Alicia said.

"And what are these babies doing?" I asked, indicating the progression of whale babies swimming away from the mother.

"They're going to the Porpoise," Alicia said. She paused to think. Ginger and I stood on either side of her, staring at her picture. Alicia pointed to the picture. "The Whale mother gave her babies to the Porpoise mother," she said.

"What a funny thing for her to do," Ginger said.

"Yes," Alicia agreed. "Why did the Whale mother give her babies to the Porpoise mother?"

"I'm sure I don't know," Ginger said. "But look, honey. Give Mama a hug. I've got to go."

Alicia allowed herself to be hugged without reciprocating.

Ginger looked at me. "I don't know what you are thinking," she said. "But you can see it just didn't work out."

"I understand," I said. "Sometimes things just don't work out."

She sighed. "Maybe I need to start all over."

"How do you mean?"

"You know. Start another family with some other kids. Try to do it right."

I was speechless.

Paul said he wanted to go with his mother to the car, and after she put on her coat, he walked out with her.

"It's a very fine picture," I said to Alicia. "Maybe we can talk about it next time you come and see me."

"Will you keep it?"

"Yes. I'll take good care of it," I said.

I went over to the couch and sat down beside Eugena who was still crying. I put my arm around her.

The Med-Ride car arrived early, and the two girls left. When he was alone in the room with me, Paul pulled a piece of paper out of his pocket, and showed it to me.

"See," he said. "It's her address – its where she'll be in Mexico."

"She gave you that?" I asked.

He nodded triumphantly. "Yes. I'll write to her every week, and when she gets all set, she'll come for me."

*****

Three progress notes describing sessions with the different children will serve to give a general idea of how things developed after the "good-bye visit." The first is Paul's next visit to me, only a week later.

Progress Note

Name: Paul Gagnon

Date: March 14, 1992

Time: 1 hour

Goal: #4, Help Paul to become reconciled to being abandoned by his mother.

Description of the session: Paul arrived in surprisingly good spirits. He told me that he had written to his mother and sent his letter to the address she gave him. I reminded him of the times in the past when she had not kept her word, and in this way I tried to prepare him for the disappointment he will feel if she does not follow through on her promise. He admitted that she sometimes did not keep her word, but said he said she would not desert him. He sincerely believes that she will abandon the girls but not him. I asked him why he felt she would choose only him.

"Because I'm white," he said.

"Why would being white make a difference?" I asked.

"Because," he said, "she's white, same as me."

Although I think it's unlikely she will come for him, there is some truth in what he says. She has treated him with favoritism because his father was white.

"If some day I just disappear," he told me as he was leaving, "don't worry. I'll be with her."

Progress Note
Name: Eugena Gagnon
Date: March 28, 1992
Time: 1 hour
Goal: #3, Help Eugena develop and maintain a sense of self esteem and self efficacy.

Description of the session: Eugena lacked animation today. Early in the session she got out the dress-up clothes and dressed herself with all the fancy jewelry she could put on, the high heel shoes, etc. She took a red skirt and put it on her head so that it became hair. Then she strutted around the room, as one would imagine a Barbie doll might act should some malevolent genie bring her to life.

"You're a glamorous woman with long red hair," I said.

"I'm a famous movie star," she said.

"And the red hair, is that to make you more beautiful?"

She came out of character at this point. "Yes," she said.

"You don't like your hair?"

"It's ugly."

"Is that why you got rid of your afro?"

She nodded.

"I think your hair is beautiful," I said. "And you are a beautiful girl. Just as you are. You don't need to do lots of things to change how you look."

"I don't think I'm pretty."

We talked more about this. Her only consolation was that she was at least lighter colored than her sister, Alicia. I did what I could to get her to see this differently, but with little success.

I plan to give her foster mother the name of a magazine that tries to help black kids overcome their heritage of spoiled identity.

In the last part of the session she talked about her devastation at having been abandoned by her mother. As she sees it, she's not desirable enough for her mother to hang onto.

At least she is talking about it.

Progress Note
Name: Alicia Gagnon
Date: April 7, 1992
Time: 1 hour
Goal #7: Facilitate transition to her adoptive home.
Description of the session: Alicia didn't want to talk much about her mother abandoning her. I allowed her to play a while. She drove a toy tractor around the room pushing other things out of its way. Then I suggested that we do a picture of the tractor, and tell a story about it. She agreed. After she did the picture, she dictated the following story:

Once there was a tractor. It lived in the forest. And it was so small that it was a little baby. And it had nothing to eat. It had no family. And he always went to plow. Then the snow went away and came back. After that the tractor found a family. Then he had some food.

I then told her a story aimed at helping her have a hopeful attitude toward finding a good adoptive family.

Progress notes are very brief thumbnails meant for public consumption. The three reproduced above are accurate as far as they go, but, as always, a great deal is edited out. Nothing, for example, is conveyed about the delight I experienced while Alicia sat in my lap listening to the story I told her.

The plot was very simple. Girl loses one family. (I had tigers eat them). Girl decides to find another family. Girl has adventures overcoming dangers in the lonely forest. Girl finds new family. The major danger in the forest was Glimmel, a fat and slimy 300 pound frog who terrorized everybody and for lunch liked to eat little girls in sandwiches.

There was no particular plot connected with her finding the new family in the forest. She just happened upon this cottage in a clearing, and it just happened to be occupied with a very nice middle-aged couple who had for many years been pinning away about their inability to have a little girl of their very own. I spent some time dwelling on all the good things they had in their refrigerator and cupboard, for they liked to eat well. As I enumerated the kinds of cookies and candies, the different types of jellies, the deserts, the breakfast foods, the wide selection of ice cream toppings, the various brands of potato chips, and all the other delicacies they stocked, her lovely dark eyes, beneath her wrinkled brow, gave me undivided and serious attention.

"But," I said. "They didn't have any celery in the house – not a single stick."

"Why?" she asked.

"Because they didn't believe in celery," I said.

*****

While waiting for Eugena to arrive for her April 14th appointment, I sat in my office and reread the letter from the Columbus Ohio Department of Human Services. It was a response to my letter to them, in which I asked about the possibility of Eugena and Alicia returning to live with their natural father:

> *Dear Mr. Fuller,*
>
> *I regret to tell you that Mr. Gagnon, the father of Eugena and Alicia, has not fully cooperated with the Department's efforts to complete a home study, nor has he indicated unequivocal interest in gaining custody of his children. In view of this demonstrated lack of motivation on his part, we are recommending to the Department of Human Services in your state that they proceed with the adoption.*
>
> *If we can be of any further assistance in this matter please let us know.*
>
> *Sincerely yours,*
>
> *Ms. Gloria Green*

Eugena had talked a fair bit about her father and her grandmother in Columbus. She, Alicia, and their mother had lived with them until Eugena was seven. Alicia was too young to remember very much, but Eugena's memories were positive.

"Daddy told me stories like you do," Eugena said during one session. And she told me of the wonderful meals her grandmother prepared for the family. But a card and small present each Christmas and birthday was the extent to which the children now heard from their father and grandmother. I had my doubts as to whether they would prove to be a resource, but at Eugena's encouragement, I wrote to the Department of Human Services asking them if they could look into the matter. This led to my telephone conversation with the father of the girls. He was a soft-spoken man.

"I hope the girls are doing okay," he said.

"They're fine kids." I said.

"I wish I could do more for them."

"Eugena has very good memories of being with you."

"We had some good times. But I couldn't get along with their mother."

"Eugena is still hoping that you could get custody of her and Alicia. She would like to live with you."

I heard a sigh. Then there was silence for a few moments. "I'd like to have the girls with me," he said, finally. "I think about it all the time. But Human Services is against me. They'd never allow it."

"You could take it to court," I suggested.

"Nobody ever wins against Human Services."

"Why do you think the Department has it in for you?"

"I've got a little drinking problem. Once when I was drunk I hit their mother. So they say I'm a dangerous person."

"Do you think you are?"

"That's the only time I ever hit anyone."

"What's your living situation now?"

"I live with my mother."

"Do you think you and she could together provide the kids a good place to live?"

"I'm sure we could."

"I think it would mean a lot to Eugena if you tried to get her back, even if you didn't succeed."

The silence on the other end of the phone line told me he was thinking about this. "Yeah," he said. "It might."

"It would probably need to begin with a request for the Ohio Department of Human Services to do a home study," I said.

He said he needed time to think about that. When I called him back the next day, he told me he had talked with his mother, and they had decided to give it a try. Eugena was thrilled when I told her this. I emphasized that it might not work out.

I reread the letter from the Columbus Department of Human Services, and asked myself why he had given up so easily. There was no way to know. The conclusion, however, was clear. The girls would not be returning there to live

*****

Upon entering the play room Eugena announced that she wanted to draw pictures.

"We can do that," I said. "But first I have some news from the Ohio Department of Human Services." I showed her the letter.

"Oh? What did they say?"

"It's not real good."

She threw herself down on the couch and crossed her arms in front of her. "Well, what is it?"

"It looks like you probably won't be able to go there to live."

"What they got against my dad?"

"Would you like me to read the letter?"

She nodded.

When I finished the letter from the Columbus Department of Human Services, Eugena slouched back on the couch, but said nothing.

"Do you have any questions?" I asked.

"It means my father isn't trying very hard, doesn't it?"

"He doesn't seem to be making every effort he could," I said.

"So I'm going to be adopted."

"That would be the plan at this point."

She let her head fall on her chest, and I felt her withdrawing, like a snail pulling back into its shell.

"I wish I could make your father do things differently," I said.

She shrugged. Then she got up from the couch and went over to the easel. "I think I want to make a picture."

She clipped a new sheet of paper to the easel, and took out the markers.

"How do you feel about the letter?" I asked.

"Don't want to talk about it." She began working on a picture. I sat with my back to my desk, and watched her draw. With painstaking care she created a picture of a princess with rosy cheeks and long blond hair dressed in an elaborate, many colored dress.

As she was putting the finishing touches on her picture I began a story. "Once upon a time there was a girl who had a Great Dane as a pet. It was a strong and handsome dog, and she was quite attached to it."

"What was it's name?" she asked.

"Hannibal."

"That's a silly name."

"Can't be helped," I said. I went over the couch to sit. "One morning the girl let Hannibal out to play and he failed to return home. She worried about him all afternoon. By bedtime he had still not returned. That night she lay awake, wondering what happened to him. For days she hunted for the dog, and couldn't find him anywhere. Then one day she got a call from a friend."

"'I know where Hannibal is,' her friend said."

"'Where?'"

"'He went to Susie's house. He's living there.'"

"'Why?'"

"She feeds him the canned stuff. He likes that better than the crunchy dog food you feed him.'"

"Stupid dog," Eugena said.

"I need your help with the story," I said. "What did the girl do then?"

"How should I know?"

"Well, what would you do with a dog like that?"

"I'd poison it."

"So the girl poisoned Hannibal," I said. "Then what happened?"

"It died a horrible death."

"So Hannibal began having terrible convulsions, and after he suffered horribly for a long time he finally died."

"Served him right," Eugena said.

"That girl must have been really angry at Hannibal to do such a thing," I said.

"Of course she was mad. That dog was supposed to be her friend. But it just threw her away for nothing."

"Does it seem like your father threw you away like that?"

"I said I didn't want to talk about it."

"Are you sort of pissed at him?"

"That's a bad word."

"I suppose it is," I said. "But no nice word can do the job."

She stared at the proper young princess with the blond hair for quite some time. "I'm pissed," she said finally.

"I should think you would be."

"I'm pissed, pissed, pissed, pissed." Her eyes began to fill up with tears. "Why didn't he try harder?" She asked. She came over and sat on the couch with me.

"I don't know," I said, putting my arm around her. She took hold of my hand with both of hers, and leaned her head back against the hollow between my chest and my shoulder.

"There must be something wrong with me," she said.

"No," I said. "I think there must be something wrong with him."

*****

Why do I not like this woman? I asked myself, as she sat across from me in my office. Her stylish dress, her excessively correct diction and grammar, even her tallness – everything about her grated on my nerves. Janet McPherson and her husband, Richard, had learned about the girls in a Department of Human Services Ad, and they had expressed a strong interest in adopting them. Janet was here to get more information. Richard was a lawyer, and Janet had a undergraduate degree in psychology. She worked in a head start program. Their credentials could hardly be better.

"I am pleased that the Gagnon girls have attracted attention so quickly," I said.

"They seem to be just what Richard and I are looking for." She punctuated her comment with a politician's smile.

"What was it about them that appealed to you?" I asked.

"We have one of our own who is about their age – just in the middle between them, in fact. We thought they might enjoy being sisters." She pulled her billfold out of her purse, and showed me a photo of her daughter. "That's our Samantha."

"I see." How does Samantha feel about the plan for the adoption?"

"We've talked with her. I think she will adjust quite well."

"Sometimes birth children are a bit jealous," I said.

"Not Samantha. She understands the plight of displaced children."

"Hmm. Yes, well, that's good." I glanced at the clock. "Well, were there specific things you wanted to know about Alicia and Eugena?"

"What were some of the themes you dealt with in your therapy with the children?"

I thought about this question. "Both the girls have shown a lot of concern about food." I said finally. I went to the file and pulled out the children's folders. I showed her some of the endless drawings of apples, bananas, strawberry short cakes, cookies, and ice cream cones executed by Eugena and then pointed out the concerns with being fed in Alicia's stories.

"They will be well fed if they come to live with us," Janet said.

"That's good. Food is important."

"Yes, in fact I've studied the impact of diet on affect and behavior."

"Oh?"

"You know about the connection between hyperactivity and sugar, of course."

"I've heard the theory, naturally," I said. "But studies on the subject have failed to give much support to the idea that sugar makes children hyperactive."

"I think the studies must be faulty," she said. "Anyone who has worked a lot with kids has seen the effects." A certain tightness in her voice told me this was a touchy point with her.

"In any case, Eugena and Alicia are not diagnosed as hyperactive," I said. "So I suppose it's a moot point."

"At the same time, we wouldn't want to give them anything that might make it harder for them to control their behavior," she said.

I picked up one of Eugena's drawings of a fruit bowl and shook it – not in Janet McPherson's face – but off to my side. "This preoccupation with food," I said, "seemed to me to be indicative of their concern about nurturance – about love and affection – not about food as such. They have enough to eat."

"Perhaps they didn't always get enough to eat. I'm told that Alicia sometimes steals food."

"Yes, she does. But again that seems to me to reflect her need to be in control of her nurturance."

She frowned. "What are some of the other behavior problems you have addressed with these children?"

"There are minor behavior problems in the home, and I have worked with the foster mother to develop some simple behavior plans there. But for the most part their behaviors aren't that problematic."

"The school says Eugena is oppositional, and isn't living up to her potential. And the foster mother says they are both manipulative."

"I see you have looked through their records pretty carefully," I said.

She nodded. "We are thinking about adopting them; we want to know everything we can about them."

I put the drawings back into the folder. "That's probably wise," I said.

In order to get through the rest of the allotted hour without arguing anymore with her, I began asking her about herself. She talked about her ideas for behavior management, and her beliefs about diet.

*****

During his appointment with me on September 17, Paul told me that on his way to the office he had seen some leaves beginning to change.

"And that stinks," he said.

"Why does it stink?"

"It means summer is over. No more swimming. School every day. No more fun."

"There must be some things you can look forward to," I suggested, weakly.

He shrugged. "I don't know. Maybe I'll get into basketball this winter."

He took out the paper and the colored markers and began working on a picture. I tried to make conversation.

"How do you like your new teachers?"

"They're okay, I guess." Then silence.

I tried again. "Have you heard from your sisters."

"Nope."

"Do you miss them?"

"Not much."

More silence.

I wasn't feeling very energized myself, so I sat back and watched him work on his picture. He had drawn a big house, with curtains at the windows, and smoke coming from the chimney. A huge tree, which was the major focus of his picture, dominated the yard. Four colored leaves lay on the ground around the tree. A fifth leaf was just separating from the twig to which it had been clinging. A little cartoon balloon indicated what the leaf was saying: "Oh no, now it's my turn."

"It's a picture about how fall stinks," he said.

Then he extricated a wrinkled letter from his back pocket, and threw it on my desk.

"What's that," I asked.

"Read it."

It was a letter that he had sent to his mother. It had been returned because the post office in Mexico could find no such address. It appeared to me that it might have been carried around in his pocket a while.

"You never showed me this before," I said.

"It's the second one I sent to her. The first one came back too."

"Why didn't you tell me about it before?" I asked.

He stood back to contemplate his finished picture. "I don't know. I just didn't want to."

"This is the address she gave you, isn't it?"

He nodded. "But it's just a mistake. She'll get in touch with me."

For a long time we were both silent, looking at his picture. "There are four leaves on the ground," I said.

"You can count."

I ignored his sarcasm. "And there is one just now dropping off the tree. That makes five."

Barf

Kit-Kats

We bob lightly in each other's awareness,
Choreographed by faint breezes,
Until he alights,
And snuggles in my lap.
He eats Kit-Kats from my hand.
He licks my stamen fingers,
Lapping the small residue
Of chocolate nectar
With his pink proboscis.

The King of the Diamond Thieves was furious. He had sent his most fierce and trusted warriors to do battle with Super Cop and one by one, in mortal combat, they had been defeated. So the most formidable villain in history came forth to personally put an end to this threat to his power. Nine year old Philip Gomez, creator and director of the drama that we were enacting, had cast himself in the role of the King of Diamond Thieves and me as Super Cop. He pulled one of the collapsible plastic swords from the play chest and whipped it out to its full length.

"Now we must fight to the death," he said.

I took a couple of shots at him with my pistol, but it was to no avail.

"You can't kill me with that," Philip explained. "You have to defend yourself with the sword."

I took the other sword from the play chest and we began slashing away at each other. Although we were both horribly wounded many times, we continued fighting.

"You have a special magic you can put on your sword that makes it able to cut through mine," he said. I put the magic on my sword with a wave of my hand. Now, every time I hit his collapsible sword, it became shorter. Finally he was defenseless, with nothing left of the sword but the handle.

"You're doomed," I said, and prepared to run him through. With a super karate kick he disarmed me, and we began wrestling, each trying to put a fatal hold on the other, but we were too powerful to be overcome in this way. "Its almost talking time," I said. How do you want this to end for today?"

"You have to get the sword back and stab me in my heart," he said. "Only that will kill me."

For the next few minutes we grappled. We each attempted to retrieve the sword he had kicked out of my hand. Finally I succeeded, and ran it through his heart. He screamed. "The blood that comes out is black" he said. "It isn't like human blood." His death agony took some time. When it was finished, I had to burn the body to make sure that no follower of his would bring it back to life by magic.

I poured Pepsi into two cups and put them on the coffee table, along with a Kit-Kat for us to share. We sat on the couch and settled into talk. He leaned back against the arm of the couch, extended his gangly legs in my direction, and put his stockinged feet in my lap. He had never done this before. I took one of his feet and massaged it through the white sock.

"I'm curious about something you do in your play," I said.

"What's that," he asked. Still flushed and disheveled from the wrestling, he ran his fingers through his dark curly hair in a cursory effort at grooming.

"When you assign parts, you always make me be the `good guy,' and you be the bad guy. Why wouldn't you want to play the part of the `good guy'?"

"You asked me that before," he said.

"As I recall you gave me no answer." I removed one of his white socks and stroked his foot gently, being careful not to tickle him. His foot was clean and smooth.

"That feels good," he said.

I smiled. "So why do you think you like being the bad guy?"

He took a sip of the Pepsi and I handed him a piece of the Kit-Kat. He appeared to be thinking about my question. "Because they don't have to go by the rules," he said.

"You don't like rules very much, do you?"

He shook his head.

"Why do you think that is?"

"Everything that's fun is against the rules," he said.

"Interesting. Could you give me an example?"

He could think of no specific thing that was fun but against the rules. As was characteristic of him, when he had reached a point where he didn't want to share any more he began responding to my questions with vague shrugs and "I don't knows."

A couple of weeks later, I received the phone call from his mother, Theresa Lacrosse. "Do you have a minute?" she asked.

The tension in her tone of voice told me that there was a problem. "You caught me at a good time," I said.

"Are you aware that Philip has been abused by an older boy?" she asked.

I racked my brain for anything that Philip might have told me that would fit the description: "abused by an older boy."

"I don't' think so," I said. "What kind of abuse are you talking about?"

"Sexual."

"No. I don't think he ever said anything to me about that. What happened, exactly?"

"Philip told me that you knew about it."

"I can't recall anything he ever told me about being sexually abused."

"Why would he say you knew if you didn't?"

"I don't know, Theresa. This information is new to me. What exactly happened as far as you know?"

"An older boy did fellatio... I think that's what its called... on him. And he had Philip do it to him."

"I see. How much older was his partner?"

"Five years. A friend of mine told me that the older boy could be charged with sexual assault for this."

"So the older boy is, what? Fourteen?"

"That's right."

"Can I ask his name?"

"Paul Murphy. He and his family are neighbors."

"Does Paul admit to this?"

"He admitted it to his mother."

"I see."

"I need to let you know, Mr. Foster, I'm not very happy about this." Her using my last name was not a good sign. She had been calling me Alex for some time.

"I understand this is upsetting," I said

"I think it should be reported to the Department of Human Services."

"Perhaps it will come to that, Theresa. But let's not move quite so quickly until we know more about what really happened."

"I'd like you to see Paul."

"That sounds like a good starting point. Does Philip know you are telling me this?"

"I'll be telling him as soon as I'm done talking with you. We don't need any more secrets."

"Good. Then I can talk with him about it the next time we get together."

"You are sure you didn't know anything about this?" she asked.

"Certain."

"Well, I have to do what I think is right. I may call The Department of Human Services even against your advise."

"It's your decision, Theresa. I'm only asking for a little time."

After hanging up, I looked through my recent progress notes, trying to locate ones that might help me view the information I had just received in the context of a larger understanding of Philip. I selected three of them as possibly significant: May 13, June 3, and July 8.

Progress Note
Name: Philip Gomez
Date: September 9
Time: 1 hour
Goals worked on: Process inner conflicts through play
therapy.

Description of the session: Philip introduced a new theme in play today. We are knights of the round table. For the first time, we are both on the same side, and also for the first time, he is a "good guy." I am his special friend. We are going to fight the evil knights because they kidnaped his father many years ago, when he was just a baby, and they are holding him in the dungeon of a castle. We are going to rescue him. After fighting many evil knights, and descending into an intricate labyrinth of tunnels under the castle, we find him and bring him back. Father and son are reunited, and the three of us together overcome the bad knights.

In our quiet time together we discussed his memories of when his natural father, Miguel Gomez, and mother were together. He remembers wonderful times with his father who took him fishing, played ball with him and told him stories. But he also remembers chaotic times when his father was drinking and his parents were fighting. He wants to go live with his father when he gets out of prison. He comments that selling drugs isn't as bad as killing somebody. "My dad never hurt me," he said.

Progress Note

Name: Philip Gomez

Date: September 30, 1996

Time: 1 hour

Goals worked on: Process inner conflicts through play therapy

Description of the session: He wanted to continue with the adventures of the wonder dog he calls, "Barf." Picking up from the last time, Barf was hidden in a secret den (behind the couch). Barf continues to provoke his master (me) by breaking various rules. He enacts the dog peeing on the furniture, and then he poops in a corner. I tell him he is a bad dog for doing this. Then he begins eating the furniture. He stops when I get after him. Then he wants to sleep in the bed with me. He has been told that he can't get on the furniture so I tell him no. He begins barfing all over everything. He finally ends up barfing on my shoe. I ask Philip what he thinks is the matter with this dog. He says it's the dog food. He's allergic to it. So we enact my taking him to the vet, who determines that he is allergic to the dog food and recommends a different brand. Then Barf doesn't hurt so much and he can live by the rules better.

During our quiet time we discuss rules, and how he

feels about them. He expresses the belief that if there weren't cops, everybody would be criminals. Then we discussed the problem of bad rules. Do we have to follow the rules of our families, our school, and our country even when we think they are bad rules? What about the rules that got his father put in prison?

Progress Note
Name: Philip Gomez
Date: October 13, 1996
Time: 1 hour
Goals worked on: Process inner conflict through play therapy

Description of the session: An interesting new theme emerged during the play session today. He was back into the role of the King of the Diamond Thieves, with me as Super Cop. As usual the King of the Diamond Thieves is out to enhance his power and steal riches. This time, however, he is after a special medicine that gives magic powers. I have this medicine. He brings me lots of gold with which to buy it. I'm not sure I want to deal with the King of the Diamond Thieves but he points out all the good things I can do with the gold. We meet in a sleazy bar to transact our business, but at the last minute he just takes the medicine and runs off with it without paying. This leads to several inconclusive fights with some of his henchmen as I try to track him down. When he takes the medicine it gives him wonderful powers, but it also poisons him. He needs an antidote, which I just happen to have. Again we meet in the bar. My position is strengthened, and I'm able to force him to pay me for the medicine as well as the antidote. However, he benefits more than I do in the long run because the power the medicine gives him is very useful to a thief. By this power, for example, he is able to turn invisible.

During the quiet time he wanted to look at a

*naturist book I keep around that shows how people look
without their clothes on. He said he wished he could go
to a naturist place and see what women looked like. He
was especially interested in their breasts.*

A section from a note regarding a collateral contact with the
mother provides some additional information that seems relevant.

*Ms. Lacrosse reported that while in first grade
Philip once got into trouble for exposing himself to a little
girl on the bus, and asking to see what she looked like.
Also she reported on a number of occasions that she
caught him engaged in games of "doctor" and other
forms of sex play with friends and neighborhood kids.
These incidents seemed quite upsetting to her.*

Given that he was an enterprising child there was nothing
that seemed especially remarkable about these sexual explorations
and transgressions, except that he apparently had a propensity for
getting caught.

After Theresa Lacrosse told Paul Murphy's parents that I
was not enthusiastic about a referral to Human Services, they
agreed to have me see their son. The Murphy couple hoped that I
might help them resolve the whole thing without the "state"
becoming involved.

*****

Paul arrived on time for the session wearing jeans,
sneakers, and a tank-top with a Loony Toon's cartoon on the front
of it. Not quite shoulder-length blond hair protruded from a
baseball cap that he wore backwards.

After we introduced ourselves, he slouched in the easy
chair, crossed his arms, and glanced around the room, avoiding
eye contact with me. Small and slender, he appeared younger than
fourteen. I opened the session with general questions. School was
OK, but boring. He liked bike riding, basketball, and Nintendo.

His favorite books were from the "Goosbumps" series. He had lived in Colesville all his life. If he found a bottle on a beach that produced a genie, his three wishes would be to go to Disney Land, to be rich, and to live in a tree house with his friends.

"How do you feel about being here?" I asked.

He shrugged. "OK, I guess."

"You don't look very `OK' about it," I said.

He squirmed down a little lower in his seat. "Well, I didn't much want to come."

"I see. So why did you?"

He raised his head and glared at me. "Cause Mom made me."

"And why did Mom say it was necessary?"

"Because of the thing with Philip."

"The "thing" with Philip'?"

He sat up and stared directly in my eyes. "Didn't Mom tell you anything?"

"She told me some things. But I'd like to hear how you see it."

"Well, you know. Something happened."

"It seems kind of hard to talk about," I said.

"Course it is."

"What makes it hard"

"Its embarrassing."

"It's embarrassing to talk about things like this with someone you hardly know."

"With anybody."

I nodded. "Let me see if I can help get things started. Philip's Mom says that you and Philip were involved in a little sex play. Is that true?"

He hugged himself more tightly, and slouched deeper down on the couch. "Why do you want to know?"

It was a good question. Why did I want to know? And what benefit might he derive from talking about it? "I'd like to see whether we can sort the whole thing out without the state having to get into it," I said.

He sat up and stared at me, trying to read from my face whether I could be trusted. "Would the State put me in foster care if they thought I did something?" he asked.

"I don't know what they would do," I said. "I feel they over-react to this kind of thing these days. There's a difference of five years in your ages. That would concern them. They might think you were taking advantage of younger kids."

"I didn't start the thing," Paul said. "Philip did. I didn't even know boys did that to each other."

"You never heard boys talk about it?"

"I guess so. But it was just talk."

"So what did he do."

"He asked me to suck his thing."

"And did you?"

He hunched his shoulders slightly.

"That means yes?" I asked.

"Yes," he said irritably.

"And then?"

He looked down and rubbed his brow with his fingers, hiding most of his face. "Then he did mine."

This last admission was mumbled. "Then he did your's?" I asked, in order to confirm that I had heard him correctly.

He nodded.

"Where did this happen?"

"In the woods, down by Bakers's Creek. We were skinny dipping and we got... boners...." He shrugged apologetically. "Whatever you're supposed to call it when that happens." At the word "that" he gestured vaguely toward his crotch.

"'Boners' is fine."

"Well, that's when he asked me to do it."

"I see. Did it also happen other times?"

"Couple more times."

"At the Creek?"

"In his bed-room once, and again at the creek."

"How did grown-ups find out about it?"

"A neighbor saw us at the creek and called his mom."

"I see. Did you like doing these things with Philip?"

This time he put both his hands over his face and rubbed his eye brows as though he had a head ache. "That's a dumb question," he said.

I shrugged. "Perhaps. But it might be helpful to me if you could answer it."

"Why do you got to know that?"

"I like to know why people do things. For example if he paid you or threatened you, that would make it a different kind of thing."

"He's not big enough to make me do anything."

"Did you pressure him in any way?"

"I told you, it was his idea."

"So it was something both of you wanted to do?"

"I guess so."

"It felt good?"

His gaze dropped. "Maybe" he said. "A little." Then he looked me in the eye, and frowned. "But I ain't gay."

I shrugged. "Lots of boys who aren't gay get into a bit of sex play from time to time," I said. "But whether you're gay or not gay or partly gay or whatever, it's all the same. It's OK. It's not such a horrible thing you and he did. But there are other's who may not see it that way. We have to be concerned about them."

*****

Paul's description coincided with what Philip told his mother on all the major points.

An incident from a Norwegian fairy tale that I once read to my daughter concerned a young hero who disarmed a potentially dangerous troll by popping a bit of bread into his mouth. It was noted that trolls could not attack people if they had once accepted food from them. I thought about this story as I poured some coffee to go with the cookies I was sharing with Theresa and George Lacrosse.

"Why do you think we should not call in the Department of Human Services," Theresa asked. She sat on the couch with her new husband, George Lacrosse, a small thin man with a pointed nose and a sharp chin. They were holding hands as a sign of mutual support. Theresa felt that it was a combination of George and the Colesville Baptist Church, to which he had introduced her, that had made it possible for her get her life together. George was a gentle and dependable man, and the church gave a welcome stability to her life, and provided some firm answers in a confusing world.

"I think the Department of Human Services sometimes does more harm than good," I said.

Theresa frowned. "What would they do with Paul?" She asked.

"I don't know." With five years difference in the boy's ages, they might refer it to the District Attorney for prosecution."

"What would the charge be?" George asked.

"It could be "sexual assault," I said. "Even if both children entered into to it willingly, they would say the younger child was not able to consent. In effect, they would accuse the older child of rape."

"I don't think Paul raped him," Theresa said.

"Nor do I. In fact it appears that Philip may be the one who initiated it."

She glared at me. "That still doesn't excuse Paul," she said. "I don't think he should just get away with this, scot free."

"Paul broke some rules," I said. "But I am terribly afraid of what can happen to a child once the state gets that `sexual perpetrator' label pinned on him."

"What worries me," George said, "is that this may tempt Philip in the direction of homosexuality."

"The evidence doesn't indicate that sex play between children – same sex or not – leads to homosexuality," I said.

"But if Paul doesn't get help he may perpetrate on other kids," Theresa said.

I sighed.

I had already tried to explain the difference between sexual attack and sex play. I had explained that consent really is a key issue, and that societal over-reaction could be as damaging as under-reaction. There seemed to be little to be gained by going over the same ground again. "Well, I've told you what I think," I said. "It's your call."

"We need to pray abut it," George said.

"That's good, " I said. "Also let me suggest that you sit down and talk with Paul's parents, to get their perspective. Would you need my help in this?"

"We can do that ourselves." Theresa said. "We've been neighbors for a long time and have always gotten along."

"Getting along with one's neighbors certainly does make life more pleasant," I said.

"Still, we have to do what's right," George said.

Theresa smiled at me. "We'll get in touch with you when we make up our minds, Alex."

Her using my first name again gave me some hope. Maybe the history of my having been helpful to Philip would have some weight with her. She once told me that he became "a different boy" after beginning to see me.

"Let me suggest that whichever way you decide, we think

of it as a permanent decision. If we don't report at first, and then someone reports it later on, that could create problems for me."

*****

A few days later I received a call from Theresa.

"We have decided to go along with your suggestion and not report everything to Human Services," she told me.

"I'm glad."

"We trust you Alex. I want you to know that. It's just that the whole thing was such a shock to us."

"Yes, I can understand it might have been."

"Paul's parents agreed that he would come to see you. That was a big part of our decision."

"That sounds good."

As long as we know he gets the help he needs, that's the important thing."

"I think Paul will be all right."

"But there's another problem that has cropped up," Theresa said.

"Yes?"

She paused before answering. "Philip says he doesn't want to see you anymore."

"I see. Did he say why?"

"No. He just says he doesn't want to have any more sessions."

I thought about this for a minute. "OK," I said. "Tell him he needs to see me one more time. Tell him that if he doesn't want to see me anymore after that, he doesn't have to."

"You would leave the decision to him?"

"I don't think the kind of work I am trying to do with him will be very useful if he comes only because he has to."

"What if he says he won't come even for one session."

"I don't know. Be your most persuasive self. If that doesn't

work, call me and we will deal with it then."
*****

When the time arrived for Philip's three o'clock appointment, I heard a timid knock. I opened the door and found Mary Gould, the secretary/receptionist.

"Yes?

"Philip refuses to come in," she said. She lifted her shoulders and turned her palms upward in a gesture of helplessness.

I looked past her into the waiting room, and saw Philip's mother standing by the door. "Thanks, Mary. I'll take care of it." She retreated to her desk.

No one else was in the waiting room.

"What's happening, Theresa," I asked.

"He says you've got to come and talk with him in the car," she said.

"All right," I said. "We'll try that."

I found Philip hunched over in the back seat of the Lacrosses' four door station wagon, with his back to me. "Why don't you want to come in?" I asked.

"We can talk here?" he said.

"It's kind of hard. There's people around. And I don't like talking to your back."

"So."

I climbed into the back seat.

"This isn't your car," Philip said. "I didn't invite you in."

"What is the trouble, Philip? You've never been like this with me before."

"You're the trouble," he said.

I reached over to put my hand on his back, and he shook me off. Then, without warning, he climbed over into the space behind the seat, pushed the back door open, and jumped out onto the parking lot. I went out the side door and started around the station wagon in his direction. He bolted across the parking lot just as car was driving in. The car screeched to a halt just a few feet from Philip. Startled into immobility, Philip stood staring at the car. I took advantage of this moment to walk over and take hold of his arm.

"I don't usually boss you around, Philip," I said. "But this time I'm going to insist you come into my office. If you don't want to see me anymore after today, that's your decision."

Perhaps the shock of almost being hit by the car, followed by my unusual firmness with him was too much for him to process. For whatever reason he allowed himself to be corralled in the front door of the counseling center, through the waiting room, and into my office. "You might turn the radio up a bit, Mary," I suggested before shutting my office door.

As soon as I let loose of Philip in the office he started toward the door. I blocked the way.

"You can't make me stay here," he said.

"I'm not letting you leave," I said. "Not till we've talked."

"Can't make me talk," he said. He glanced around the room, and then crawled under the couch. I sat down in front of the door.

"Why are you being this way?" I asked.

There was no answer.

"It's important that we talk about what's happening."

Again he didn't answer. For perhaps five minutes I sat in front of the door, trying to think of a new strategy while he lay on the floor under the couch, humming little tunes.

"How can I know what is the trouble if you won't tell me?" I finally asked.

There was another long silence. But then he answered."You have to guess," he said.

"Ah," I said. "A guessing game."

I made an occasional "Hmmm" sound to indicate I was

trying to think of something to guess.

"If I guess correctly, will you let me know?" I asked.

"I might."

"Well, I'll give it a try."

He began humming again.

"Let me think. You got into trouble for breaking rules about sex."

The humming stopped.

"It seemed like everybody thought you were real disgusting."

I thought I heard a faint growling noise.

"So then what might happen? Hmm. Maybe you got to thinking that I would think you are disgusting. Maybe you would even think that I would hate you."

No noise at all came from under the couch. I barely breathed. And I waited.

"You do hate me," he said, finally. It was a small hurt voice, full of conviction.

"I don't hate you, Philip," I said. The impulse to cry caught me by surprise and I choked on my words. "I don't hate you at all."

"I broke the rules."

"Those aren't my rules."

Another long period of silence followed, and then he asked, "what are your rules?"

"Ah, I'm glad you asked that," I said. I knew he wouldn't bolt now. I went over to the easel, and found a clean sheet of paper. "I've been meaning to tell you about what rules I think are important. I'll write them down up here. The first rule is that you shouldn't hurt people."

I wrote, "1. Don't hurt people." I then stated and wrote down two more rules. "2. Don't make other people do things they don't want to," and "3. Don't do things that could be dangerous to yourself or others."

"Those are the main ones," I said. "So far as I can tell, you didn't break those rules."

I glanced over my shoulder and saw him peeking out from behind the couch at the rules that I had written on the board. When he saw me looking at him he pulled back.

"There's something about all this I'd like to ask you," I said, addressing the couch.

"What's that?"

"Your mother said that you told her I knew all about what happened between you and Paul."

He stuck his head out from behind the couch again. "I thought you did."

"You never told me about it. How could I have known?"

"I don't know."

"Sometimes I can guess what you might be thinking. Maybe that makes you think I can read your mind," I said.

"It seems like you can."

"I can't. I only know what you tell me."

"Sometimes you know things that I didn't tell you."

"That's because you have told me something in your stories, or by how you act, or because I know a lot about how boys think about things. I really can't read your mind."

"OK"

"When I talked on the phone, I told your mom I didn't know about you and Paul. Did she tell you that?"

"Yes."

"Maybe it was then that you thought, 'Now that he does know he's going to hate me.'"

He pulled his head back behind the couch. A minute later I heard barking sounds. He came out, crawling on all fours. It was Barf. He lifted his leg, and made the motion of peeing on the couch, accompanied with a little hissing sound.

"That's how dogs mark their territory I commented."

He nodded. Then he came over to me to me and rubbed his head against my leg. I scratched him behind the ears.

He stood up. "Can I go now?" he said.

"I think we've done what we needed for today," I said.

"I've got a new idea for next week," he said.

"What's that?"

"Barf gets a family."

"Cool. I can't wait."

"You'll like it."

"One other thing," I said. "For now, why don't we keep this conversation about rules just between us."

"OK," he said.

*****

The day of his next session was cold, rainy, and blustery. Philip's feet were wet from stomping in puddles. He took his socks off and I laid them on one of the base board eclectic radiators, hoping to dry them a bit before he had to put them back on. He said he was tired from playing outside and wanted to rest. I poured us each some Pepsi, and took the Kit-Kat candy bar out of the drawer. We took our places.

"Let me warm your feet," I said.

"OK."

He leaned back on the arm of the couch and parked his feet in my lap.

"Hmm! They're really cold," I said, rubbing them.

"Yeah."

I handed him a piece of a Kit Kat, and took one for myself. "I think a lot about why you always wanted to be the bad guy," I said.

"It's because it's more fun," he said.

"Right. Because anything that is fun is bad. That's what

you told me."

"Yeah."

"Give me an example."

"Nintendo."

"Nintendo?" I raised my eyebrows. "Are Nintendo games bad?"

"Not all of them."

"But some of them?"

He nodded.

"I don't know too much about Nintendo," I said. "What makes some of them bad?"

While he thought about this, I massaged one of his feet, warming it up.

"Don't know," he said.

"Here's some brain food," I said, handing him another piece of Kit-Kat. "I'll bet you can remember."

"Remember what?"

"Why you said some Nintendo games are bad."

He looked me in the eyes, the way he does when he wants to read my reaction to something he's about to say. "I saw one where a guy had a dink that became a big club." He giggled. "He killed people with it."

"Wow. What a crazy idea!"

"Yeah."

"Of course dinks never are that hard," I said.

"When you get a boner it's hard," he said. He continued staring at my eyes. He had never talked about boners before.

"Yeah." I said. "They stand up and get kind of hard. But even then they're not that hard – like they could never hurt a person."

"It would awesome to have a big dink like that – one you could smash people with."He laughed.

"Maybe," I said, laughing with him. "But I don't think that's what dinks are for."

"It looked funny in the Nintendo game."

"I'll bet it did." I changed his feet and began warming the other one. "Do you remember that session in which the King of the Diamond thieves made a medicine that gave him magic powers?" I asked.

"Yeah, like making him invisible, and turning his finger into a laser sword."

"Right. That one. And you remember how the medicine turned out to be a poison as well?"

"Yeah. It could kill you if you didn't have the anklidote."

"Right. ell, I think that's a little like your dink."

He looked puzzled. "I don't get it."

"Well, your dink is something that gives you wonderful feelings, almost like magic, but it has also got you into a lot of trouble."

"Its nasty," he said.

"I don't think so," I said. "But it has got you into a lot of trouble."

"Sometimes I wish I didn't have one," he said.

"But you always want to be one of the bad guys."

"Yeah."

"I think you want to be the bad guys because bad guys still have their dinks."

He laughed. "But they get into too much trouble," he said.

I handed him another piece of Kit-Kat. "Still, every guy does need to have his dink," I said. I twirled the second toe on his left foot back and forth between my fingers while we thought about this.

"Yeah," he said finally. "I wouldn't really like it if I didn't have one."

"Maybe a person could learn how to have a dink, and still not get into so much trouble," I said.

"How?" he asked.

"It's not always easy," I said. I rubbed his foot, gently. "But it's something we can talk about."

The Sex Offender

The scar began on his cheek and extended down the side of his neck and onto his shoulder. It stood out pale and wrinkled against the brown of his skin. Nine years ago, when he was two, he pulled a pot of hot grease, in which his mother was preparing French-fries, down on himself. This was the first of several disasters that plagued the Joslyn family after they adopted him.

I wanted to touch the scar tissue. I felt that if I rubbed it with sufficient gentleness I might magically smooth it out and return his skin to its original color. I did not, of course, give in to this absurd impulse. It would have disrupted the play, and God knows how he would have interpreted such a gesture. So I contented myself with asking him about the drama he was enacting.

"Where are Mom and Dad going?"

Kyle made loud motor noises and steered the pink plastic car at breakneck speed across the rug.

"To an auction," he said.

"What kind of auction.?"

"A baby auction."

"Who's selling babies.?"

"Parents."

"Why?"

"They don't want them."

"Why is that?"

"There's something wrong with them." The car came to a screeching halt at a little enclosure he had built out of blocks.

"Something is wrong with the babies?" I asked.

"Yeah."

"Maybe something is wrong with the parents," I said. "Why would they sell their babies?"

"These two aren't selling a baby," he said. He took the doll parents out of the pink car and leaned them against the wall of the enclosure. "They're here to buy one."

Kyle went to the box where I kept the accessories to the play house and took out one of the babies. "This is the one that's for sale now," he said. He then selected an adult doll and returned to the enclosure he had built. He placed the baby within the enclosure. The new adult stood on the wall. He was the auctioneer.

Auctioneer: Do I hear seventeen?

Person from the crowd: Seventeen.

Auctioneer: Do I hear eighteen?

The father: Eighteen.

Auctioneer: Do I hear nineteen?

Person from the crowd: Nineteen.

Auctioneer: Do I hear twenty?

The mother: Twenty.

Auctioneer: Sold to Mr. and Ms. Johnson for twenty dollars.

"So Mom and Dad are named Mr. and Ms. Johnson?" I asked.

"Yeah."

"And they just bought this baby?"

"Yep. They were the highest bidders."

Kyle put the baby in the back seat of the car, and Mr. and Ms. Johnson in front and the new family drove to the play house.

When they tried to take the new baby into the house a girl child in the house named "Sissy," objected.

Sissy: That's an ugly baby. I don't like it.

Mr. Johnson: We bought it at an auction. It was real cheap.

Sissy: Take it back.

Mr. Johnson: OK.

Ms. Johnson: "You can't take it back. That would hurt its feelings. (Pretty soon everybody in the play

house is arguing and screaming. This wakes up Kirk, a sixteen year old boy who had been taking a nap.)

"They got Kirk just like they got this new baby," Kyle explained to me.

"You mean he was bought at an auction too?"

"Yeah. A lot of years ago."

"When he was little, eh?"

"That's right.

"What about Sissy."

"That's their kid."

"They didn't get her at an auction?"

"Nope. She was their real kid."

"OK. So what happens next?"

"Kirk doesn't like all this arguing," Kyle said, and returned to directing his play.

Kirk: There's too much noise in this house. I'm leaving.

Mr. Johnson: You can't take the car."

Kirk: Why not? I know how to drive.

Mr. Johnson: You're grounded."

Kirk: For what?

Ms. Johnson: For all the bad things you do.

Kirk: It's no fun in this house. (Kirk climbs up to the roof of the house and starts jumping around. The mother looks out the window.)

Ms. Johnson: Come back in Kirk. You can't play on the roof. It's against the rules. (Kirk continues jumping around on the roof, defying his mother. Then he slips and falls off.)

Ms. Johnson: (Rushes out and looks at him.) Oh. look. Kirk is hurt.

Mr. Johnson: What's the matter with him.

Ms. Johnson: His back is broken.

Mr. Johnson: Serves him right.

Ms. Johnson: We have to take him to the hospital. (They pile him into a car and rush him to the card board box which serves as the hospital. He is put into a bed there and Kyle selects a young woman from the accessories box, to be a nurse.)

Nurse: We're going to fix your back, Kirk.

Kirk: (Reaches up and feels her breast.) You're pretty.

Nurse: (Slaps him.) You're not supposed to do that.

Kirk: (Jumps up.) My back is OK now.

Mr. Johnson: (To Ms. Johnson.) See how bad he is. We can't take him home."

Kirk: I don't even want to come home. So there. (He goes and gets into the car and drives off.)

"I think our time is just about over, Kyle," I said.

As we straightened the play room we talked about the overnight canoe trip that we were planning for his family.

"Can we go swimming?" He asked.

"It's still a little early in the year," I said. "But if the waters not too cold we can."

"Wow. I can't wait," he said. He fluffed his afro with a hair pick.

"Me too," I said.

*****

"The department has decided that Kyle's visits to Henry and Glenda Joslyn will be limited to once a month," Phyllis Black announced. She glanced around the small conference room. The foster parents, Helena and Pierre Oulette, looked down. The Joslyns and I stared at Phyllis. I zeroed in on a point between, and just a little above, her penciled eyebrows – the place where her third eye would have been, had she had one – and I did my best to drill a hole in her cranium with my gaze. She smiled apologetically.

"I'm not sure I understand," I said. And truly I didn't. Phyllis had never before dealt with the team in such an autocratic manner.

"I talked to Peggy Price, my supervisor, and that's what she said needs to happen," Phyllis said.

"But the team worked this out," I said. "We felt that the visits should be more frequent, so long as Kyle's behavior showed he really wanted them."

"Ms. Price feels that's too confusing," Phyllis said.

"She feels it's too confusing?" I shook my head. "What does that mean?"

Phyllis shrugged apologetically.

I looked around the room, and tried to make eye contact with the foster parents. Pierre Oulette took a sudden interest in a picture of some flowers that was hanging on the wall. Helena stared at the floor. Then I looked at the adoptive parents. Making eye contact with me, Glenda raised her eyebrows and lifted her shoulders slightly in a nonverbal question mark. She was tall, and gaunt. Henry, who sat beside her, was shorter with softer features. He looked at me and tilted his head just slightly to one side as if to say "what can we do?" The conversation fell into an abyss of silence.

"I guess I'm the one who's confused," I said, finally. "I thought we had all agreed that decisions would be made by a team process. In fact I thought there was a cooperative agreement between Mid-State Counseling and Human Services to this effect." I directed my comment to Phyllis.

" Human Services has the final say in matters of visitation," she said. "We are the child's guardian."

"I'm not debating that point, Phyllis," I said. "But we never even discussed this change."

"I'm just telling you what my supervisor told me to say," she said. "It's not really open for discussion."

I continued staring at her missing third eye with the hope that a hole would open and her brains would ooze out onto her nose and chin. "For Human Services to come in and simply give orders like this isn't quite my understanding of how a team approach was supposed to function," I said.

Phyllis squirmed uncomfortably in her chair. "I suppose you and my supervisor, Peggy Price have somewhat different ideas of what a team approach means," she said.

"Would she be willing to come and discuss this?" I asked. "For the whole last year we have been making the major decisions in the team here, and it seems to me that it has worked very well."

Phyllis frowned. "I'll talk with Peggy about it, but I don't think she'll like it."

Glenda leaned forward. The twitch in her eye was conspicuous. "Does this mean that Kyle won't be coming home for a visit this weekend?" She asked.

Phyllis picked up the leather case in which she carried her papers and held it against her chest. "I'm afraid it does," she said.

"He won't like that very much," Glenda said.

"Maybe Mr. Foster can help him see the reason for it in his therapy session with him," Phyllis suggested.

"That will be a little difficult," I said. "I'm pretty fuzzy on the reason for it myself."

*****

I caught Henry and Glenda Joslyn in the parking lot. "Hell of a meeting," I said.

The skin of Glenda's gaunt face was pulled tight with tension. "Helena Oulette's in her glory," she said.

"What does that mean?" I asked.

"She's Peggy Price's first lieutenant now."

"There might be something to that," I said. "I think the Oulettes knew what was going to happen in this meeting,"

"They did. I'm sure of it." Glenda said. "Helena and this Peggy Price are on the phone all the time, plotting out what's going to happen next."

"How do you know that?"

"Kyle told me."

I shook my head. "Ever since Peggy Price got on this case, the team has been by-passed," I said.

"You can forget your team, Alex," Glenda said. "Peggy and Helena are the only team now."

"The team worked well for over a year now," I said. "Even Kyle was getting a sense that he had some control over his life by meeting with us. Maybe we can still get it back on track."

Glenda rolled her eyes. "Alex, you're so naive. How can somebody as smart as you are not see what's right in front of him. The reason Peggy Price was put on the case was to squash the team. Can't you see that?"

"Why would they want to squash the team?" I asked. "It was working."

"Control, Alex. Control. You've got these dreams in your head about how life should be. It blinds you to how things really are. DHS wants control. The team was a threat to that."

The sun was low. I was tired. I wanted to get into my car and go home. "I hope you're wrong," I said.

Glenda stepped closer to me and put her hand on my shoulder. I instinctively pulled back just a few inches. She had never touched me before. She either did not notice, or she ignored my involuntary reflex. "You're good, Alex." she said. "You have helped us and you have helped Kyle. But let me tell you what will happen. DHS will get Kyle away from us, because sometimes I go against what they say." She paused. "And so do you, Alex." She dropped her hand and stepped back.

"So you think they'll try to get rid of me?"

"You're the enemy, now," Henry said. "That's how DHS sees you."

Glenda nodded in agreement with her husband.

"We've got to try to fight this thing," I said.

Glenda sighed. "I suppose so," she said. "It's just that they wear me down."

*****

During our next session Kyle returned to the play house where he continued the adventures of the Johnson family.

Mr. Johnson: You're a bad baby." (He mercilessly beats on the baby they bought at he auction. The mother comes into the room.)

Ms. Johnson: Father. Why are you beating on the baby?

Mr. Johnson: Because he's so bad. I caught him playing with matches again. He could burn our house down.

Ms. Johnson: He is bad.

Mr. Johnson: I told you we should take him back.

Ms. Johnson: Nobody would want him.

Mr. Johnson: Where's his real mother?

Ms. Johnson: She's an old drunk.

"Then the baby gets some steroids and swallows a whole bottle of them," Kyle explains to me.

"Steroids," I said, not hiding my astonishment. "Where'd this kid get steroids?"

"At the drug store."

"But where did he ever hear about them?" I asked.

"On TV. They give you those big muscles and make you strong."

"So they make the baby strong?"

"Watch," he says.

Baby: I'm not going to take this shit any more. (He stands up and hits the father and then the mother. Then he grabs Sissy and throws her out of the window. After this he spends some time tearing the whole house apart. The steroids have given him super powers, so no-one can stop him.)

With the house turned upside down and all the furniture and dolls strewn around him, Kyle looked up at me. "That's it for today, folks," he said. "Tune in next week for the further adventures of super baby."

"Some baby," I said. "You want a snack?"

"Sure."

"Popcorn?"

"Yeah."

I put a bag of popcorn in the microwave that I keep on a cabinet beside the couch. "We can share a Pepsi," I said.

"That's OK with me," he said. He dragged the easy chair up to the coffee table. I took the soda and a couple of paper cups out of the cabinet beneath the microwave, put them on the coffee table, and settled on the couch opposite him.

"Seems like that baby was a little angry about something," I said.

"He thinks nobody wants him," Kyle said.

We sat silently for a while, listening to the corn popping. Finally he spoke. "What happened to my home visit?"

"Human Services canceled it," I said.

"Why?"

"They think the visits are confusing to you."

"What does that mean?"

"I don't know."

He climbed over the side of the easy chair and went to the shelves where the toys are kept. He took a can of red Play-Do off the top shelf and brought it back to the coffee table, where he climbed back into the easy chair.

"What did Mom and Dad say?"

"They were upset. They thought you had earned your home visit."

"I did." He took the top off the Play Do can and dumped the contents out on the table.

"You did," I said.

"It's not fair," he said.

"I agree."

"Why didn't you make them let me have my home visit?"

"I tried, Kyle. They have the final say about things like that. They got more power than I do."

He looked down and became absorbed in working the somewhat crumbly Play Do into a single mass. When the popping of the pop corn became less regular I went to the microwave and took it out. After opening it on the coffee table I poured us each some soda. While I was making these preparations he was forming the red Play Do into an irregularly shaped ball.

"It's an apple," he said, holding it up for my examination.

"I can see that."

"Is the camping trip still on?"

"Yes," I said. "I asked DHS about that and they promised me that we would be able to go."

He nodded his approval. The he pushed his finger through his Play Do apple. When it came out the opposite side, he wiggled it at me.

"Hello," the finger said.

"Well, hello. Who are you?"

"I'm Willy Worm."

"I see. Do you live in the apple there?"

"Yes. That's my house."

"It's a nice house."

"I'd like to be friends with you."

I reached out and shook the worm-finger, as though I were shaking his hand. "Yes, that would be nice, Willie," I said. "I'd like it if we were friends."

*****

"So when did things change?" I asked. I didn't direct the question at either of them, but Glenda answered. She was generally the spokesperson for the couple.

"You mean with Kyle?" she asked. She scooped a teaspoon full of sugar into the coffee I had prepared for her and looked over at Henry, who was sitting beside her on the couch.

"Right. You describe how fun Kyle was to be around, how he was everything you could want in a son, how charming he was with everybody at your church and so on. Then all at once I'm hearing about this holy terror who is turning your house upside down. That's a big change."

"He changed after Lisa was born," Glenda said.

"I remember it being after the fire in the stable," Henry said.

Glenda turned slightly away from Henry. "That's when you changed," she said.

Henry reddened just slightly. "Kyle changed first," he said. "I changed because he did."

"Maybe," Glenda said.

Henry nodded. "It is so," he said. "When a kid is calling you names, and swearing, and refusing to do anything you ask, it's hard not to change."

"I can see that," Glenda said. "He could be pretty nasty with me too at times."

Henry's color returned to normal and he took a sip from his coffee. "Anyhow," he said. "the fire happened pretty close to when Lisa was born."

"So Lisa is what... four years old now?" I said.

"That's right," said Glenda.

"So more or less four years ago things seemed to take a turn for the worse," I said.

They both nodded.

"And one of the things that happened back then was that your stable burned," I said

"That's a sore subject," Glenda said.

"Why is that?"

"Human services thinks that Kyle did it," Glenda said. "We're afraid that if they prove it, they won't let him return to live with us."

"And what do you think about the fire?" I asked.

The redness came back to Henry's face, and I noticed the area under Glenda's left eye begin to twitch. A silence followed.

"I agree with Human Services," Henry said, finally.

"That Kyle ought to live somewhere else?" Glenda

snapped.

"No," Henry said. "Just that he was responsible for the fire."

"We don't know he did it," Glenda said. She scooted away from him on the couch.

Henry crossed his arms in front of himself and looked away. "I feel that I practically know it. We know that Kyle was always playing with matches." He turned to me. "He had a fascination with fire, Alex. And he was outside when it happened."

"That doesn't prove it," Glenda said.

"No, I suppose it doesn't actually prove it."

Glenda looked at me. "The fire was devastating for Henry," she said.

"What made it devastating?"

Glenda glanced at her husband. "You tell him," she said.

"There's not a lot to tell," he said in a matter of fact tone. "I had a horse in the stable."

"It was a horse that was very special to Henry," Glenda said.

"Well, yes, I was fond of Jumper," Henry said.

"Fond of him hardly says it," Glenda said. "He was your life."

"I said I was fond of him," Henry said. "You make it sound weird."

"I don't mean to," Glenda said. She turned to me. "By the time we got to the stable, it was already too much on fire for us to go in. We could hear Jumper neighing."

"Where was Kyle during this?" I asked.

"He watched the fire from behind a tree in the yard," Glenda said.

"He never came up to us while it was burning," Henry said. "That's why even then I thought that he did it."

"That had to affect how you felt about Kyle," I said.

Henry slouched down. "It was kind of hard to want him around after that," he said.

"And that was when things began to get out of hand?"

"Up until then Kyle just worshiped Henry." Glenda said. "Now it seemed all they did was holler at each other. Henry never hit him, or anything like that. But Kyle was always being punished. Henry seemed like he hated him."

"I didn't hate him," Henry said. "He was just being such a pain in the ass. It didn't make you feel like you wanted to be near him."

"And how did you respond, Glenda?"

"I cried a lot. And I turned my attention to Lisa. I was afraid all this conflict was going to mess her up. And I was afraid I was going to have a nervous breakdown."

"You went to Human Services for help about a year or so after Lisa was born, is that right?"

Glenda nodded.

"Nobody reported you or anything like that?"

"No," Glenda said. "We went on our own. We felt we needed help. They told us that they couldn't help us unless we said we were abusing or neglecting Kyle. So we signed a statement to that effect, just to get the help. They did an investigation, and removed him from the home. They've been treating us like criminals ever since."

"Phyllis Black has been supportive, at least until this last meeting," I pointed out.

"She has. I admit that. But you see how that's turning around, Alex. You can't trust them."

*****

Peggy Price twisted her body around in her chair trying, without much success, to find a comfortable position. But the arms of the chair pressed too tightly against her thighs. I visualized these chair arms as being the jaws of the great white shark on the verge of biting her in two. "The department is thinking that perhaps Kyle should be refereed for participation in a sexual perpetrators group," she was saying.

Phyllis Black sat beside her supervisor. She had contributed nothing to the meeting, and generally avoided eye contact with everybody.

"I'm concerned about your use of the term "perpetrator," I said. "Is there something I don't know about?" I looked at Helena Ouelette. She looked away.

Peggy Price thumbed through a heavy notebook on her lap. "Last month when he was in his respite home he took off all his clothes and went swimming in their pool." she said. "There were three other children — ages five to thirteen — a boy and two girls — in the swimming area with him at the time."

"That sounds harmless enough," I said.

"The Respite foster mother didn't think so." Peggy tried to lift herself out of the chair a bit so as to settle back in more comfortably, but the chair came up with her. She and the chair banged back down onto the floor noisily. "One of the other children was her seven year old natural daughter." she continued. "She doesn't want her daughter exposed to that kind of thing."

"So you are calling that sexual perpetration?'" I asked.

"At this point we are just saying that we want an evaluation done. There are enough red flags, certainly."

"What 'red flags'?" I asked.

"He has abused two other boys that we know of.

"The other two boys were about the same age he was, and I don't think he forced anything on them."

"But our report indicates that he did initiate the contacts." Peggy pointed to something in her notebook that nobody else could see.

"Perhaps so," I said. "But I think `sex play,' would be a more neutral term to describe what happened."

"Perhaps we should hear from other people in the group,"

Peggy said. "Helena, what have you observed?"

"Well, sometimes when he gives me a hug he makes me feel very uncomfortable," Helena said. "It feels very sexual."

"What exactly does he do?" I asked.

"It's hard to say, exactly. He just rubs up against me in a certain way." She crossed her arms in front of her chest, rubbed her upper arms, and shuddered. Her face puckered as though she had eaten something very sour.

"Also there were the bus incidents when he was in kindergarten," Peggy said.

Glenda sighed deeply and rolled her eyes. "Why do you keep dredging that up?" she asked. "That was years ago."

"Years or not," Peggy said, "it's one of the red flags."

"I agree with Glenda," I said. "We simply don't have anything that justifies pinning a sexual perpetrator label on this kid."

"Mr. Foster, there is a pattern here, whether you want to look at it or not," Peggy said. She attempted to twist herself around to face me more directly, but the jaws of her chair held her firmly, and she had to content herself with turning her face toward me and glaring. "We're not labeling anybody. We just want an evaluation so we can see that this child gets the help he needs."

I shook my head. "I don't like it, I said."

"With all due respect," Mr. Foster, this is neither your decision nor the team's decision, " Peggy leaned forward slightly in her chair. "The Department will be making a referral for this evaluation."

"So team process means nothing," I said.

"The team is not Kyle's guardian," Peggy said. "The Department of Humans services is."

*****

In response to this meeting I drafted a memo which I sent off to Peggy Price the following week, with carbons to all the other treatment team members, and to my supervisor, Estelle

Turner.

To: Peggy Price, Supervisor
Protective Services Division
Department of Human Services
From: Alex Foster
Re: Last weeks team meeting
Date: May 23, 1992
Two items emerged in the team meeting last week that I found somewhat disturbing. First, I worry about the term "sexual perpetrator," being used in conjunction with Kyle. I realize that he is a bit rambunctious, and that he does not always comply with society's norms with regard to how children should behave as far as sex and modesty are concerned. However, to the best of my knowledge, we have no report of his forcing himself on a weaker or younger partner. The only actual sex play that I am aware of occurred with boys of approximately his own age. Surely for the term "perpetrator" to be used appropriately there must be some finding of coercion. For the label "sexual perpetrator" to become attached to this child could be a very damaging thing for him with regard to his social and personal identity.

My second concern relates to team process. I understand your Department has custody of Kyle, and that, within the guidelines supplied by the court, you have the final say about most matters in his life. Yet for the last year this did not prevent a cooperative team approach developing in which decisions emerged out of an open discussion with all the care givers, with Kyle himself also having a significant role in the process. This has worked well. Phyllis Black, as the representative of your agency, was competent and flexible and provided good leadership in this process. Kyle is functioning better in all spheres of his life. I now sense that a more unilateral approach is being implemented by the department, with a lot of decisions being made by you alone, outside the context of a team discussion. I feel if things continue in this direction, it will prove harmful to the working relations between the various care givers in Kyle's life, and ultimately harmful to Kyle himself.

I am confident that these issues can be worked out to everyone's satisfaction. I look forward to discussing all of this with you in more depth.

cc. Estelle Turner

*****

"It's better since you been working with us," Henry said. "But Kyle's still got an attitude." He poked the fire with a stick to get the logs to settle, sending a little spray of sparks up into the night sky.

Glenda sat in the lawn chair I had brought along, with Lisa snuggled in her lap. Kyle and I sat on a log together. He was toasting his fifth marshmallow.

I was pleased with how the day had gone so far. Paddling to Neptune Island early in the day had presented just enough of a challenge to keep everybody interested. Swimming was a hit, and Glenda had planned excellent meals which we had all pitched in to help prepare under her supervision. But I knew from adventure based trips with kids that everything could blow up when difficult issues cropped up in sharing times.

"What do you mean by "an attitude?" I asked.

He sat back down and leaned against the granite boulder that rose to a height of about five feet a few yards from the fire. "Like when I need some little job done around the house he acts like it's a big insult — like he shouldn't have to do anything to help out."

"He's getting better with that," Glenda said.

"I little bit," Henry said. "But that's due to the point

system."

"So the point system seems to be working?" I asked.

"I suppose it is," said Henry. "But I was hoping for something more."

"Like what?"

"Like maybe he'd just see that because he's a member of the family, he ought to help out."

"That he would help out because of a sense of duty to the family." I said.

Henry reached into his shirt pocket and took out a small plastic jar of bug repellent, squeezed some out in his hand, and rubbed it on the back of his neck. "Like maybe he would even want to help," he said. "That's what I mean by attitude."

"That's your idea of what it means to be a part of a family," I said.

Henry nodded. "I guess so," he said. "That's a lot of it."

"If I'm a member of the family, how come I hardly ever get to come home," Kyle asked.

"It was the Department of Human Services that changed the home visit plan," Glenda said. She shifted her weight in the chair, and repositioned Lisa in her lap.

"But it was you and Dad that called Human Services in the first place," Kyle said, pointing his marshmallow stick at her. The marshmallow had just caught fire. He raised it close to his mouth and blew it out.

"We were desperate, Kyle," Glenda said. "We didn't know what to do."

Kyle stuffed the marshmallow into his mouth. "It's cause you didn't want me," he said.

I noticed that he was looking at his father as he said this.

"How can you think that?" Glenda asked. "We did everything we could. We love you Kyle. We have always...."

"Wait a minute, Glenda," I said, interrupting her.

"We always wanted him" she said to me.

"I understand that," I said. Then I turned to Kyle. "Who didn't want you?" I asked.

"Them," he said with a sweeping motion of his marshmallow stick that took them all in.

"But you were looking at your dad when you said that," I said.

He chewed his marshmallow slowing and finally swallowed it. Then he licked his fingers methodically. "Especially him," he said.

"Me?" Henry asked. "Why do you say that?"

"It just seemed that way."

"Why would I not want you at home?"   .

Kyle looked at the fire and began poking it with his stick. He said nothing.

"Your dad asked you something," I said.

"I heard him," Kyle said. He continued to poke at the fire a while longer. "Jumper," he said finally.

"Jumper?" Glenda said, sitting up so suddenly that Lisa almost fell out of her lap.

"Mama, be careful," she said.

Kyle looked directly at Henry. "You don't want me because of Jumper."

"You mean when Jumper died?" his mother asked.

Kyle nodded without taking his eyes off Henry.

"That was a long time ago," Glenda said.

"It may still be something that's on people's minds," I said.

"You think I killed him," said Kyle, still addressing his adoptive father.

Henry turned his head away and scratched the back of his neck. "Well, I guess I do think you started that fire," he said.

Kyle lifted his marshmallow stick out of the embers and

stared at the burning tip. "I didn't mean to," he said. It was hardly more than a whisper.

I was astonished at this unexpected confession, and stared dumbly with the rest of the group at Kyle, wondering if they had heard. Kyle pushed the stick back into the embers and avoided looking up.

Unable to understand the sudden silence in the group, Lisa looked inquiringly from one member to the other. "What did Kyle do?" she asked.

When she received no answer she turned to Kyle. "Did you kill someone?" she asked.

"Hush," said Glenda, patting her daughter's lips for emphasis.

When the silence continued Lisa pulled her mother's head down to her and whispered in her ear. "Why can't we talk?"

"You did start that fire then," Henry said.

Kyle looked up. "I played with fire in the stable earlier in the morning," he said. "I thought it was out."

Henry shook his head. "I guess I've always known it."

"I didn't know until I came back and found you watching the stable burn."

"I never expected to hear you say this," Henry said.

"I'm sorry," Kyle said. He lowered his head and rubbed his face with the palms of his hands.

"What did he do?" Lisa whispered to her mother.

"Hush," said Glenda.

"Just tell me what he did," Lisa persisted.

Kyle looked up. "I stared a fire," he said.

"Oh," said Lisa.

"It burnt down a stable and killed a horse," he said. "Dad's horse."

"That was bad," Lisa said.

"No kidding," Kyle said.

"Will they put you in jail?"

"I don't know."

"Nobody's going to put him in jail," Glenda said.

"I'm glad you told," Henry said.

"Do you still want me?" Kyle asked.

"Of course we still want you," Glenda said.

"I'm asking Dad."

Henry nodded. "Yes. We still want you," he said.

"OK," Kyle said.

For some moments the family sat around the campfire, avoiding eye contact with each other, and waiting for someone to give them some direction.

"Sometimes, when people make a breakthrough, they give each other a hug," I said.

Henry looked at Kyle. "Come here," he said.

Kyle broke his marshmallow stick in two and threw it into the fire. Then he stood up and went over to his father. Henry pulled him down, settled him into his lap, and put his arms around him. "I want you," he said.

*****

"Bambi's mother ran and ran and ran," Kyle said. He galloped the little plastic deer across the rug. "But there were too many hunters." Behind the leg of a chair, he hid two plastic army men, that served to represent the hunters.

Bam. Bam.

Bambi's Mother: Oh they hit me. I'm dying. (She falls over.)

"They killed Bambi's mother," I observed.

"Yes, but Bambi doesn't know that yet," Kyle said, picking up another deer that he identified as Bambi.

(Bambi begins to search for his mother.)
Bambi: Where's my mother? I want my mother.
(He comes across Ms. Bear.)
Bambi: Have you seen my mother, Ms. Bear.
Ms. Bear: Leave me alone, stupid. I'm not your mother.
(Ms. Bear kicks Bambi. He moves on and pretty soon he comes to Ms. Horse.)
Bambi: I need my mother. Have you seen my mother, Ms. horse? (Ms. Horse kicks him.)
Ms. Horse: Leave me alone, stupid. I'm not your mother.
Bambi: Oh, I want my mother. (He begins to cry and then encounters Ms. Buffalo.)
Bambi: Hello, Ms. Buffalo. Have you seen my mother?
Ms. Buffalo: Go away. I'm not your mother.
Bambi: Where is my mother?
Ms. Buffalo: Your mother's dead. The hunters shot her.
Bambi: No! It can't be. I need my mother.(He cries harder.)

"Bambi's pretty upset at losing his mother," I said.
"Yes, he is. He's crying. There's so many tears he can't see."

(Bambi stumbles along a little further and then falls into a mud hole.)

Bambi: "I can't see. Where am I?"

"Now he's fallen into a big mud hole because he can't see," I said. "I think Bambi needs a mother. Maybe someone else will be like a mother to him." I pick up Ms. Buffalo. "Here's a different buffalo mother. She's nice. She want to help Bambi. In the next sequence I act the part of Ms. Buffalo.

> *Ms. Buffalo: Hey. What are you doing in the mud? Let me help you out. (Ms. Buffalo pulls Bambi out and takes him to a river where she washes him off.)*
> *Ms. Buffalo: Who are you?*
> *Bambi: I'm Bambi.*
> *Ms. Buffalo: Where's your mom?*
> *Bambi: I don't have a mom. The hunters killed her.*
> *Ms. Buffalo: Maybe I can be your mom.*
> *Bambi: No, you're not my real mom. I want my real mom.*

*****

I had picked him up very early to take him on his home visit. I noticed that his head was nodding like a bobber with I fish nibbling on the hook.

"Looks like you're still in dreamland," I said.

He smiled sleepily. "I stayed up late watching a horror movie. It was awesome."

"Cool," I said.

"They let me stay up late on Friday night."

"You can sleep in on Saturday if you want," I said.

After he tried to find a comfortable position, sitting up, I moved my seat back to make room, and suggested he stretch out and put his head in my lap. After a moments hesitation he did so. With his back to the back of the seat and his legs curled up toward his chest, he fit nicely into the available space.

I asked him a few questions about last night's movie, which he answered listlessly. Then I caressed his head and the side of his face. He closed his eyes and put his thumb in his mouth.

"Sometimes I still suck my thumb," he mumbled in a halfhearted apology.

I shrugged. "Nobody else seems to be using it," I said.

He smiled around his thumb, and relaxed.

"You looking forward to the visit?" I asked.

He took his thumb out of his mouth. "I don't know why I can't go every weekend," he said.

"Well, you're going this weekend," I said. "I hope you enjoy it."

He put his thumb back into his mouth and closed his eyes. I couldn't tell when he went to sleep, or even if he actually did, but he hardly stirred as we continued down the turnpike for perhaps an hour. I continued to run my hand over his hair and cheek.

The need to stop rather quickly at a light as we came off the turnpike roused him. He sat up, looked around, and said, "I'm hungry."

"You're always hungry," I said.

He grinned. "I didn't have much breakfast."

"What would you like?" I asked.

"Look, there's a Dairy Queen," he said, pointing it out to me.

"Ice cream for breakfast?"

"He shrugged his shoulders. "Why not?"

After I bought us each a small cone with jimmies we continued on our way.

"Are you interested in Bambi?" I asked.

He looked at me and licked at his cone. "Why do you ask that?" he asked.

"Because of your play last time."

"Oh, yeah."

"Did you ever see the movie?"

"Yeah. It was one of my favorites."

"Ever see the book?"

"No."

"Maybe I'll get it sometime. I'd like reading it to you."

"The movie was sad," he said.

"The book is too."

"Especially where his mom gets shot," he said.

"Yeah. Especially there. Do you ever wonder about your natural mom?"

"My real one."

"Yeah."

"Sometimes."

"What do think about when she comes to your mind?"

The cone was melting a little faster than he was eating it. He licked at the melted parts, especially around the rim of the cone, until he had it under control. "I think she was pretty."

"Come on, now," I said. "How could she be pretty and have such and ugly kid as you?"

He laughed "Least I'm not as ugly as you," he said.

"That's cause I take ugly pills," I said. "When I was younger I was so charming to the girls I had to do something to keep them away. They were always chasing after me."

"I still got that problem," he said. "I guess it's 'cause of my good looks."

"Seriously, you are a nice looking guy," I said."

"You think so?"

"I do."

He smiled and took a big bite out of the cone. "My mom – my real mom – was dark like me."

"When you think about her, does it make it hard to let anybody else be your mom?" I asked.

He looked puzzled. "How do you mean?"

"Like in your Bambi story. Ms. Buffalo wanted to be like a mom to Bambi, and he pushed her away."

"Yeah," he said. "Cause she wasn't his real one."

"His real mom was gone from his life forever."

"I'm going to find mine when I grow up."

"What are you going to do for a mom in the meantime?"

"I've got my adoptive one."

"But you keep pushing her away."

He stuffed the remainder of his Ice cream cone into his mouth. "She does things that make me mad," he said.

"Of course she does. Real moms – whether they be natural moms, or foster moms, or adoptive moms – are just ordinary people. Sometimes we get mad at them."

He wiped his mouth off with some napkins that had been supplied by the Dairy Queen. "I guess Glenda's been pretty good to me, mostly," he said.

"She has."

I wondered whether I should push the conversation further and talk also about fathers, but I decided that would be too much for one session. Or maybe I just wasn't ready to talk about people who could be like a father to him.

*****

The call that was to end my relationship with Kyle came two days later. It was from Peggy Price.

"The Department has decided to cease visitation," she announced.

I was startled. "Why?" I asked.

"We feel it's in Kyle's best interest?"

"Did you ask Kyle about that?"

"No. But we feel the relationship is abusive," she said. "Sometimes kids aren't able to get themselves out of abusive relationships. Also we are afraid he may further abuse Lisa."

"Further abuse? I hadn't even heard that he abused her at all."

"We had Lisa evaluated by a therapist who specializes in sexually abused children."

I sighed. "Was that June Deprey?" I asked. This was the therapist that the Department generally used when that wanted to confirm sexual abuse.

"Yes. Lisa disclosed some abuse to her."

"I see. Exactly what."

Lisa disclosed that Philip showed her his penis and asked her to touch it. Also he asked to see her private places."

"That was it?"

"June thinks a lot more happened."

"June always thinks a lot more happened."

"I don't think you are interested in looking at the facts, Mr. Foster. Kyle has abused at least three boys that we know of. And he has been inappropriate with his foster mother."

"The boys were his own age. It was consensual. And he didn't actually do anything with his foster mother. She just said she felt uneasy."

"I realize that you don't consider these things to be a problem, Mr. Foster. But it goes past what most people would consider normal. We are concerned that Kyle may represent a risk to children around him. It isn't responsible to wait until after the fact. The Department's mandate is to protect children – not wait until they are abused."

"So what are you saying?"

"We are sending Kyle to a residential sex offenders program for evaluation."

"I don't think he's done enough to justify that."

"It's the Departments decision."

"I understand that. But I'm the boy's therapist. Isn't that a reason to check with me first?

"We're taking you off the case, Mr. Foster. You are no longer Kyle's therapist."

I was too dumbfounded to know how to respond. "You can't," I said finally.

"We can, Mr. Foster. The Department is Kyle's guardian."

"Why would you do this?"

"Frankly, Mr. Foster. We find that you are too difficult to work with."

It shortly became clear that further conversation was pointless, and I hung up.

*****

I had trouble believing that Carol Price could simply terminate my involvement with Kyle without further justification. Hopeful that I could effectively challenge her move in this situation, I wrote a memo to the Director of Protective Services in her area, and sent a carbon to my own supervisor.

To: Robert Morris
From: Alex Foster
Re: The management of the Kyle Joslyn case
Date: June 16, 1994

It is my understanding that you are Carol Price's supervisor. I am writing to you to submit a complaint about the manner in which she is handling the Kyle Joslyn case. I presume she has informed you regarding some of the issues that surround this 12 year old boy.

Ms. Price became actively involved in the case only a month or so ago. Since that time she bypassed the team process that had been previously established between all the providers of services, and began making important decisions unilaterally, often without even consulting with other key professionals. Arrangements were made, for example, to send Kyle to a sex offenders program for evaluation, and to discontinue visiting with the adoptive parents, without consultation with me.

Finally I was informed last Monday that I have been pulled off the case, because I was "hard to work with." This is not good professional practice. I believe Kyle will suffer from the simplistic manner in which he is being understood, and the autocratic manner in which the Department is handling this case. I would request that appropriate members from your agency and from mine sit down together to discuss this matter and seek some resolution of the conflict. I have concerns both with the process of decision making and the content of some of the decisions.

cc. Estella Turner

*****

In a phone call from Glenda Josyln a couple of weeks later I was told that after Kyle learned that he was to have no more home visits and that he was not going to see me anymore, his behavior both in his foster home and at school deteriorated. He began making suicide threats and ended up being hospitalized.

A few days later I received a memo from my supervisor:

To: Alex Foster

From: Estella Turner LCSW

Re: Communications with The Department of Human Services

Date: June 28, 1998

I received your memo of June 16, and have had a chance to look into the matter. After talking with Carol Price from the Department of Human Services, I am persuaded that the Department acted within its rights in the situation you complained about. They are the child's guardian, and are paying for the services we are rendering. Professional differences of opinion do crop up from time to time in this business, and I think it is a part of your professional responsibility to take it in stride when things do not go your way. I know this can be difficult in situations where you have strong convictions.

In the future I am asking that you clear it with me before going over the head of any person from the Department you are working with to make a complaint. When such complaints are made, it becomes an administrative concern that has ramifications beyond the clinical dimension of the situation. I'm afraid I need to warn you that should you persist in pursuing administrative matters unilaterally, as you did with you June 16th memo, it could lead to a letter of reprimand.

*****

I was checkmated. If rage by itself were able to produce real effects in the world, a hole would have opened under the Department of Human Services and the agency would have fallen into hell. But there was nothing to be done. A few days later, when I was able to calm myself down sufficiently, I wrote Kyle a note. Being afraid that either the department of Human Services or the treatment Center where Kyle was sent might screen my note, I sent it by way of his parents who were permitted to visit him once a month.

Dear Kyle,

I am sorry that I won't be able to work with you anymore. I want you to know that this was not my choice.

I liked working with you very much. I hope things

will go better for you in the future.
I think of you often.

Your   friend,

Alex

Allah Saves Me From the Jaws of Death

I have heard the mermaids singing, each to each.
I do not think that they will sing to me.

From "The Lovesong of J. Alfred Prufrock"
T.S. Eliot

"I like big boobs," Justin said. "I don't know why. I just do." He pressed the nudist magazine we were looking at into his lap, in order to hide the bulge in his pants.

He looked up at me. I still wasn't quite used to his left eye. It matches his real eye fairly well, but of course it doesn't move. His curly red hair is beautiful despite the fact that it's never combed. But his artificial eye may make it more difficult to find a girl friend. Girlfriends is one of the things we talk about.

"Most fourteen-year-olds like big boobs," I said.

He scooted over so that he was right up against me on the couch, and turned the page to a large picture of people swimming and playing naked on a beach.

"I wish I could go somewhere like that," he said.

"Like a nudist beach?"

He nodded.

"We'll see," I said. I would like to take him, but am not sure whether I want to take the risk. I used to take one of my clients skinny dipping from time to time. We both loved it. If human services had known about the skinny dipping they would have assumed I had engaged in sex with him. I had not, unless just looking was sex, or unless it was sex to wrestle with him in the water, to have him ride piggy back on me while I swam, to teach him to dive off a rock, and to find joy in these activities. But to actually have sex with him – to masturbate him or have him masturbate me, to take his penis in my mouth, or to do any of those things I had read about – these were not things I had ever done. I had never done them with Scotty with whom I went skinny dipping, nor with Justin, whom I have known for about six months, nor with eleven year old Neil, who I think may be in love with me, nor with any boy. I am a married man with two daughters. I like women. I've been faithful all my life, so even with women I'm not what you would call experienced. But with my other love, that is to say, with boys, at 52 I was a still a virgin. When I was with boys I loved, I couldn't seem to break through the shared fiction that our feelings had nothing to do with sex: in short, I was afraid.

"What does 'we'll see' mean?" he asked.

"I don't know," I said. "Maybe some day you will be able to go to a nudist beach."

He looked up at me and grinned. "Yeah! I'd like that. A lot." I noticed that his teeth were a bit crooked – not decayed, but crooked. His mother doesn't have the money for orthodontics. Because she works, she gets too much money for Medicaid and too little to attend to any but the most urgent dental and medical needs.

"You'd have fun in a nudist scene," I said.

My right arm was resting against the back of the couch. It was getting uncomfortable in that position, but I felt that lowering it around his shoulders, and pulling him in closer to me, might be too forward. With the nudist magazines, the atmosphere was already pretty charged. I pulled my hand back and ruffled his red hair.

He looked back at the magazine and turned the page. "That one's kind of fat," he said," indicating a heavy-set woman sitting on a beach.

"You see all kinds of shapes on a beach like that," I said. "Most of us aren't movie stars."

On the next page, he saw some children jumping into a swimming pool. "Sometimes when I swim at the lake, I just wear my shorts," he said.

"They look enough like swimming trunks you can get away with it?"

He nodded. "They're boxer shorts." He pulled up his T-shirt so that I could see his belly. It was soft, with a little fat on it. "Like... these," he says, indicating the tops of his plaid shorts where they extended past his blue-jeans.

"I see," I reached over with my left hand and playfully patted his belly. He grinned, let his shirt fall back down, and turned his attention back to the magazine.

"Sometimes when I swim, I jump up and down in the water, and my shorts come off. It feels good."

"Of course it does," I said. "That's the only way to swim. Unless there are others around that don't like it."

"They can't see. I'm under the water."

"Right."

"I step on my shorts so they don't get away."

I laughed. "You sure don't want them to get away," I say. "Not at a time like that."

"I'd have to walk back naked."

"And that would be embarrassing."

He nodded his head in agreement. "People would laugh."

"Don't you wish you could go skinny dipping anytime you wanted to, and nobody would mind?"

He nodded, and pointed to a photograph of a teen-age girl. "That one's got hair down there."

"She does. She's pretty."

"I've got hair down there." He lifted the magazine from his lap and pointed to his pubic area. The bulge in his pants was conspicuous. I was sure that he wanted me to notice.

"Do you?"

He looked up as me and smiled. "Lots."

"Can I see?"

"Sure."

He stood up and unfastened his pants. He pulled them down to his knees, along with his boxer shorts. His erect penis was larger than a little boy would have, but it had not yet attained its full growth. A thin fringe of very short reddish hair curved around the base.

I reached out and touched the hair. "You do have hair there," I said. "That's nice."

"Do you have lots of hair?" He asked.

"Do you want to see?

He nodded. "If you want."

I unfastened my pants and pulled them down. I liked this intimacy, but for whatever reasons – my age or my nervousness – I was only a little aroused.

"You've got more hair than me," he observed.

"I'm older." I reached over and took his penis in my hand. He smiled and nodded. I moved my hand up and down a couple of times.

"That's how I do it," he says.

Our hour was up, and I was quite anxious. "Well," I said. "Let's get dressed."

I hugged him briefly before he left.

I was told once by a supervisor that I had a "problem with boundaries." I guess this is what she meant. I wasn't sure whether I was happy with what had just happened. It was such a mixture of things. But I did know that a watershed had been crossed.

I had to use the bathroom. As I was walking down the hall,

a woman who works in the office next to me came out of the lady's room. She said, "Hi" as she went by, but her attitude seemed cool. I felt, irrationally, that she may have heard something through my door – that somehow she knew what I had done.

*****

Rachel stabbed another bundle of spaghetti from the bowl, and dropped it on her plate. "I shouldn't do this," she said, and scooped up a liberal helping of spaghetti sauce.

"Live it up," I said. She is a bit overweight by conventional standards, but I don't mind. It would be hard to get used to a thin Rachel.

"Are you going in tonight?"

She nodded.

"What unit?"

"They still have me in pediatrics."

"Leave the dishes alone," I said. "I'll get them later."

"That would help," she said.

She broke off another piece of garlic bread. "Ran into a really weird story on the net today."

"Yeah?"

"It took place in Afghanistan," she said. "I guess they have a super repressive group of Moslem fundamentalists running the country. They caught this guy for sodomy. That's a crime there. In fact it's a capital offense."

"How old was his partner?"

"It didn't say. But over there it doesn't make any difference. If they catch you doing what they call "sodomy," they kill you."

"Sounds like our fundamentalists."

She shook her head. "It makes our Christian fundamentalists look tame," she says.

"Maybe," I said. "But we don't know what ours would do

if they ran this country."

"I don't think they would be as bad as the Muslims," she said.

I shrugged. "So what did they do?"

"They decided to push a big stone wall over on him to crush him to death."

"Incredible!"

"Yeah. So get this. They carry out the execution. They use a big military tank to push a wall over on the guy. When they are done they dig him out and send him to the hospital. They figure he's dead, but he's just unconscious. He's got broken bones and head injuries and, of course, he's in a lot of pain. But somehow he survived."

"I guess it just wasn't his time."

"'Allah saved me from the jaws of death.' That's how he explains it. He claims that his miraculous escape vindicates him. It proves that he never was guilty of sodomy."

"So maybe they'll just push another wall over on him – a bigger one this time."

"They can't. Somewhere in their holy laws it says that if anyone survives an execution, they can't execute him again."

"It's different here," I said. "I read about a guy in this country who survived being executed in the electric chair. When he recuperated they electrocuted him again."

She finished the last of her spaghetti. "I've got to get ready to go," she said.

"How's things at work?"

"Pediatrics is hard," she said. "You get close to the kids, and then they leave."

I put the last of the spaghetti on my plate. "We professionals aren't supposed to get too attached to our clients," I said.

After Rachel left for work I relaxed in my easy chair

listening to a CD of the *St. Thomas Choir Of Boys and Men* singing Benjamin Britten's *Rejoice In The Lamb*. Eventually I got up and gathered the dishes. As I washed them, I thought about whether I should tell Rachel about what had happened with Justin. She's my best friend and up until now I have told her everything. She knows how I feel about boys, so that part of it wouldn't shock her too much. I don't think she would be jealous, but she would worry. They don't push brick walls down on us here for doing things like that. But they might as well. And figuratively speaking, some of the bricks would land on her as well as on me.

*****

It was 2:30 in the morning. Rachel was on night shift. Heidi was in her bed. She sleeps soundly. I had been tossing and turning in my bed for almost an hour. I couldn't find a comfortable position. Fantasies intruded into my consciousness, like a procession of images in a *La Dia de los Muertos* parade on its way to the local graveyard.

I am naked with Justin when the police barge into my room, kicking the door open. I am in court being chastised by the judge. All my neighbors have come to watch. My daughter is mortified. I am in prison. Three men come to rape me in my bed.

I knew that I was not going to get to sleep soon, so I got up, went downstairs to the kitchen and fixed a cup of hot chocolate. I took it into the living room, where I settled into the easy chair and picked up a novel I'd been reading. It wasn't very good, but it distracted my mind. After a while, I heard Heidi moving around upstairs. I heard the toilet flush and shortly saw her feet and legs as she came part-way down the stairs. She looked down at me. "Are you OK, Dad?"

"Yeah. I had a nightmare, and thought I'd let my mind calm down."

"I saw the light on down here."

"Go back to bed. I'm fine."

I listened to her steps padding to her bed room, and heard the mattress creaking and rustling as she got back into bed.

All this I could lose just for touching Justin's penis. I must be mad.

I tried to read some more as I finished the hot chocolate. Eventually I became sleepy and went over the couch. I lay down and covered myself with the quilt. I felt peaceful there, and soon drifted off to sleep.

*****

"Neil says he doesn't want to come to any more sessions."

I pulled the receiver away from my ear for a moment while I tried to make some sense of what Neil's mother was telling me. My anxiety about what had happened with Justin was already more than I could handle. The last thing I wanted was serious problems on another case. "Neil doesn't want to come to any more sessions," I repeated. "Does he say why?"

"He says you are stupid and boring,"

"He's put up with my stupid boring personality for over two years now," I said. "Does he give any other reason?"

"I tried to get something more out of him, but he clammed up. You know how he does."

"I do."

I thought back to the last time I saw Neil, remembering how he began the session:

He bounds into the room, dashes over to the toy area, and grabs a four foot length of cardboard tubing that came with a rug I recently bought. He straddles this tube, and begins rubbing it vigorously. "That's my super dick," he says, and gallops over to the couch where I am sitting. He presents it to me.

I put my hand on the end of the tube and begin to rub it tentatively. I look at him, and smile weakly. It's a question. He laughs, drops the tube, and pulls back.

"What happened in the play room last week?" Sandra asked.

"Nothing out of the ordinary."

"Well, he came out of there upset. I could see it. You looked upset too."

"It was a hard session."

Neil throws his sinewy body at me and we fight. I enjoy the contact. Clearly he does, as well. But I am anxious. When he presses his slender buttocks against my belly as he extricates himself from my effort to subdue him, I enjoy it too much. He breaks free and dashes back to the far corner of the room. There he straddles the tube once again and rubs it vigorously. "I'm super criminal, he says. Nobody can stop me. You're a cop."

"In what way was it hard?" Sandra asked. I smiled at the unintended double entendre.

"Nothing special," I said. "It's just that he wouldn't open up to me – was very distant."

After twenty or thirty minutes of wrestling, chasing, catching, escaping and killing, to the tune of his super-criminal fantasies, it's difficult to get him to settle down. He throws himself into the chair on the opposite side of the coffee table rather then joining me on the couch as he usually does. I bring out a bag of chips and a Pepsi. I tear open the bag of chips and dump some of them on the coffee table for us to share. Then I pour about a third of the Pepsi into my own cup, and give him what remains in the bottle.

"I was interested in how you pretended that the

tube was a huge penis," I say.

"You talk stupid," he says.

"How do you mean?"

"Penis sounds dumb. It was a dick. A super dick."

"Dick, then. But what was interesting was how you pushed it toward me, like you wanted me to rub it too."

"This is boring," he says, and takes such a big mouthful of Pepsi that some of it overflows at the edges of his mouth.

"It makes me wonder whether maybe some of your sexual feelings might have to do with me."

He glares at me. "Maybe you're a faggot," he says, "but I'm not."

"Having different kinds of feelings doesn't mean somebody's a faggot – whatever that is".

"It's somebody like you."

"People have all different kinds of feelings." I say. "Everybody does..."

"Boring! Boring! Boring!" He chants the words in a singsong voice.

"Why is it so hard just to talk about this?" I ask.

"It's stupid."

"In your play you show a lot of interest in dicks and what they can do, but when we try to talk about it, you say it's stupid.

He glances up at the clock. "When's this session over?"

I sigh. "You wish it would end soon?"

"It's boring in here."

"Did you try to get him to deal with some things he didn't want to?" Sandy asked.

I had promised Neil that I won't disclose what he says and does in our sessions without his permission. "I don't know," I said.

"Usually he loves to see you."

"Maybe he was still angry at me for going on vacation. Sometimes that makes kids feels you have deserted them, and it takes a little while to get over it."

"He liked getting your card, and seemed OK with it," Sandy said.

"Well, we've been talking about the possibility of discontinuing therapy. Maybe its easier to leave people around a big blow up."

"Do you think now is the time to end the sessions?" she asked.

"I don't know. They can't go on forever."

"Hank and I were talking about the same thing."

"It's hard to know when it's the right time to stop," I said. "But if he is saying that he doesn't want to come any more, maybe we should just accept that."

"I agree. I don't think we should force him. He's doing OK in school now."

"Tell him I want at least one more session with him to wind it up. And that from then on it's his choice."

"OK."

"If the session is boring to you, we could end it early," I say.

He ignores my remark. "Its really boring here," he says. "I wish we could do something interesting."

"Like what?"

"Why don't you get a Nintendo game?"

"'Cause I think that would get in the way of what we get together for."

During the rest of the session he refuses to engage with me in any significant conversation. The time drags painfully for both of us, but he does not take me up on my offer to let the session end early. Finally it's over. When we go out into the waiting room we find Sandy and Hank. Neil and I are both lacking in animation. Our few remarks are stilted and forced.

"I could tell that something was wrong as soon as I saw you and him come out of your office" Sandy said. "I wish I understood what it was."

Well, let's give it some time," I said.

*****

I was lying in bed trying to recall a dream. Rachel was asleep in the bed beside me, snoring faintly. The dream was about sucking my thumb. I was doing it very vigorously, and was wondering whether a person could get an orgasm doing it. It felt very good. I thought this must be what babies feel – it's not just the food and the cuddling. It's also that the nipple in the mouth is very exciting. I don't know, of course, whether that's true.

Heidi had gone to stay over at a friend's house, so I had no competition for the bathroom. While I sat on the john, I read an article in *Naturally* on Caravaggio. In the accompanying photos, I noticed the similarity between angels and cupid. Light and dark angels. The ambiguity of Eros. Interesting. In Caravaggio's painting, Eros was trampling civilization under his feet. I thought about Caravaggio's life – his brawling, his flamboyant self assertion, his making love to his boy model. We may share certain aesthetic tastes, I thought, but there our similarities end. He was a brawler. I, on the other hand, have measured out my life in coffee spoons.

When I finished with my business, I went downstairs and made a cup of coffee, which I brought up to the bathroom. I filled the tub with water that was as hot as I could stand, and lowered myself into it slowly. I balanced the coffee cup on the edge of the tub where I could easily reach it with my right hand. This was the good life. I thought about Justin's penis, and felt a slight stirring in my own. I fantasized about taking a shower with him. I was scheduled to see him later in the day. I thought about Goffman's book on stigma. Some stigmas are out there for all to see. Justin tells me how the other boys at the junior high tease him about his eye. Other stigmas are private, and there are disclosures that could be catastrophic. Suppose people knew how I felt about boys. Suppose Justin told someone about my holding his penis.

If I felt attracted to boys and also to adult women, but not very much to adult men, did that make me a homosexual? I didn't know. I supposed it depended on how one defined the term. I sipped my coffee. It was just right.

My hemorrhoids were acting up. I wondered what anal sex would feel like. Even if I didn't have hemorrhoids, I didn't think I would want somebody doing that to me. Would I want to do it to a boy if it were safe? I didn't know. That wasn't where my fantasies took me. The bath water was beginning to cool so I got out. After drying off I inserted a Preparation H suppository.

I flossed my teeth carefully that morning. During our most recent encounter, I had noticed that Justin's breath was not good. It seemed to me that he didn't brush his teeth well, and that he was careless about bathing. I wondered whether I should mention this to him.

My beard needed trimming, especially on the neck. I soaped it and got out my safety razor. Justin was preoccupied with body hair. During the third time we got together, he proudly showed me how he was getting hair in his armpits. Very faint, almost transparent hairs were beginning to grow there. He also pulled up his shirt to show me that he was getting hair on his chest, around his nipples. His nipples were slightly enlarged, as sometimes happens with pubescent boys. I didn't actually see any hair around them. But he didn't give me long to look.

I went to the bedroom and began selecting my clothes. It was a cold day, but I decided not to wear long-johns. Justin wears boxer shorts. I never found boxer shorts that comfortable, but he seems to feel they make him sexy. I put on a fresh pair of blue-jeans, and found a shirt that would match the last pair of socks I had in the drawer. I was giving a lot more thought than I usually do about whether I was color-coordinated.

*****

It was about ten minutes after the hour. I admitted to myself that if he hadn't arrived by now, he probably was not coming. I went to my shelves, took out a book on humanistic economics, and tried to read. Right then, I didn't care exactly where Adam Smith went wrong. When it became clear that I couldn't concentrate, I put the book down. Why did he not come? Maybe he had told somebody what happened. Maybe the police were already on their way to my office to confiscate my computer, charge me with sex abuse, and defame me in front of everybody I care about. Maybe I had misread what seemed like an invitation. Perhaps he had been astonished and distressed at my holding his penis. His erection spoke clearly enough about his desire, but perhaps he had felt that I and his body conspired together to betray his higher self. I couldn't bear the thought of picking up the phone to inquire. Suppose his mother should answer the phone? I might have been able to hear from the coldness in her manner of speech that my worst fears were realized.

In any case, I had to admit that Justin wouldn't be seeing me that day. He wouldn't see that my socks were coordinated with my shirt, or that I was wearing jockey shorts. Did I really think that we would undress together during the session? I didn't know what I thought would happen when he arrived. I just wanted to be clean and attractive for him – and make sure my breath didn't smell.

I remembered his first disclosure of forbidden sexual behavior. It was a couple of months ago that he told me about it.

I have just discussed my version of the "love map" with him. I diagram this on a sheet of drawing paper. The diagram consists of two vertical rows of circles on either side of the page, with a stick figure representing the self in between. Each row contains three circles. The row on the left represents males and the row on the right, females. From top to bottom, they represent someone significantly older than we are, a peer and someone younger. The paper sits on the table between us.

"What I am trying to say with this diagram is that we might love all kinds of people. This one on the upper right could be your aunt." He listens to me without comment. But he appears to be attentive so I continue. "Here it indicates younger boys. See, it's on the male side of the page and being on the bottom shows it's someone younger than us. That's like your little brother." He is still listening so I point to the middle circle on the left. "Here's boys who are peers. That's like buddies your own age. These are all people you love," I say, and then take the final leap. "And with any of them, the love could at some point be expressed in a sexual way."

He says nothing. I have made my point and don't want to ramble on, so we sit in silence. I am afraid that I have pushed it too far – that he might be turned off, or even shocked.

Finally he speaks. "A friend might come to your house and go into your bedroom."

"Yes," I say, "that might happen."

"You and him might take off your clothes."

"And then...?"

"He might suck on your dick."

"That happens with lots of boys your age who like each other."

"It's bad."

"I'm not sure it's all that bad."

"It's not too bad if you like each other?"

"That's what I think."

He looks at me and smiles. "Me too."

"Did that ever happen with you?" I ask.

"You won't tell Mom?"

"I promise."

"Pinky promise?" He puts out his hand with his little finger extended. I haven't made a pinkie promise in ages, and am a little surprised that someone his age would want to seal a contract in this manner. But I have no problem with it. I offer him my hand, with the little finer extended. He takes it and our promise becomes sacred.

"Who did you do this with?" I ask.

"David."

"I remember you telling me about David. He's your special friend."

"I have a girl friend too."

"That's like I was saying in my diagram. A person can feel many different kinds of love."

During the weeks that followed that session, Justin told me more about his love life. His aunt likes for him to give her back rubs, and sometimes she lets him rub her breasts as well. Once he masturbated when his little brother was sitting in his lap. Another time, he let his friend David "stick his dick in my butt." As we discussed his sexual exploits, I told him how much trouble he could get into if people found him being sexual with his brother, and suggested that he limit himself to kisses, hugs and horseplay there. And I cautioned him about the health risks of anal penetration. We talked about everything. It was understood that our "pinkie promise" covered all this material. But we had made no "pinkie promise," about his not telling about things I did or said. Suppose he told a friend who told...

I didn't really think he would tell what happened between us. But why did he not call if something got in the way of the appointment? Why would he leave me hanging? If you allow yourself to love seriously disturbed kids, sooner or later they will cause you to suffer. You imagine that their bond with you is as deep as your's with them. That's the fatal illusion. By and large they do not see who you are, do not focus on your needs, and do not sense your pain. Therefore they are capable of anything. Justin and Neil had this in common.

*****

Neil spun around and around. He was sprawled in the large stuffed rocking chair that is constructed to rotate a full 360 degrees. Each time he came around he shot at me. He had decided that I was a police officer chasing him in a police car. This was his compromise. I told him this couldn't be a regular play session, and asked him to sit down and talk with me. He was sitting down... sort of.

"Bam, bam, bam...bam. BAM. Ha. I got you that time. You're the driver. The car flies off the road and crashes into a tree." With a jerk of his head he flipped his blond hair out of his eyes, and spun on around.

"We need to talk, Neil."

"Talk, then."

"It's hard to talk when you are playing with that gun."

"I can play and listen too."

"But you need to be able to talk, as well."

"What do you want me to say?"

"What happened at school today?"

"Mom told you that, didn't she?"

"She told me something. But I'd like to hear it from you."

He stopped spinning. I felt maybe I was making headway. He took careful aim. "Bam. Right in the heart."

"Neil, put the gun down."

"Are you my boss too?"

"Is that what it's about? Everybody wants to be your boss?"

He dropped the gun. "I know what. Lets finger paint."

"That's not what we're here for."

Our time was already half over. At his mother's request I

had squeezed him in between two other appointments. We had only a few more minutes to try to get things sorted out.

He spun the chair around so that I was facing its back. All I could see of him was his leg hanging over the arm. "What are we here for?" he asked.

"I thought it was your idea to come here. That's what your mom told me."

"I just wanted to get out of school. It's better here than there."

"That's something. But the idea was that maybe you and I could sort out what happened at school."

"I'll just get the magic markers and draw while we talk." He jumped out of the chair and went over the shelves where I keep the toys and art supplies.

"I need your attention, Neil."

With his back to me he began speaking in an imitation adult voice. "He just does it for attention." I could hear some teacher evaluating the cause of his behavior after he had done something outrageous.

I couldn't help laughing. "All right. That's funny. But I still don't want you drawing. I do need your attention."

He came back to the chair without the art materials and sat down again. "You sure do need a lot of attention, Mr. Alex."

"So what happened at school?"

"I called Ms. Purcell a bitch. That's all."

"So what got you to that point?"

"I didn't say it to her face."

"Who did you say it to?"

"Lewis."

"Lewis?"

"He's the one who sits beside me. I was talking to him — not to Ms. Purcell."

"So she overheard you."

He shrugged. "I guess I said it a little too loud."

"Why did you call her a bitch?"

"She wouldn't let me go to the bathroom."

"You needed to go bad?"

"I was going to explode."

I looked at the clock. "We only have a couple more minutes Neil. I'm not sure this was all that helpful."

"It got me out of school."

"Are you mad at me, Neil?"

He swung the chair around so that its back was to me once again. There was a long pause. "No," he said finally.

"You told your mom you didn't want to see me any more."

"I changed my mind."

"You want us to continue?"

"I guess so."

"You say you want to continue our sessions. And I do too. But when you come, you do everything you can think of to avoid talking with me."

He spun around again so that he was facing me. "Sometimes we talk."

"Sometimes." I said. "But not very much."

He shrugged. "Some things are private."

"Why is it so hard, Neil, for you to tell me about the things that bother you?"

He spun the chair around a couple more times and when it comes to a stop, the took careful aim at me with a finger that had again become the barrel of a gun. "Bam." The he looked down. "Because you might tell," he said, very quietly.

Ah! The session was worth while, after all. He had told me the important thing. It might not be the only important thing, but it was the ice-jam that prevented our talking about anything else.

"Good," I said. "That's important." I glanced at the clock again. "Our time is up now, but I'll remember that."

"I'll see you Thursday," he said.

*****

I was sitting in my office doing some paper work, when I heard a noise in my waiting room. I went to the door of my office and looked out. It was Justin. It was four days since he missed his last appointment and three days before his next scheduled one.

"Justin! Come in."

"I was just wandering around."

"Fine. Good. I had a cancellation, so I'm free this next hour. Come in and lets talk a minute." I ushered him into my office.

"I've got my friend's pants on," he told me, and pulled up his T-shirt to show me a pair of baggy blue jeans that rode low on his hips so that about a fourth of his plaid boxer shorts were visible.

"They're nice," I said.

"He gave them to me."

"Well, sit down." I gestured toward the couch. He sat down, and I positioned myself across from him in the rocking chair.

"I just wanted to say hi."

"That's fine. I'm glad to see you." I rummaged through the books and other clutter piled beside my chair and pulled out the paper with my weekly schedule on it. "You missed your last appointment."

"When?"

"It was scheduled for last Monday. At 2:30."

"I forgot."

"Well, I'll give you a card next time. And do call if you can't make it in for some reason. OK?"

"Sorry."

"It's all right. It's fine. I'm glad you came in today."

We sat staring at each other without saying anything for a few moments. Then he said, "I walked from school."

"Well, I'm glad you did. Would you like some popcorn?"

He nodded. "Good."

I pulled a dollar out of my billfold and handed it to him. "Run down the hall and buy a soda we can share. I'll get the popcorn started."

He was back with a 20-ounce bottle of Pepsi before the popcorn in the microwave had stopped popping. As he began to unscrew the top of the soda, it fizzed all over his hand and dripped on the rug. "Screw the top back on," I said. He did, and the fizzing stopped. "Now, undo it just a bit at a time, and let the pressure out," I said.

"Sorry." He followed my suggestion and successfully removed the cap.

Soon we had the popcorn bag torn open between us on the coffee table. I poured a little of the Pepsi into my coffee cup and put the bottle in front of him.

"I hope you weren't upset by what happened last time," I said.

He looked a little puzzled and didn't answer.

"I mean when I held your dick in my hand."

"It felt good," he said.

"It felt good to me, too. But I wouldn't do something like that if you didn't want me to."

"It's what I do myself."

"I guess most 14-year-olds do that," I said. "Probably all of them. Probably most people of any age, too, as far as that goes."

"It feels more good if someone else...." He ended his sentence there, and helped himself to some popcorn.

God! That certainly sounded like an invitation. *Do I dare*? "It feels better if someone else does it to you," I said.

He nodded faintly.

"Yes. I suppose it would." My stomach was full of knots.

He washed down a mouth-full of popcorn with a gulp of Pepsi, and helped himself to another handful."

"Would you want me to do that to you?" I asked.

He shrugged and smiled at me.

"I could do that," I said.

He nodded. "If you want."

"Like now? There's time."

Again he nodded his agreement. I got up and closed and locked the door to the waiting room, and the door to the inner office. Then I took off my shirt and pants and hung them on the coat rack.

He got to his feet and pulled his T-shirt up. I could see the bulge of his erection. It was clear that he wanted me to remove his pants. I undid the button of the blue jeans and unzipped the fly. As I pulled his pants down his penis popped out through the opening in his boxer shorts. I took hold of it and rubbed it briefly, but he still had his boots on. "Maybe it would be better if we got those boots off," I suggested.

He almost fell over the coffee table as he and I together struggled with his boots. When they were finally off I pulled his pants and underwear the rest of the way off. Then I removed my own underwear.

"Maybe if I lie down, it would be good," he said.

He stretched out on the couch on his back. I pushed the coffee table back out of the way and knelt down beside him. I took hold of his penis and kissed it. Then I pushed his shirt up and rubbed his chest. I played with his nipples for a bit and then returned to his penis. I wasn't sure what he would like. I took his penis in my hand and stroked it for a little bit, then, very gently, I felt his testicles. Then I put his penis in my mouth and sucked on it.

"That feels good," he said.

It felt good to me too. I explored it with my tongue. Then I sucked on it some more. I remembered my dream — sucking on my thumb. After a little bit he pulled away from me. I thought he was coming close to a climax and didn't want to go off in my mouth. I wasn't sure whether I wanted him too or not, but I finished doing him with my hand. A small amount of semen came out on his belly. He seemed a little embarrassed about this.

"I had to pee," he said.

"It's not pee. It's semen. Or cum. It's what would make a girl pregnant."

I took some Kleenex out of the box that I keep on the coffee table and cleaned him up.

He sat up on the couch, and I sat beside him. He looked at my penis. It was only partly erect.

"Do you want to touch it?" I asked.

He felt it gingerly. "It's not much a boner," I said, apologetically. "I think I'm too nervous. I never did this before."

"I'm not scared," he said.

I reached down, worked myself up into an erection, and came to a climax.

"You had to pee, too," he said. "A lot."

We dressed without much talk. Before he left, I made out a card for his appointment next Monday and gave it to him.

*****

It was one of those three o'clock in the morning times – 3:20 to be exact. I had wakened about a half hour earlier with a thought in my head and a feeling in my belly. The thought was "my God, what have you gotten yourself into?" The feeling was a hollow, cold, dreadful emptiness. Very quietly, so as not to wake either Rachel or Heidi, I got out of bed and slipped down stairs. Sitting cross legged in my easy chair, I wrapped my blanket around me.

"God, what have you gotten me into?" I said. I noted the apparent shift of responsibility in my new question. Was this a variation on the "Devil made me do it" ploy? I didn't think so. I was not trying to "blame" God (or Buddha, Allah, Earth Mother, Creative Matrix, Ground of Being or whatever other alias He/She or It might be traveling under). But I didn't create my own penis, nor the beauty of boys. Of course one might point out that it had been my choice to actually put my lustful hand on his eager penis. Well, perhaps. But neither did I create this impulse nor its sense of rightness. Was it possible that my penis (and his as well) might be right and the world around us wrong about these things? Did my penis hear the will of the creator more accurately than all those shrill moralists who dominated the written word? But they do dominate the written word, and more. Those moralists determined who went to prison and who was free to walk among the wild flowers. *Do I dare disturb the universe?* Which brought me back to my original question. God, what have you/I gotten me/myself into?

The dreadful hollowness crept out into my extremities and threatened to swallow me whole. I tried to make myself still – first my body, then my mind, then my emotions. None of my efforts worked very well. As I tried to find a refuge of quietness in my center, I discovered that an ice monster had taken possession of the place, and would not be dislodged by my meager efforts to comfort myself. All the natural bird songs and water flowing sounds in the world interlaced with the most soothing flute music imaginable wasn't going to melt this monster. But I did the best I could.

No answer came to me, so I rephrased the question. "What am I to do?" Still nothing came. I felt very cold. Then it popped into my head. I was suspicious of this question/answer process. Is the word of Allah something that just "pops into one's head?" I wondered. Lots of things pop into peoples heads and most of them aren't Allah. But I was too desperate to argue the point.

What popped in was: "Tell them."

So I said: "Who? What?"

"The boys. What your problem is."

I knew, Allah or not, that this is what I had to do. *I love you but I am afraid.* It wasn't that complicated really. *If you tell others about this I will be killed.* Maybe it would be all right. I felt the ice beginning to melt. Soon I would be able to sleep.

*****

I was sitting on the couch with Neil. We were reaching the end of the popcorn. He sat sideways with his back against a pillow that rested on the arm, and his legs draped over my lap. He was a bit disheveled from our roughhousing. I removed his socks and massaged his feet.

"Did you know I would betray you?" he asked.

He was referring to the game we played earlier in the session. He had assigned to me the role of a bad guy who was in cahoots with him. Then, after we stole all the money, he had abandoned me to the police — handcuffed me and left me where I could be found.

"You caught me by surprise," I said.

"I thought so." He smiled.

I took aim at his mouth with a piece of popcorn. "Open up."

He opened his mouth and tried to catch the popcorn which I threw. It hit his chin and bounced off onto the floor.

"I remember something you told me last time," I said.

"What was that?"

"You said you didn't tell me important things because you were afraid I would tell."

"Oh, that."

"Well, you know, that works for me too."

"How?"

"There are things I would like to tell you, but I am afraid to."

"I wouldn't tell anybody," he said.

"Some of these things could get me into a lot of trouble."

"What kind of things?"

"I'll tell you what," I said. "Lets make a deal. Neither of us will share the things we tell in here. What I say will be private just like what you say."

"Except if we ask permission to tell," he added, remembering the rule I had previously set up about confidentiality.

"Unless the person has permission to tell. That's the deal. OK?"

"OK."

"Shake?"

We shook.

"The thing that's hard for me to talk about is partly about sex," I said.

He looked at me with interest. He said nothing, but his calm, attentive waiting said, "yes? go on." I was massaging his legs, gently.

"Well, some of that play that you do makes me think that sometimes when you are with me, you feel like masturbating."

"I'd never do that in front of you," he said.

"The thing I'm trying to say is that sometimes I have similar feelings about you."

His head fell slightly to one side, and his mouth drooped open just a bit. He said nothing. But his face was a question mark.

"You remember those love maps I showed you?"

"Yeah. About how people can love different kinds of people."

"Right. And about how everybody has his or her own love map, and how that's all right."

"I remember."

"Well, my love map is very strong in two places. Women is one place. And boys about your age is another. Does that mean I'm gay? I don't know. I think people can feel lots of things, and we don't need to call them anything in particular. Like take somebody your age who loves another boy. We don't need to say 'he's gay,' or 'he's not gay.' He's just whoever he is with his own particular love map."

We were both silent. He leaned back with his hands behind his head, reflecting. I continued to massage his legs.

"Like me and Tyler."

"You and Tyler?"

"Sometimes we jerk off together."

"Lots of boys do that."

"Once we did it to each other."

"That's a way to show love to each other," I said.

"Jerking off?"

"I can be a kind of love," I said.

"Me and Tyler's blood brothers."

"Good. You know the kind of love you feel for him? I think that's probably pretty close to what I feel for you."

He looked at me with slightly widened eyes, and smiled faintly. Then he snuggled his legs more closely up against me." I want us to get together *twice* a week," he said.

"We'll see. At any rate you want the sessions to continue."

He nodded.

I looked at the clock. "The time is getting away from us." I said. "We have only about five more minutes. Probably your mom is already in the waiting room."

"Can she hear us?"

"No. That's why I keep some music going in the other room."

Neil sighed. "I wish I could live here," he said.

*****

My experiment with a new kind of honesty could hardly have gone better than it did with Neil. With increased confidence in the words I had received from Allah, I looked forward to Justin's visit. When he arrived for his session, I intercepted him on his way to the couch. "Sit down in my chair," I said.

He stopped, but did not follow my instruction. "Why?"

"Because you are the counselor today."

"I'm just a kid. How can I be the counselor?"

"It's just pretend," I said. "Sit down."

He flopped down in the rocker.

"Don't slouch. It will give me the feeling you're not interested in what I'm saying."

He sat up. I put my reading glasses on him, and handed him my pad of paper and a pen. "Here. You'll need these to take notes."

He balanced the glasses on the end of his nose and said in a very self important way, "Hello there. I'm Doctor Foster. What's your problem?"

I took my place on the couch. "I really need to talk to someone," I said. "See there is this kid I know. He's really neat. Gentle. Got a nice sense of humor. All kinds of good things about him. Well he and I got to messing around the other day and I ended up playing with his dick."

"Did he like it?" he asked

"I think so. I wouldn't do that unless I thought he did."

"What's the problem?"

"Well, I've got this counseling business, and a family, and friends, and all kinds of things I like. And if it ever came out the I played with this kid's dick, I'd lose all that, and they would probably send me to prison for the rest of my life, and everybody would think I was a creep. That's a lot of bad things. On the other hand I like this kid a lot, and I like playing with his dick. If he likes it, I want to be able to do that."

"I have to write this," he said. He turned with total absorption to the task of making his notes. It required his full attention and took about five minutes. Finally he placed the pad of paper face down on the floor beside him and looked up. "I think it's OK," he said.

"Why do you say that?"

"He won't say anything."

"Why not?"

"Because he likes you."

He wanted to be naked again. We fixed some popcorn, and got ourselves a couple of sodas. We both took our clothes off and sat on the couch. I put my arm around him and he cuddled up against me. I smoothed his hair, rubbed his chest and played with his penis while we watched a video of a nudist event.

"It's doing it," he said, toward the end of the hour. I rubbed his penis more vigorously and he ejaculated a small amount of semen.

When he left I picked up the pad on which Justin wrote his "therapist notes." It had two numbered questions:

1. Does he like it when you play with his pinis?

2. Does he like to play with your pinis?

*****

The Playboy magazine was open on the coffee table in front of us. Neil had concealed it in his book bag in order to bring it to his session with me. He wanted to show me his favorite pictures.

"See how big her boobs are?" he said, pointing to the centerfold. "That's what I like!"

"That's a pretty awesome magazine," I said. "Where did you get it?"

"Tyler gave it to me. He gets them from his dad. His dad has hundreds. So he never misses a few."

Then he pointed to the pubic region of the woman. "But she's got a lot of hair down there. I don't like that," he said. His ideal seemed to be a woman with huge breasts and no pubic hair.

"Why don't you like hair down there?"

"I don't know. It's yucky."

"Maybe as you get older it won't seem so yucky," I said.

He shrugged, and then began flipping through the magazine, showing me some of his other favorite pictures. "I jerk off to all these," he said.

"I guess a lot of kids do. Grown-ups too, for that matter."

"It's nasty," he said.

"I don't think wanting to see people naked and jerking off are nasty."

He looked down and leaned away from me. "I might go to Hell," he said.

"Where'd you hear that?"

"Dad's going to this new church. That's what they say. It's in the Bible."

"That kids go to Hell for jerking off?"

"Yeah."

"I don't think that's in the Bible," I said.

"Dad thinks it is."

"Some churches teach really bad things," I said. "They teach us to be afraid of God. They teach us that God can send His children to a place where they will be tortured forever. Nobody who loves his children could do that, whatever the children did. So really they teach us that God doesn't love us."

He stared at me, his mouth open a bit in surprise. I don't usually express myself with quite this much vehemence when I'm with him. Then he looked down at the magazine. He stared at the woman's pubic hair again. "I'm not sure," he said.

"Look, God made dicks, just like he made faces and hands. And He made the kinds of feelings we have about dicks and boobs and vaginas. He didn't make everything else except our dicks and then send us to the Devil and ask him to finish the job."

Neil laughed.

"You laughing at me?" I asked, pretending to be mad.

"It's funny, what you said."

"What?"

"God made dicks!" This got him going again and I began laughing with him.

"Well, He did make our dicks, don't you think?"

"I guess so," he said. "I don't know who else could of." He was still laughing.

I picked him up off the couch, set him on my lap, and gave him a hug. He put his arms around my neck and kissed me on the cheek.

Suppose some day Neil offers me his dick, I wonder...

Do I dare to eat a peach?

Well, perhaps.

Ungame

From behind the two glass doors I watched Elizabeth in the parking lot. Her body, heavy, and insufficiently responsive to the wishes of her mind, struggled forward between the supporting arms of two community integration workers. She was determined to negotiate the distance between the car, few yards away, and the door without the use of her wheel chair. Her struggles brought to my mind beetles I overturned as a child so that I could pass the time watching them strain to right themselves.

Her nose was running from the chilliness in the air, and perhaps from her efforts as well. A piece of mucus clung to her upper lip. She was meticulous about her appearance and would have been embarrassed I saw her in this condition, so I returned to my office.

My office and Elizabeth's day program are in the same building. I had gone up the hall because she was late, and I wanted to see what was keeping her. I now knew that after the workers helped her clean up her face, she would go the bathroom, and that she would be joining me in about five minutes. As I waited, I thought about her coming to my office last week – on the day of my panic.

*****

My panic had been precipitated by a phone message that I found on my answering service the first thing in the morning:

"Alex. This is Justin. They found out about us. Sorry."

I was metamorphosed by Justin's message on the answering machine. In the afternoon I lay on my couch like Kafka's beetle-man, paralyzed. My clandestine identity was exposed, and would soon be visible to the entire community. I would be found guilty of unforgivable crimes – crimes against children. They were tender crimes of love – for the most part committed only in my imagination – but there were many of them. And with Justin my forbidden impulses found expression in reality more fully than ever before. I would be driven from the community – possibly imprisoned, perhaps for life. As I thought about my losses, past, present and potential, I began to cry. It's unusual for me to actually cry, but I was lost in the huge shadow that has fallen all my life between my love and it's fulfillment. Several times I tried to pull myself together to do something useful, but I always fell back onto the couch, and cried again. It was while I was in this state that I heard the hum of Elizabeth's wheel chair. I collected myself as well as I was able and met her at the door to the waiting room.

"I'm sorry I had to cancel the appointment today," I said. "I had an emergency come up." We spoke to each other from the doorway, as I did not invite her in. She looked up at my face and said, "Are you all right?" Despite her serious speech defect, the words were unmistakable. She actually wanted to know.

"I'm OK," I said.

She knew I wasn't. "Your mother?" she asked.

"No. She's OK."

"What then?"

"I can't tell you, Elizabeth. I wish I could, but I can't."

"I'm sorry. Big mouth." She pointed at herself.

"No. It's OK. I appreciate your concern. But it's private."

She shook her head. "You're not OK."

"I'll see you next week, Elizabeth. I'll be OK by then."

"I go now."

I returned to the my office, threw myself back on my couch, and began crying again, but now I found some comfort in my tears. I felt Elizabeth actually cared about my upset.

*****

I heard her wheel chair coming down the hall. This time I was ready for our appointment. I had left the door to the waiting room open. As I got up to go and greet her I heard the arm rest of her wheel chair scrape against the waiting room door. There is a scratch about a foot long in the door from her coming in this way every week.

"I'm late," she said. She was breathing hard and the movements by which she controls the chair were jerky.

"Relax, " I said. "We can run over a few minutes. We'll have most of our usual time."

Once she managed to get settled on the couch, she took her teeth out and put them in her purse. Even without her teeth, she is very hard to understand, but it's a little better this way.

"You all right?" she asked.

"I'm fine this week," I said.

She studied my face to see whether I was telling the truth, and seemed satisfied. "Game?" she asked, gesturing toward the book case where I kept my therapy games.

"Sure," I said. "But first let me take your picture."

"Really?"

"Really. And with the camera I just bought, I'll be able to let you see yourself on the monitor right off."

"Yes," she says. Her face brightened and she sat upright.

"It's a camera I got because I need to make web pages," I said. I went to the desk and pulled my new digital camera out of the drawer.

I had no plan except to take a couple of shots of her sitting on the couch, and then to show the picture to her on the monitor. I was interested in trying out my new camera, and I thought she would find this amusing.

"Wait,"she said. "My teeth." She fumbled through her purse until she found them, and hurriedly stuffed them into her mouth.

I took a couple of shots with her smiling at the camera. Then, unexpectedly, she leaned over and assumed the pose of a provocative woman stretched out on her bed of pleasure. I laughed. "Yes, that's great."

I took two shots of her in this pose. Then, as I positioned myself for a third shot she rolled off the couch. She moaned as she hit the floor. She was helpless. I put my camera down, moved the coffee table, and got to her as quickly as I could.

"Are you OK?"

She moaned again.

"Let me help you."

I helped her sit up and then, with one hand behind her back and the other and holding her hand, I struggled to pull her up. She was very heavy and at first did little to help. I made a grunting noise, and strove to get a better grip on her. This seemed to motivate her to make more of an effort. Like an eight-limbed beast suffering from Cerebral Palsy we struggled to our feet and fell back onto the couch. I pushed her into an upright sitting position.

"You all right?" I asked.

"All right," she said.

Thinking it would help calm us both down, I offered to go up the hall and buy us a Diet Pepsi. She agreed that she would like one. I was back with the soda in less than two minutes.

I divided the Pepsi between us, pouring some into my coffee cup, and the rest into a big cup with a large handle I keep in the office mainly because it is one she can handle pretty well. As she leaned over the coffee table to grasp her cup she inadvertently drooled on the table. I ignored it at first, but she called attention to it by wiping at it with her bare hand. "Sorry," she said.

"It's nothing," I said, and got a paper towel to wipe it up.

*****

At about five in the evening of the day that Justin left his message on my answering machine, the phone rang. I could feel the adrenaline surge through my body. I was sure it was the police. I dragged myself off the couch and grabbed the receiver after the third ring.

"Alex here."

"Alex Foster?

"Yes."

"This is coach Pierson. Russell Pierson"

"What's on your mind?"

"Well, um... it's Justin Colinas."

"I see... what about him?"

"Well, something he wrote."

"Yes?"

"It's... you know..."

There was a long silence. "I guess I don't know," I said.

"'Course not. ...um... maybe I could come by," he suggested.

"OK. When?"

"Now?"

"Yes."

"I'll be by in fifteen minutes."

I wasn't sure how I would survive that quarter of an hour.

*****

I went over to the shelf get the Ungame. "We'll look at those pictures I took when you get back into your chair and ready to go," I said

"On the TV?" Elizabeth asked.

"Yes."

I returned with the game. I set up the board and let her pick the counter she wanted. I chose the #2 cards, which asked more intimate questions. On her first roll she landed on the square that said "If you have been lonely this past week, go to the lonely area." I read it to her. She didn't seem to understand what she was supposed to do.   "Have you felt lonely anytime this last week?" I asked.

"No. Not lonely."

The game proceeded though a few more turns without very much that was productive coming up. Then she landed on an Ungame square, drew the card and handed it to me to read. It said, "To whom can you turn if you need to be comforted." She looked at me with a blank expression.

"That means like if you really feel unhappy about something, who can comfort you? Who can tell you something that makes you feel better or hug you? Things like that."

"You," she said.

"It's nice of you to say that."

"Remember you hug me?"

She referred to an incident that occurred almost a year ago.

*****

I had been working with Elizabeth and Peter to help them with their relationship. Peter had not really wanted to continue with her, but could not bring himself to say so. Consequently he kept leading her on, and then pushing her away. It kept them in a state of emotional turmoil, and was the original reason for the referral to me. I saw them both jointly and individuality. When I became clear what was going on, I told Peter he needed to be honest with Elizabeth, both for his own sake, and for her's. The session during which he finally told her what he felt was devastating to Elizabeth.

"I don't want to go with you anymore," Peter said to her. It did not follow logically from anything we had been discussing at that moment and consequently took both Elizabeth and me by surprise.

"What?" She couldn't believe he meant it.

"Like boyfriend and girlfriend," he said. "It's no good."

"But why?" It was more of a cry than a question.

He was flustered now. "No good," he said. "Doesn't work."

When it became apparent that he really meant what he said,

and that he could not be talked out of it, she began crying. It was an uncontrollable expression of grief that made Peter very uncomfortable. "What can I do, Alex?" he asked.

"You did what you had to do," I said. "You probably can't do anything much to help her with this now."

"Should I go?"

"I suppose you might as well, Peter. I'll be in touch with you later."

After Peter left, Elizabeth continued to cry. I wondered whether the frustration of an illusory relationship might not be better than this despair. I could see that there was nothing I could say that would help much, so I went over to the couch and sat beside her. I pulled her over to me and hugged her and rocked her for some time, saying, "I'm sorry Elizabeth. I know it hurts."

*****

"I remember that, always," Elizabeth told me. "You hug me.".

"You helped me to," I said.

"Me?" Her eyes were wide. "How?"

"Last week when you asked if I was all right."

"Big mouth," she said.

"No," I said. "I couldn't tell you what had me upset. I still can't. But it helped me to have someone who could see that I was upset, and who seemed to care about it."

She beamed. "You OK now?"

"I'm a lot better now."

I landed on a "question or comment" square and asked her, "What dream did you have last night?" I asked.

She looked at me with wary eyes, then smiled shyly and looked down. "Nothing," she said.

"Nothing?"

She nodded.

"I don't believe you."

"Why?"

"Because you looked... well... like something went through you head when I asked you."

"Bad dream," she said.

"A nightmare?"

She shook her head negatively.

"Ah," I said. "One of those dreams. A sexy one, I'll bet."

She smiled uncertainly. "A man hold me."

"In a good way?"

"I don't know," she said.

"You don't know?"

There is a pause while she decided how to respond. "Am I a whore," she asked. She knew what my answer would be. We had been over this ground before. But she needed the re-assurance.

"You know you're not a whore. Our dreams are our dreams. Just as our feelings are our feelings. There's no right or wrong about them."

"He did things to me."

"Sexual things?"

She nodded

"Well, was he nice?"

She hugs herself and grins. "Oh, yes."

"Well, you know what you should do about dreams like that?"

She looks alarmed, as though she feared I might take her dreams away from her. "What?"

"Enjoy them. And consider yourself lucky to have such nice dreams."

"I'm not a whore?"

"Elizabeth, dear, everybody has dreams like that.

Everybody has dreams and fantasies about what they'd like to do with people they would like to love."

She looks down, then raises her eyes to peer at me slyly. "You too?"

I laugh. "Yes, of course. Me too."

"You too old," she says

"I may be old," I said, "but I'm not dead."

We both laughed.

*****

After the call from Coach Pierson I fell back onto the couch. I wondered whether his coming over to see me was a setup. Had he already told the police? Would he arrive with some local version of a swat team that would present me with a search warrant, and arrest me? I thought about calling my wife but my paralysis was complete.

As I laid on the couch my attention focused on the door. I realized now that had left it locked but took no steps to remedy this situation. I was not anxious to welcome my persecutors. Scenarios of who I might encounter at the door crowded into my mind. Court scenes, explanations to loved ones, encounters with contemptuous neighbors, dealing with attacks in prison – image after image, none of them reassuring, filled my brain.

I was jarred out of my reveries by the sound of a real knock at the door. I had not heard footsteps. Maybe they are trained to approach quietly, I thought. I lifted myself off the couch and went out into the waiting room. I paused a moment, and then unlocked and opened the door.

Big-boned, muscular and lanky, the six-foot-seven frame of Coach Russell Pierson filled the doorway. I could barely see around him.

"You're alone?" I asked, foolishly.

He looked behind himself. "Yeah."

"Well, come in."

He ducked slightly to clear the doorway. I led him through

the waiting room into my office. I noticed as we went through my rooms that he didn't bend over just at the doorways – he walked always in a slightly hunched over position – as tall girls who are determined to minimize their height sometimes do. As he sat on the couch, his knees sticking awkwardly up in from of him, he reminded me a giant frog. In contrast to his huge muscular body, Coach Pierson had a rather boyish face framed with blond hair that was beginning to recede from the forehead.

"What about Justin?" I asked.

"I don't know," he said, pulling his billfold out of his back pocket. He removed a irregularly folded piece of paper from it, and tossed it on the coffee table between us.

I stared at it, afraid to pick it up..

"It's to you," he said.

I unfolded the note. It showed evidence of having been labored over by someone who is not used to writing as a means of communication. There were many places where the text had been crossed out with a heavy hand. Minus the smudges and the crossed out places, the letter read as follows:

Dear Alex.

I want to see you. I like to be nakid with you. You are hairy and I like your pinis. I like it when you touch mine. When can I see you?

I miss you.

XXXXX Justin.

Despite being an a state approaching terror, I could see that it was a love letter, and I was touched. He wanted to see me. How impossible that was, yet how much I also wanted it.

"Jesus" I said.

Couch Pierson rubbed the back of his neck and looked down, carefully avoiding eye contact. I knew I had to come up with some sort of explanation.

"It's some sort of fantasy;" I said.

"That's what I thought," the coach said.

"He didn't want our sessions to end," I said. "I doubt that he ever intended to send this." It was true about his not wanting our sessions to end.

We had talked about terminating our sessions together. I had very mixed feelings about this. I wanted to continue seeing him, but at the same time was in a panic about our sexual activities being discovered. He was in a "Teens" class, and it seemed he was surrounded by adults with nothing better to do than wonder whether he might have been touched in a not all right place. I wasn't sure about his judgment.

I looked at Coach Pierson, trying to read how he was taking this.

He looked up at the picture up on the wall behind my back. "I don't know," he said. "Kids that age, well, you know. All those juices."

"How did you find it?" I asked.

On the locker room floor. Last period yesterday. I guess it fell out while he was changing up for gym."

"And you asked him about it."

He nodded.

"What did he say?"

"Not much."

I couldn't see a way out. "You're a mandated reporter, aren't you," I said.

"I guess so," he said. "We had an in-service on that." He squirmed around, trying to find a more comfortable position on a piece of furniture that was just too small.

"An allegation does a lot of damage, whether anything gets proved or not," I said. 'It can pretty well mess a person up."

"Coaches too," he said.

I looked at him but he still avoided eye contact. "It's

dangerous to work with kids at all these days," I said.

"It is," he said. "You pat a boy on the butt, and say, 'good job,' and it's all over."

"Pretty scary," I said.

"Well, I got to go."

"Can I ask what you plan to do about this?" I said.

"Its your note," he said. "It's not my business."

"So you don't feel you need to report his?"

He shook his head.

"That would help me." I said. "A lot."

He nodded. "Well, see you 'round."

I stared at the note on the desk. Then, as the coach ducked through the door to my office and started through the waiting room. I turned. "Thank you," I called after him.

After the door to the waiting room closed, I picked the note up and read it again. "When can I see you. I miss you." Perhaps, I thought, if he called or just came by, nobody would have to know. Then I told myself that these thoughts were suicidal. I went over to the couch and fell back on it. Alex, I said to myself, you've got to be crazy. You must never see this boy again.

I did see him a few more times, but avoided any sexual involvement. I told him it was too dangerous for both of us. Gradually our relationship came to an end.

*****

"I wait and wait, and nobody comes."

We were talking about the loneliness she felt at night. I took advantage of landing on a "question/comment" square to ask her whether she thought she would ever have her dream come true – would she ever find a man who would love her and hold her, and not just one night for sex.

"At night then, you find yourself waiting for someone."

"Yes. I listen. I want someone to knock on the door."

"So you do feel lonely."

"A little." She smiled sheepishly, aware that this contradicted what she told me earlier about never being lonely.

"You want someone to come so you won't be so lonely."

She nodded.

"I know how that feels," I said.

"You do?"

"I certainly do," I said. "Its happened lots in my life."

She nodded her head in an understanding way. I couldn't bring myself to tell her that I knew the knock she waits for will never come. On some level I am sure she must know this. Nor could I tell her about Coach Pierson knocking on my door. That knock may not have brought Justin back, but at least for now I may still hope for a life that is worth living.

"It's very hard to wait and wait," I said.

"Yes," she said. "I wait and wait, and nobody comes."

A Fleeting Wisp of Glory

In the Colesville High School auditorium, many of the children waiting for the play were sprawled between the stage and the front row of the folding chairs. As I negotiated a path through the children someone called my name and ran to me, arms outstretched. It was Henry. I dropped to my knees and engulfed his small body in a firm hug. His arms squeezed my neck so tightly, and he pressed himself against me with such force, I almost toppled over backwards.

"Will I see you again, Alex?" He asked.

"No," I said. "I can't see you any more." I tried to think of a way to explain. They won't let me. It isn't good for you. What could I say? "I miss you," I said.

"I miss you," he said. He was not one to lie about such matters.

Arms came around my shoulders from behind. I turned and recognized the ten-year-old girl smiling at me.

"Hey, Janet. You were great in last week's performance," I said.

"Thanks."

By the time I turned back, Henry's green eyes were preoccupied. I had lost my connection. "I wish I could..." I began. But he pulled away and escaped in the confusion. It would not be seemly to follow him in order to continue our conversation. What could we, in any case, talk about in this public place?

I found my seat and studied at the Program. "The Colesville High School Players present: Camelot." Camelot was spelled in large Old English letters. I looked over the list of the personae, hunting for people I knew. I found several in addition to Janet's brother and sister, Earl and Amanda. I had known the Salines children for some years. They participated in virtually all the performances the Children's Theater put on, and I had directed a number of these. They were afraid that I would miss seeing them perform in a play I was not directing. Earl was a senior with a good singing voice and was playing the part of Lancelot. Not being a senior, Amanda had a smaller part, but was still anxious for me to attend. They had called me to make sure I remembered the play, and had secured me a good seat. So of course I went.

The audience hushed as the pit band began to play. I was surprised at how good they sounded. As I listened to the familiar overture, memories of my encounters with Henry came to me in scattered bits – fragments that did not represent a coherent sequence as it actually unfolded in any given play therapy session.

I remembered him acting the part of the devil and forcing me to do his evil will, which usually involved some diabolical torment of babies and other innocents. I remembered him sword fighting with me. How many times I was vanquished? I remembered his fascination with poop and pee, and his pulling at the front of his pants in obvious sexual arousal when he changed the diapers of a doll, or when he asked me to pretend he was the baby who needed his diapers changed. I remembered the day he became a baby tiger. He had me cuddle with him under the table that had been converted by pillows, blankets, and whatever he could find, into a tiger's den. We were nestled in a squalor of weapons and pretend food. We had been eating humans all day and were tired, so we had gone to sleep. He awoke and had me feed him from the bottle. I knew then that we were reaching the most protected burrow of his being – the place that he defended so strenuously with his outlandish behavior – the place of vulnerability that would hopefully be the home of his re-birth. I was as thrilled to lie there cuddling him, feeding him, petting him, as he was to be fed and petted.

I remembered wondering whether it was wrong that my heart too had been lost, and that I was finding it with him? But how else would I have been so perfectly attuned to his hurts and bizarre strategies of self preservation?

I remembered my hopes that one day he would accompany me on some of my adventure based group excursions into uncharted waters. And I remembered his green eyes – so full of cruelty, need, confusion, and love.

The curtain raised on act one. I was transported to another place and time: a hilltop near the Castle at Camelot where a light snow is falling. It is afternoon.

*****

Ms. Williams, the High School Music teacher, had made some adjustments in the play in order to scale it down, and make it more manageable both for the cast and the audience. She knew there would be many younger children in attendance so she divided the play in to three acts to allow for two intermissions. The first act, as she divided the play, ended with the scene in which they sang the wonderful "Lusty month of May." With the music fresh in my mind I was singing, under my breath:

Whence this fragrance wafting through the air?
What sweet feeling does its scent transmute?
Whence this perfume floating ev'rywhere?
Don't you know it's that dear forbidden fruit!
Tra la tra la. That dear forbidden fruit!

A frumpy teenager with thick glasses and a substantial harvest of ripe acne on her face waved at me enthusiastically. At first I did not recognize her. But then a younger face peered through the changes and I realized it was Rachel. I waved back with equal enthusiasm and made my way through the crowd to greet her. After all these years – it had been about four since I had last seen her – we were still on hugging terms, and we did.

"Rachel! How good to see you."

"Yes." She beamed.

"Are you still in the same home?"

"Yes."

"That's wonderful." Any sort of stability was usually a good sign.

"You want to see my report card?"

"I'd love to."

She pulled a crumpled paper from the pocket of her blue jeans and handed it to me. The grades listed for the first term were all passing. In my heart I thanked whatever benign special education teacher it must have been who made it possible for her to be successful.

"Do you remember the canoe trip?"

She grinned. "Of course."

"I remember you sitting in the canoe when we were ready to start out, and saying you didn't want to go." I smiled at the recollection.

"I was scared."

"Of course you were. But you got over it and we did make it to the island." The image of her sitting helplessly in the canoe, beginning to cry, and refusing to budge, came to my mind. We had the canoes packed up, and the children were waiting in eager anticipation for the adventure. "What the hell am I going to do with this?" I remember muttering under my breath.

"Do you still see or hear from any of the girls on the trip?" I asked.

"Margaret."

"Great."

It was on this trip that Rachel first had the experience of actually belonging to a group. Despite her glasses with the thick lenses, her physical awkwardness, her total lack of social skills, her lisp, and the odd twists in her thinking and expression, she was accepted. Her peculiarities were noticed to be sure – but each girl had her "problems." Rachel was neither a mascot nor an unfortunate Martian to be handled with tolerance and kindness.

She belonged as fully as any of the other seven girls.

"Do you still see Ms. Fiori," I asked. This was the therapist to whom I had transferred Rachel when the adolescent hormones beginning to flood her body made me feel she was more than I wished to handle in individual therapy.

"Yes."

"You and she getting along well together?"

"She's nice."

"Great.

The conversation threatened became a bit strained. We knew each other too well to talk about the weather. But we could not discuss the therapy sessions or more personal matters in this setting. I made a vague excuse that I had to see somebody about something and withdrew.

I saw Janet. In order to give some plausibility to my claim about needing to see somebody, I tracked her through the crowd.

"What do you think of your brother and sister," I asked when I caught up with her.

"They're great. I can't wait until I get to high school."

"Figure you'll be in the musicals?"

"What else?"

"I'm sure you will do well."

And, of course, unless the proverbial Mac Truck comes out of nowhere to put an unseemly end to her promising life, she will do well, in drama as in most of her other endeavors.

As I waited for the curtain to go up on act two I remembered my sessions with Rachel. She loved to pretend that she was a witch, and together we made witches brew. The essence of it was finding the most foul things imaginable to mix into a watery concoction. We pretended that a bit of red paint was snake blood; marbles were baby eyes, etc. The resulting brew was "milk" that was fed to babies. Needless to say it poisoned them and caused them to die horrible deaths. Always with my more disturbed clients we came back to this issue of milk and breasts.

My task in therapy was to help her identify with the baby rather than the witch, and to find some good milk in life.

During the last stages of my therapy with her she started bringing in an old record player, and some old forty-five rock and roll records. She wanted us to dance. I believed this would facilitate the integration of some of the new juices flowing in veins, and would encourage her live more in her body, which was a thing she carried around more like an old suit case than a home where she lived. The problem was that I had always had trouble living in my body as well, and was perhaps the world's worst dancer. My office had a window that opened onto the parking lot and I worried that someone might be able to look through the thin curtain and see us. I think we would have looked like a spider trying to have sex with a Mexican jumping bean. But to ourselves we were the King and I.

The curtain rose to Act Two (which was really scene six of act one.) Pelenore and Arthur are playing backgammon. Arthur is winning the world.

*****

When the curtain fell on Act Two (really Act II, scene 1), Ms. Williams came to the stage and began talking about what an honor it has been to work with such a fine group of students etc. etc., and naturally my mind wandered. Inwardly I listened again to the song I had just heard:

> *If ever I would leave you,*
> *How could it be in springtime,*
> *Knowing how in spring*
> *I'm bewitche'd by you so?*
> *Oh, no, not in springtime!*
> *Summer, winter or fall!*
> *No, never could I leave you at all.*

Earl had sung it well. I thought about Camelot. Camelot –

an epiphany of Eros incarnate in a community – a moment of perfect equipoise containing already the seeds of its imbalance and destruction. Perhaps the gods consider too much happiness to be a matter of hubris. I thought of times when I was unusually happy.

On Sandy Island one day last summer I was left with three eleven-to-thirteen year old boys, Michael, Timmy and Raymond, while the rest of the group with the other counselors went off on a exploration of a near-by lake. We had the responsibility of preparing supper, but that left us ample time for play. Play meant skinny dipping. Whose idea it was I don't recall. It just peculated up between the four of us.

We had not been in swimming long when Timmy yelped. He was standing in water that came up to his waist. Anxiously, as though in a dream in which one is being chased but cannot make ones legs move because of an inexplicable heaviness, he pushed against the water toward shore. I followed, thinking he might have stepped on something sharp. I caught up with him on the beach.

"What's the matter?"

"Something bit me?"

"Where?"

"There." He pointed to a small mole on the outside of his thigh.

I laughed. "It was the sun-fish. They will nibble at anything dark on your body that catches their attention. They can't hurt you."

"It scared me."

"Don't you swim in lakes much?"

"Not like this."

"Just at regular beaches, and in swimming pools?"

He nodded. "I don't think I want to swim here."

"It's safe."

"What if there was a bigger fish?"

"What would it do?"

"It might bite... my thing."

I laughed. "I know how you feel. But it really won't happen. Bigger fish are too afraid of you."

"Are you sure?"

"Positive. I've been swimming like this for years, and never had a problem, except for the sun fish."

"What about turtles?"

"They'll never let you get close to them."

It took some time, but he allowed himself to be talked out of his fear, and we returned to our romp in the water.

That was the day we found the five legged frog. Later I read about such frogs becoming more common, and being an indication of something profoundly out of kilter with the ecosphere. But that day we know nothing of this. We knew only that the frog was the most amazing thing any of us had ever seen.

Michael caught the creature on the shore while we were swimming, and called excitedly to us. "A five legged frog! Come and see." We thought he was putting us on, but when we came to look, it was indeed the monstrous thing he promised. A fifth leg, fairly well developed, protruded from the side of the frog. Closer examination revealed in addition a missing eye. For a moment the four of us stood ankle deep in a naked huddle, literally struck dumb. It was as though we were in the presence of the Holy of Holies speaking to us in this omen of disarray.

"Awesome," Timmy said, finally.

There was nothing any of us could add.

Michael put his find in an orange juice jar he retrieved from the trash, and brought it back to the beach where he guarded it possessively. Timmy and Raymond ran off to see if they could find others.

When we were alone Michael said, "I'm growing hair down there."

"That happens at your age," I said. "Can I see?"

He was standing at the edge of the lake, facing the water.

He nodded. I came around and looked more closely. There was an arch of blond fuzz beginning to sprout around the base of his penis.

"Can I feel it?" I asked.

"If you're careful."

I ran my fingers over the soft growth. "Very nice," I said. "Do you have any down below?"

"A little."

He allowed me to lift his penis, and caress his slightly fuzzy scrotum briefly. Then this became too much.

"Hands off the merchandise," he commanded.

"You're the storekeeper."

He looked at me and could see I was becoming aroused. "You like me, don't you," he said.

"Yes," I said. "The feelings I have are similar to those you have about Timmy." He had confessed to me on a previous trip that he was in love with Timmy. We had that kind of relationship. He could tell me anything. I think their love was never expressed in anything more than horseplay, sharing, and hugs, though he was clearly aware of the strongly sexual quality of his feelings.

He smiled and lay down on his stomach in the sand. "Give me a back scratch," he said.

I complied. With his permission, the back scratch included a "butt massage," as well. This was my "lusty month of May." It was the first time I had been that familiar with him.

I shared a tent with Michael and Timmy. Michael would never have allowed it to be any other way. That night Michael insisted on sleeping between me and Timmy. Both boys accepted a back massage from me and then, opening their sleeping bags so they could be used as blankets, they cuddled up together. I had trouble getting them to settle. They giggled, whispered, poked, and teased each other into the wee hours of the morning. When they finally fell asleep in each others arms I felt lonely, and a little jealous.

When he returned from the camping trip, Michael, in his exuberance, bragged to his foster parents about the skinning dipping. The foster parents told the Department of Human Services worker, and that was the end of my leadership in the adventure based group. It was also the end of any individual psychotherapy I was doing with children who were in DHS custody. I could not be trusted. My judgment was faulty. DHS workers can smell Eros like police dogs can smell marijuana.

Ms. Williams was naming the seniors, one by one, and having them come to the stage for a special certificate. I watched as Earl came up to receive his award. He deserved it. His singing and acting of the part of Lancelot was the best I have ever seen in a high school performance. He may have the talent to become a professional entertainer. But he wants to go into Physics. I guess he's a prodigy in math. He's a nice looking boy as well, though a little short. That detracted some from the Lancelot role and I think it may be of concern to him. But it closes no doors to his future.

Suppose my only deficiency was that I was a little short.

I identify with the broken ones – with the miss-fits, the unacceptables, and the foster kids – with the over-achievers who still don't achieve much – with children who have lousy pasts and even less promising futures. This does not mean I'm not also fond of Earl and his sisters. They carry their many' talents with grace. I have never seen them treat anyone with contempt or flaunt their superiorities. I wish them well. It's just that my wishing seems a little superfluous.

I looked around at the parents gathered in the gym. They were solid people, for the most part, and good hearted. I felt afraid of them. I visualized myself dangling overhead, like the spider Jonathan Edwards preached about. I, "a sinner in the hands of an angry God," was suspended above a fiery hell. Only a thin thread prevented me from falling into the condemnation of these good people. This thread was fragile indeed. Michael only had to mention my touching his private place, or the butt massage. He did not have the sense to keep quiet about the skinny dipping. How could I be sure he would not mention the other transgressions? Perhaps one day in a group in which the leaders harangued about bad touchers he would be tempted to have his moment in the limelight – his moment of glory. Would he be taken in by the lure of victimhood? It seemed unlikely. But I wasn't sure.

"Mr. Foster, did you or did you not touch Michael on his penis, his testicles, and his pubic hair (the little bit of it he has), and rub his buttocks with your hands."

I retreated back to reality. The last of the seniors received her award and we were dismissed for a break before the beginning of the last act. I felt hot and restless. Avoiding anyone I knew, I spent the break outside breathing in cool air and trying to quiet my nerves.

When I returned they were blinking the lights. I looked up past the first row of seats and saw the teen-age son of Henry's foster parents sit him down roughly and say something stern to him. Henry turned his back and pouted. I worried also about Henry. Could something that had happened in my play therapy with him be mentioned and misconstrued? Men, after all, are not supposed to be breast-feeding boys his age. The flames licked at my heels.

The curtain lifted for Act III. Arthur and Guenevere are together in a quiet and domestic moment. Arthur complains of feeling old...

*****

The curtain fell and the cast received one of the few fully deserved standing ovations I have participated in giving. For a high school amateur performance, it was superb. I wanted to hide my tears and dribbling nose. In a town of lumberjacks such a display might have been seen in a negative light.

The words and the music were fixed in my mind.

I loved you once in silence,
And mis'ry was all I knew

And yet when they broke the silence it led to

Twice the despair,
Twice the pain for us
As we had known before.

They were damned either way.

As I squeezed through the crowd to find Earl and Amanda to congratulate them on their performances, I caught a final glimpse of Henry exiting with his family. He would soon be getting a new therapist. I knew the woman. She was a prim and proper no-nonsense type. I knew they would be trying to get a new therapist for Michael as well.

I thought about my dog dying when I was a boy. His name was Trixie, a black and white mongrel that wandered into our lives by accident one day, apparently after having been abandoned by someone. And it was a "he" despite the name. I was still a little vague on matters of gender, and the important thing to me at the time was that he would be able to learn tricks. He did learn to sit – sort of. At times it was necessary to push his rear end down a bit for him to remember the command, but if he ended up sitting I was satisfied. If we had been more persevering in our teaching, he might have learned more.

He chased cars, a habit we could not break, and once was hit by a car. When he re-cooperated he ran with his body turned at a peculiar 30 degree angle to the direction he was moving.

Trixie went everywhere with me during the summers of my childhood.   This gave me great comfort and a feeling of importance. He was killed in a second car accident when I was twelve. Sensing the depth of my grief, my father, with the best of intentions, promised to buy me another one. It was the first time I realized that the ones we love are replaceable – a fact that has left me lonely ever since. I never really took to the replacement, though he was by all ordinary standards a better dog.

I found Earl with his family.

He was glowing with pride, but trying hard to be modest. This was his moment of glory. "I'll bet you are proud of him," I said to his parents, "and of Amanda too."

"I'll get a bigger part next year," Amanda said. "They gave all the big parts to the seniors."

"Probably as it should be," I said. They won't get a chance to do it again."

"I guess you're right. But next year I'll still be just a junior."

"Don't wish your time away," I said. "You'll be a senior soon enough."

As we chatted about Earl's college plans for the next year I noticed that Rachel was hovering a short distance away, trying to get my attention. She was waving a piece of paper at me. When there was an opening in the conversation I excused myself and joined her.

"Here," she said, handing me the piece of paper.

"Thanks," I said. "How did you like the play."

"Yes."

"Yes?"

"I liked it."

I sang to her. It was Arthur's instructions to Tom, which we had just heard, so it was fresh in my mind.

> *Ask ev'ry person if he's heard the story:*
> *And tell it strong and clear if he has not:*
> *That once there was a fleeting wisp of glory*
> *Called Camelot.*

"Do you think I should have had the part?" I asked.

She giggled. Anyone could tell that my voice didn't merit such an honor.

"So you laugh," I said, pretending my feelings were hurt.

"You don't sing as good as they do," she said.

"I'm afraid you're right. But tell me, what do you think of Guenevere's idea of running around naked in the castle? Would that be fun?"

She giggled again and then nodded impatiently at the note in my hand. "Read it," she ordered.

"Ah, yes." I unfolded the crumpled paper and read the words that were scrawled in a labored, child-like hand:

> **Dear Alex,**
> **Write to me.**
> **Love, Rachel**

"Yes," I said. "I will."

Her community integration worker, ever watchful for the dreaded stranger, came over and stationed herself beside Rachel. I introduced myself to her in order to put her at her ease.

"I once took Rachel and some other girls on a canoe trip," I told her. "She was great."

"I see." The worker smiled politely.

"Did you never tell her about the canoe trip, Rachel?" I asked.

"I don't know."

"Don't know? How can that be?"

"Can't remember."

"Well tell her now."

Rachel turned to her worker. "It was fun. We stayed on an island."

"Rachel overcame all her fear and paddled to the island," I said. "And we listened to the frogs and the loons at night. It was a magic time."

Rachel smiled and nodded agreement. "Yes," she said.

The worker said they had to go. As I watched them

disappear through the door I was already planning the note I would write to Rachel. I would buy her a card with some silly picture of an animal on it. And I would write:

> **Dear Rachel,**
>
> *I often think about the canoe trip, and about the things we pretended in the play room. We had lots of fun.*
>
> *I hope you are getting along real well with the counselor you now have.*
>
> *I hope you have a good life. You are a wonderful girl.*
>
> *Your friend,*
>
> *Alex*

And if I think of one, I will tell her a joke.

Jesus Vs. the Buddha

"Children are the vessels into which adults pour their poison..."

>Salmun Rushdie
>"Midnight's Children"

Ah

As I walked down the pink fleshy corridor I was
  oppressed by a weightiness —
An opposition to my walking, seeing, hearing —
A refusal of things to focus.
Was this a dream, or the hall,
Or some strange hybrid fused within the space
  between sleeping and waking?
My father woke me as I urinated in the corner of the
  bathroom.
What are you doing?" he asked.
What could I say?
I was being born, I think.
I was trying to awaken from the other world.
Today I awoke again.
A honey bee weaved in and out of the bars at the
  window.

Idly I pictured myself following her to the flowers, the
    open fields and the hive.
What then?
Could I steal a little honey?
I sat up.
"Ah." I said.
"A prison."
"Ah."

The indictment will appear in the newspaper tomorrow morning. I mention that in order to tell you why I am up at 1:30 AM. 1:27 to be exact. I want you to know who I am and where I am and maybe even a bit about why I am the person I am. So I will be as precise as possible. Words are an inadequate bridge from my world to yours. Words — strung together into sentences — may convey the idea of the dread I am feeling, or the idea of that hollow sensation in the pit of my stomach, but the dread itself, along with the stomach sensations, falls out along the way, as packages might fall out of a carelessly loaded wagon. They never arrive at your doorstep. Still, words are all I have.

I am sitting at my computer in the room I call my "study." I am alone. The window directly in front of me overlooks my backyard and the backyards of several of my neighbors. A sliver of moon illuminates vague shapes without detail. Color is bleached out by the dimness; the world is painted in black, white, and shades of gray. Left of center, I see the smoke stacks of the paper mill belching out their poisons. Slightly to the right of them the pointed steeple of the Full Gospel Baptist church rises into the sky. It is not so tall as the smoke stacks, but because it is closer, it appears to reach an equal altitude. To the right two huge elm trees dominate the sky. Below these forms silhouetted against the sky, the houses of my neighbors merge indistinctly with garages and smaller trees. Nothing defines itself with precision at this level.

I am thinking of Stephan.

I am thinking of his shorts — their whiteness. I am thinking of the whiteness of the socks, the tennis shoes and the T-shirt he was wearing the first day I met him in front of the Fish and Game Club where we were gathering for our three day canoe trip. His hair too was white. No, it was blond, actually. I am trying to be precise. But it was bleached almost to whiteness by the summer sun. His skin was pale. Even his eyes provided no sharp color to contrast against the whiteness — they were not blue, as you might expect, but gray. I am thinking of Stephan's shorts. They were new and a little too large. They descended to the middle of his thighs and emphasized the thinness of his legs. His shorts were white — white like the whale that captured Ahab in a tangle of lines — the improvised net by which the giant mammal scooped the man out of the air and dragged him into the deep void of the sea.

*****

I went to bed last night at about 11:30. I was too hot — then too cold. When I lay on my stomach my neck cramped. On my back I felt exposed. My mind was a kaleidoscope of dark images — a dance of shadows. Briefly I fell asleep and was swallowed up in a dream of falling. I looked down. I could see nothing — only blackness — a void. I awoke with my heart racing.

*****

When I was about eleven a peculiar vision of the void haunted the region between waking and sleep. As I lay in bed, I thought about the concept of space being infinite. It went on forever. As I tried to imagine this unimaginable state of affairs, my mind always tried to put an end to this "foreverness." I would establish a boundary and fortify it by filling it with furniture — chairs, couches and tables. But then I could not escape the question of what lay beyond my fortress of furniture. More space, of course. Even China could not have built a wall big enough to protect me from this threat. It was not the threat of anything in particular — but precisely the threat of nothing — and more nothing — going on forever. Whatever walls we build against it, the void will still insinuate itself into our hearts.

I remember once when I struggled futilely for what seemed

like hours to solve the problem of going-on-forever and then tried, again without success, to simply exclude the notion from my mind. My stomach became upset. It was telling me, "this is bigger than your brain can solve and more dreadful than your heart can tolerate." So I crawled out of bed and went to find my father. He was still up so perhaps it was not quite so late as I had supposed.

"My stomach hurts," I told him.

He put his book down and leaned forward in his easy chair. "Come here," he said.

I came and stood in front of him, and he felt my head. "You don't seem to have a fever," he said.

"I don't think it's that."

"Maybe it was something you ate."

"I don't think so," I said.

He ran his fingers through my hair, and patted it gently. "What do you think it is?"

I edged a little closer to him, hoping that he would pick me up and put me in his lap. I waited. Finally I said, "Dad, how can space go on forever?"

He furrowed his brow like he did when he was thinking, and then said, "I don't think anybody understands that."

"Nobody?" I asked.

"I don't think so, " he said. I edged a little closer to him and stood looking at his knees.

Finally he sighed. "There doesn't seem to be anything seriously wrong," he said. "Maybe a little baking soda mixed with water will help." I didn't think so, but I followed him into the kitchen. He prepared the concoction — a heaping spoonful of baking soda mixed into half a glass of water — and I forced it down. It didn't taste too bad.

" Well," he said, "I think you need to get back to bed."

"Can I stay up with you?"

"It's late," he said. "I think the baking soda will do the

trick."

So I returned to bed and continued my struggle with foreverness until I fell asleep from exhaustion.

*****

I want you to know me. That's why I am writing this.

I subscribe to an Internet discussion group on the subject of reincarnation. One of the participants shared a message recently about our getting to know each other in a more personal way:

> *We have shared so much with each other about our thoughts, but very little about who we are. It occurred to me that the very least we could do is describe where we are as we type. I have a stereo behind me playing a Beetles tape. On the wall to my left I have a large print of Wyeth's "Christina's World." In front of me I have taped up an assortment of my daughter's art work — she is six. On my left there is a window. Most of the view from this window is taken up by a large oak tree. My cocker spaniel, "Snort" sleeps at my feet. Behind me there is an overstuffed chair on which I sit and try to remember my past lives.*
>
> *Don*

The idea was popular and others followed his example. From one participant we learned that she was usually nude as she typed. From another I discovered that his "den" was a veritable green house. From still another I found out that she sat at her kitchen table amidst a lot of clutter. These are telling bits of information to be sure — but can I say I now know Don and the others any better? Do you? I don't know. But perhaps Don is right. Perhaps it would be good to tell you about my room — the "outer space" within which I live much of the time.

I already mentioned the window. My computer sits on an old table, the top of which is constructed out of thick boards. On top of the monitor of my computer I keep a small brown Buddha carved out of soapstone. The table is an antique. The Buddha I don't know about. I picked it up in an antique shop, but for all I know it may be one of those cheap trinkets prepared for American tourists by underpaid workers in Taiwan. I have a couch on my left. This is where I sit when I read. On the wall to my right I have a Gauguin print. It is a picture of two Brenton boys, one in red shorts and one in blue. They are wrestling. Behind me I have a cabinet that contains my stereo, VCR, TV, CD player etc. I like to listen to music — mostly classical but some blues and jazz as well. Also gospel music. So that says something about where I am as I write these words. I don't know whether that helps.

You, of course, can't tell me where you are. I can imagine you on a bus, or in an easy chair, or sitting at a desk or at a cluttered kitchen table. But I can't know. You are the void into which I am writing.

*****

I am thinking of Ackroyd...

But first I think I owe you an explanation. What was a boy named Ackroyd doing in the north woods of the United States — in Colesville? The biographical material was as unusual as the name suggests. Ackroyd is an eleven year old Dravidian boy, (he must be twelve by now) born in Bombay and largely educated by a Buddhist uncle. Ackroyd didn't live in Colesville, actually, but was from a nearby city where his parents owned an Indian restaurant. Ackroyd's maternal uncle, Arivinda, served as bookkeeper for the restaurant. According to the report I received on the referral to the program, Ackroyd's parents fought a great deal and the father drank. When it came to light that the father beat boy on several occasions, he was removed from the home and placed in foster care. According to the Human Service's plan, Ackroyd was to go live with Arivinda as soon as his uncle established himself in a separate apartment. Presently Arivinda was living in a room above the restaurant.

Ackroyd came over to the U.S. with his parents when he was five years old. He speaks English quite fluently, but with just a tinge of an accent. The Department of Human Services felt that

Ackroyd was not fully acculturated to America, and hoped that an intensive adventure based experience with peers might help the process along. Hence the referral to my program. The camping trip that I will be describing presently was the last one I took kids on before the Department of Social Services discontinued using any of my services because of my offering to take a boy to a nudist beach.

So everything has an explanation, even Ackroyd's presence on our canoe adventure. Still, every time I had my attention on other things, and would then suddenly become aware of Ackroyd, I was startled. It was as though I had seen a giraffe wandering through the neighboring cow pastures and potato fields.

I am thinking of Ackroyd.

I am thinking about his beauty — his rich dark brown skin — the dark wide-set eyes that framed a narrow and slightly hooked nose — his straight black hair that came over his ears and touched his shoulders — the soft rounded contours of his legs, his arms and his belly. I think about his uncircumcised penis and his round little buns which I saw only once. But most of all I think about his smile. It made me want to tell jokes, make a fool of myself, do anything that might produce it. It gave me such joy as... But I'm telling you about my reactions to it. I set out to tell about the smile itself. Well, it melted my heart... Ah, this is difficult. How can I tell you about his smile? His teeth were white and strong and clean, but they were crooked. It has something to do with their crookedness. But that's not entirely it either. I give up. I can't tell you about his smile. It gave me happiness. There. You will have to make do with that.

*****

It probably seems improbable that two of the most beautiful boys I have ever seen showed up for the same three day canoe trip. I thought so at the time. But is was the very improbability of this happening that made me come to view it as probable. Let me explain. A thing, if I understand what our physicists are saying, is most of the time seriously lacking any definiteness. It is any number of possibilities waiting to collide with an obstacle that will force one possibility to leap to the forefront — to become an actuality. Now it is true that most often the possibility that leaps suddenly into actuality is a highly probable and therefore plausible possibility. But it is equally probable that some of the time highly improbable and therefore implausible possibilities will leap into actuality. Therefore improbable events are probable. At least a certain number of them are. The rest of the events on the canoe trip were more of the probable kind. Therefore the improbable actualization of not one but two boys of rare beauty coming on one trip was statistically to be expected. In all this deliberation about probability it may seem that I have slipped into some other language. Certainly this is not ordinary English. And indeed, it's not. This is philosophy — the most fickle of all disciplines. One minute it is the Queen of all knowledge domains, and the next it becomes a lowly sycophant, serving whatever human prejudice that happens to be dominant.

What I would draw from the idea of probability curves waiting to be actualized, is that Reality is a vast and emerging network of possible experiences, of varying degree of probability. But some other philosopher would conclude from the same data that life is like a bunch of billiard balls. Take your pick. I certainly can't prove my point. So don't worry whether you follow the intricacies of my argument. Argument has little to do with our ultimate beliefs in any case. It will suffice if your grasp my conclusions. There are three of them:

1. It was almost inevitable that Stephan and Ackroyd should both come with me on the same trip.

2. Whatever we think will happen in the future probably won't. Though it may.

3. Stephan was the obstacle into which that particular conglomeration of possibilities that I was at the time of the canoe trip was about to collide.

*****

I want to tell you about the indictment — what led up to it — when it all began. It's always hard to say when anything begins.

But I'll never get underway with my account if I stop to dwell on that. I'm the one telling this story, so I suppose arbitrariness is my prerogative. I begin then with Stephan in his white shorts running down a path. Something is about to happen — something that will change me.

He falls.

Try to see this. The path winds through the woods, down a hill. It connects the beach where the canoes are parked with our camp site about thirty yards back in the woods. It is 9:00 AM and has been raining — not hard, but steadily — for about twelve hours. You can't see the white shorts yet. You see a poncho, and bare legs starting at about the knees and going down to dirty socks hanging in folds over his ankles. And you see tennis shoes, once white but now very muddy. You see these bare legs pumping along like soft pale pistons. He trips on a root and sprawls face forward into the mud. The poncho flaps forward and you can see (through my eyes — try) the still clean white shorts. Two other boys are between me and Stephan. They stop to see if they can help, and one of them, a skinny red head named Melvin, calls back to me.

"Mr. Foster, Stephan fell."

"See if he's hurt," I say.

I saw him fall myself, but I appreciate the boy's concern. The second boy is big and wears glasses with thick lenses. He helps Melvin pull Stephan up into a sitting position. By the time I arrive at his side Stephen is perched at the edge of the path with the muddy water soaking into the seat of his pants. I hope that he brought other pants that are still dry. He begins to cry.

"Thanks Melvin... Zack," I say to the two boys who tried to be of help.

I arrange my poncho under me, sit down beside Stephan, pick him up, and put him in my lap. "Are you hurt," I ask him.

He nods, and buries his face in my poncho.

"Where?"

"My head."

I push the hood of his poncho back and gently lift his face so that I can see. A blob of mud covers part of his forehead, above and slightly to the left of his left eye. His hands, forearms and elbows are also muddy as are his knees, this pattern of mud being a faithful record of his five point landing. Gathering clear water off my poncho and from a little pool in the grass beside me, I wash off his forehead and see that it is not scraped or badly bruised.

"I don't think your head hit a rock when you landed," I say

"Look at my knee."

I rinse off his right knee, and see that it is slightly scraped. "We'll fix that up when we get back to camp. But it doesn't look too bad."

Then, as we talk, I rinse off his other knee, and his hands and forearms and elbows.

"Every thing's gone wrong this morning," he says. I see now that his tears are more a matter of anger than of physical hurt.

I run my fingers through his hair, and pat it gently.

"What else went wrong?" I ask.

"Everything," he says, flinging his arm in the air with impatience.

"Like what for example?"

"My eggs," he says.

"Eggs?"

He glares at me. "You remember," He says. "I dropped them in the dirt."

"Ah, yes."

"And you told me I couldn't have any more."

"We had already rinsed the frying pan out with soapy water," I remind him.

He shakes his head in disgust. "And my toad got away."

"Probably you'll find others," I say.

"But I'd made friends with this one."

"Yes," I say, "that does make a difference."

"It does," he says.

"Did anything else go wrong this morning?" I ask.

He buries his head again in my poncho and is silent. Finally I feel his head nodding an affirmative answer to my question.

"What was it?" I ask

"I peed the bed last night."

I look down at the child sitting in my lap, and I think about his wet and muddy white shorts, his wet sleeping bad, and his wet whatever he wore to bed last night. I look up at the steady onslaught of the rain and wonder what the chances are of ever getting him dried out.

"It's OK," I say. "Kids do that sometimes, especially on camping trips."

"The other kids know," he says.

"They make fun of you?"

"Some of them did." He looks up at me. The little trails in his dirty face created by his tears are being washed away by the rain. "Vincent peed his, too," he says.

I sigh. Our camping trip is drowning in a mixture of piss, mud and rain. "So some of them made fun of you?" I say.

He nods. "Especially Peter."

"That's a lot of things to go wrong," I say.

"It is," he says.

"Your toad escaping. The eggs. Wetting the bed. Falling down. Kids making fun of you. All in one morning," I say, thinking I have summarized all of his little catastrophes.

"Yeah. And my warm sweat shirt — the Star Wars one — got wet."

"How did that happen?"

"I left it outside the tent last night, on the ground."

I think about the behavioral patterns I have noticed with this child since the trip began yesterday morning. Whether it was a matter of putting up a tent or piling up a plate of food, I observed that he would fling himself against his task with enthusiasm and energy but never with care or planning. Between the impulse and the action there was never a thought. It was not that he was mentally slow. My impression was that he was very bright. But all his thoughts just floated around in his head. They never seemed to connect with what he was doing.

"I don't think any thing's going to be right on this trip," he said.

This, I think, might be the naturally occurring teaching moment. "When things go like this — one bad thing after another, do you ever wonder why?" I ask.

"Yes," he says.

"And what do you think?" I ask.

He looks down. Then he glances at Melvin and Zack who have hunkered down near us. Finally he looks up at me. "It's because God hates me," he says.

*****

At the time I held Stephan in my lap and listened to him relate his litany of disasters, I felt we would probably have to return home early. If too many things got wet, and there was no way of drying them, everybody would be too miserable to make it worth while to continue. But by mid morning it began to clear, and by noon the sun was bright and warm.

We had dry wood in time for an evening campfire.

Seven boys and two counselors gathered around the fire. Shoes were leaned against the stones, drying. Sleeping bags were hanging from clotheslines near enough to absorb some of the heat, but out of danger. They would be dry by bedtime, and the smell would be negligible.

I mentioned to the group around the fire what Stephan had told me earlier about God hating him, and asked the boys whether they had ever had similar thoughts. A small thin boy with a ragged homegrown hair cut raised his hand.

"You don't have to raise your hand on this trip, Timmy," I said. "Long as you aren't interrupting anybody, you're free to speak up."

"Maybe it's true," Timmy said.

"What's true?" I asked.

"Maybe God does hate him?"

The other group leader, John Dumas, waved his still sticky marshmallow branch in Timmy's direction, as though he were fencing. "God doesn't hate Stephan," he said. "Why would He?" I motioned to John with the palms of my hands to back off and be a little less assertive of his own views. We had discussed this. But Timmy did not understand John's question to be rhetorical.

"I don't know...," he said. "Maybe... maybe... I don't know... maybe he swears."

"I heard him swear," Melvin says. "I heard him use God's name in a swear."

A tall thin boy blows out the flame on the charcoaled exterior of the marshmallow he holds on a stick, and says, "that ain't nothing. I heard him say the "f" word." This is Peter Boutelle. He stuffed the marshmallow whole into his mouth.

"That ain't as bad as using God's name in a swear," Melvin said.

"Why not?" Peter asked, mumbling a little because of the marshmallow. "My mom says the "f word" is the worst of all."

"It ain't," said Melvin.

"Why not?" Peter asked.

"Cause you go to hell for using God's name in a swear," Melvin said.

"I doubt if you would go to hell for just using a bad word," I said. "But I guess that's between Stephan and God." I looked at Melvin. "What about you?" I asked. "Have you ever had the feeling that God hates you.".

"You go to hell for using God's name like that," Melvin said. "For the 'f word' God might forgive you."

"I feel same as Stephan," Zack says.

"How's that," I asked.

"God hates me."

"Why would God hate you?" Vincent asked. He was the other boy who wet his bed. His sleeping bag was hanging on the line just behind him. He picked marshmallow goo out of his braces, and stared it Zack out of his big owl-like eyes while he waited for an answer.

"Cause I'm bad," Zack said.

"If you're bad, God hates you and sends you to hell," Timmy said.

Zack stares at Timmy. "So?" he said, and shrugs his shoulders.

"So you got to try to be good," Timmy said.

"It ain't that easy," Zack said.

"It ain't 'cause He hates you that He sends you to hell," Melvin said. "Pastor Rooney — he's pastor at Faith Baptist Church where I go — he explained that. God don't hate nobody. He sends you to hell on account of His great mercy."

"Jesus! What kind of mercy is that?" John Dumas asked. He stood up and spread his arms in a gesture of disbelief. John is huge and bearded. I think the boys are a little intimidated by him. If I didn't know that he would never hurt anybody, I would probably be intimidated myself. "Just what kind of goddamn mercy is that?"

All the boys stared at John. No one spoke or moved a muscle. John looked around, and then stared at the ground. "Sorry," he said, and sat back down.

"Maybe Pastor Rooney said it was because of his justice," I suggested.

John shook his head but refrained from speaking.

"Loony Rooney," mumbled Zack.

I stared at Zack, and was unable to totally suppress my

smile. "What was that?" I asked

"Nothing," he said.

"Whatever," Melvin said. "The main thing is you don't have to go to hell when you get washed in the blood of Jesus."

"I don't believe in no Jesus," Peter said.

"That's 'cause you're Indian," Timmy said.

"Ain't supposed to say 'Indian,' Vincent said. "Supposed to say 'Native American.' Right Peter?"

"Don't make no difference to me," Peter said.

"What I mean is Indians is from India like Akerloid." Vincent said.

Ackroyd corrected him. "Ackroyd," he said, pronouncing his name carefully. "Ackroyd."

Timmy stood up with a big piece of wood in his hand. "It's because he's an Indian," he said, and threw the log on the fire. Sparks flew in all directions. "Hey, watch that," Zack said, and several other boys joined in with their complaints.

"Sorry," said Timmy. "But what I'm trying to say is this: it's 'cause he's an Indian."

"What's because he's an Indian?" Vincent asked.

"That he don't believe in Jesus. He believes in the Great Spirit."

"Don't believe in no Great Spirit, either." Said Peter.

"What do you believe in?" asked Vincent.

"Nothing," Peter said. He pushed some embers on the ground back into the fire and looked from one group member to the other until he went most of the way around the circle. "Maybe it's cause I'm only half Indian," he says. "My dad's French. So I ain't Indian, not really. And I ain't white. I ain't nothing."

"Maybe you can take what's good from each of your backgrounds, and put together something new," I suggested.

He shrugged and threw his marshmallow stick into the fire.

Ackroyd had been lying on the ground with his head propped on a log up until this point. He stood up, brushed himself off, sat on the log, and leaned toward the fire. "I'm like Peter," he said. "I'm Indian — that is really from India. But now I'm part American. Dravidians — that's what I am — got stomped by white folks in India, just like what happened to Indians here. Only a lot longer ago."

"So what do Dravidians believe," Vincent asked.

"Different ones different things, I guess," Ackroyd said. "But I believe in the Buddha."

"The Buddha is a devil," Melvin said.

Ackroyd glared at him. "He's not," he said.

"What's the Buddha believe?" Vincent asked.

"My uncle explained that to me," Ackroyd said. "He can explain things better than me."

"But your uncles not here," I said. "So you'll have to explain."

"My uncle says that most everybody's in hell. He says that this life here – with us spitting on each other and killing each other and all that kind of thing – is hell. He says the Buddha doesn't send anybody to hell. He just tries to help people get out of hell."

"Sounds good," Said Vincent. "Maybe I could believe in the Buddha."

"You'll go to hell if you believe in the Buddha," Melvin said.

"Will not," Ackroyd said."

"Will," said Melvin.

Ackroyd shook his head.

"This is really interesting," I said. "But I want to come back to a point that was made earlier." I looked at Zack. "You said you thought God hated you. What could you have done to make God hate you?"

"Bad things," he said.

"Yes, but like what?"

"Like not doing what Mom says. Or cheating in school."

"Anything worse that those things?"

"Well, fighting."

Then I turn to Stephan. "What about you? What might you do to make God hate you."

He looked down. "Don't want to say."

"That's OK," I said. "You don't have to share anything you don't want to."

"Why don't you want to say?" Vincent asked.

"Leave 'em alone," said Timmy. "Maybe he's too 'shamed."

"Yeah," said Peter. He stands up and points his marshmallow stick at Stephan. "Maybe he plays with his thingy."

Everybody except Stephan laughed. They laughed uproariously, and joined in the teasing:

"Yeah, he plays with his thingy."

"When he can find it."

"Ooooh, Stephan."

Comments of that sort continued despite the efforts made by John and me to get them to stop.

"Do not!" Stephan screamed, and he bolted from the group and headed toward the Lake. John followed him, and I stayed with the group.

*****

After Stephan had been comforted and the other boys reprimanded for teasing him, we were finally able to settle in for the night. Stephan, Melvin and Ackroyd shared a tent together. Zack and Peter were with John. I had Timmy and Vincent in with me. We were all tired. After I gave Timmy and Vincent each a back scratch, they soon fall asleep. Yesterday's rain had not cooled things off. The air in the tent was hot and moist. All three of us slept on top of our sleeping bags. Vincent had actually brought pajamas. Timmy wore only a pair of jockey shorts and a T-shirt.

I was lying on my back, listening to a heated conversation carried on in urgent but hushed tones in the tent shared by Stephen, Melvin and Ackroyd. I was not able to make out anything they are saying. Since they were making an effort to keep the volume down, I did not try to get them to be still. I wished I was in there with them – especially with Stephan and Ackroyd. I wondered whether they knew how beautiful they were. They can study their faces in a mirror, as I did when I was their age, and wonder whether they are handsome. But they cannot see their own beauty. They have to learn that from another person. Do they see each other as beautiful? I don't know. They did beg to share the same tent, and included Melvin only as an afterthought. Perhaps they would have to have my eyes to see that they are masterpieces. It's probably best that they can't see this for themselves. Look what happened to Narcissus.

I imagined Ackroyd and Stephen in each others arms. Dark and light. East and west. Yin and Yang. A perfect sphere. Here was the eight limbed primeval man Aristophanes spoke of in the Symposium – a creature so powerful it was a threat to the gods themselves.

I drifted off to sleep.

At about 2:30 or 3:00 in the morning, I woke up needing to pee. The tent was hot and steamy. I did not want to make the effort to get up to and go relieve myself. Then I became aware that my discomfort with the air is not just because of the temperature and the humidity. There was an odor as well. At first I thought that it was just gas. Someone has farted, I told myself, and tried to make myself think that's all there is. But I knew better. It was the smell of shit.

I was between the two boys. Vincent was sprawled out on his stomach, wedged down into the space between the side of the tent and his sleeping bag. Timmy was curled up in fetal position with his back to me. I wondered which one had the accident, but decided to wait until morning to deal with it. I went out and relieved myself. Then I opened all the flaps on the tent in order to give us the maximum amount of air before I settled back down. My efforts didn't help much as there was no breeze to blow the stagnate air out and replace it. I was very tired and, despite the humidity, the heat and the smell, I eventually fell back asleep. I awoke again just before the sun came up. With the extra light in the tent I could see that the seat of Timmy's shorts were lumpy and that there was some brown showing through. I shook him.

"Timmy. Wake up."

"Huh?"

"You need to wake up. You've had an accident."

He reached down and felt the bottom of his shorts. "Oh, no." He looked over at Vincent. "Is he awake?" he whispered.

"Shh. Just get what you will wear today and we'll get you cleaned up. Nobody needs to know."

He located a clean pair of underpants, and the shorts and shirt he planed to wear for the day, in his pack. I grabbed my shaving kit, and we sneaked out of the tent and down to the lake. We walked down the beach a ways so we wouldn't be in the area where we swim or wash dishes. He took his underwear off and handed it to me. I dumped his underwear out in the woods, and then washed them out as best I could while he tried to wash himself with the bar of soap I gave him. I walked behind him as we waded through the shallow water back toward the beach where he had his clothes. I could see brown streaks running down his legs and realized he had not done the job very carefully. I stopped him.

"You need a little more washing," I said.

He twisted around and looked at the back of his legs. "Gross," he said. "I thought I got it all."

"Bend forward a little," I said.

He complied and I cleaned him up.

"Don't tell anybody," he said.

"I won't," I said.

A little later, while Vincent and I were in the tent alone,

straightening it up for the day, he said "I smelled something in the tent last night." He looked out the front door of the tent to make sure nobody was there. "Did Timmy... make... have... you know... a problem?"

"If he did, he wouldn't want anyone to know," I said.

Vincent nodded. "OK," he said.

*****

During breakfast I learned that my fantasy about Ackroyd and Stephen sleeping in each other arms did not reflect what actually happened in the tent.

"Ackroyd and Melvin kept me up half the night arguing," Stephan complained." He was sitting at the end of the picnic table, slurping his somewhat slimy oatmeal. He looked up at me and wiped a dribble of milk off his chin with the back of his hand.

I was frying French-toast on a camp stove on the other end of the table.

"What were they arguing about?" I asked.

"Jesus and Buddha," he said.

"Jesus and Buddha?"

"Yeah. Which one is better."

Melvin was sitting on the end of the table across from Stephan waiting for "seconds" on French-toast. Ackroyd was sitting under a nearby white pine pouring syrup on his first helping.

"Jesus could heal sick people, couldn't he, Mr. Foster?" Melvin asked.

"Well, there are reports in the Bible that he did," I said.

"See. What did I tell you?" Melvin waved his sticky fork in Ackroyd's general direction.

"I didn't say he couldn't," Ackroyd said. "I said the Buddha could too."

"He says he knows about someone who got cured of liver cancer by the Buddha," Melvin said.

"It's true," Ackroyd said. While he was talking, the bite of French-toast he was about to eat fell off his fork into his lap.

"I don't think so," Melvin said.

"How would you know?" Ackroyd asked. He picked the piece of French-toast up off his lap with his fingers and popped it into his mouth, and then wiped his hand on his shorts.

"Only Jesus can do that," Melvin said. He stood up and came over to me to get the piece of French-toast that I had just finished frying.

"The Buddha can do anything," Ackroyd said. "He went a thousand days without eating."

"So can Jesus," Melvin said. "He can go a million days without eating." He looked up at me as I plopped a piece of French-toast down on his plate. "How many days did Jesus go without eating, Mr. Foster? You remember when he was out in that desert?"

"I think is was forty days," I said.

"See," Ackroyd said. "Only forty days."

"He could go a million if he wanted," Melvin said.

"The Buddha can levitate," Ackroyd said.

"What's lebitate," Melvin asked.

"It means just be sitting somewhere and then rise into the air with no propeller or nothing."

"Jesus could do that, easy."

"Sure," said Ackroyd.

Melvin sliced off a huge piece of butter and watched it slip off onto the ground before he could get it onto his new steaming-hot piece of French-toast. He picked the blob of butter up out of the dust and pine needles, and tried to wipe it off. He succeeded only in spreading the dirt and needles over the rest of the blob. He looked at the whole mess of butter, pine needles and dirt in his hand with disgust and threw it back onto the ground. "I'll tell you how powerful Jesus is," he said. He wiped his hand off on his shirt and sliced off another piece of butter for his still steaming French-toast. "He can just point at something and say, 'you're dead,'" and it will be dead." He put his hand on his hip, looked at Ackroyd and nodded his head. "He did that to a tree, once."

Along with the rest of the group, John had been watching this exchange of ideas from the sidelines. Suddenly he put his plate down and stood up. "Jesus Vs. the Buddha," he said. "The final show down. It's the biggest thing since Godzilla vs. King Kong." He beat his chest a few time, growled, and began stomping, super-monster style, toward the picnic table.

"That dude over there frying French toast is Jesus, and I'm going to break him in two. I'm the Buddha." John explained.

I put the spatula down. "You think so." I said, backing off. "Well, what if Jesus rips a huge pine tree out of the ground by the roots and uses it as a club, and attacks the Buddha with it." I pantomimed the actions that I described.

John backed off, holding his arm defensively in front of him. "The Buddha easily fends off the blows, and picks up a mountain." He makes the motions of picking up a mountain and flinging it at me.

"But Jesus is too quick," I said, ducking. "He grabs hold of the edge of North America, and pulls the whole continent like a rug, out from under the feet of the Buddha.

John falls. "Ah, I'll get you for that, Jesus," he said, standing back up. "The Buddha grabs the moon our of the sky and throws it – straight at Jesus' head, as though it were only a baseball."

"Get him, Buddha," Peter screamed with delight.

"I'm betting on Jesus," Vincent shouted.

"No way he's going to win," said Peter. "The Buddha is twice as big and hairier."

This was true. John is twice my size, and harrier as well. He plays tackle on his college football team. On that level I'm no match for him.

"But Jesus has got magic," I said. "He suddenly levitates

and the moon misses him by a mile. Then he gathers together the fire from a million suns and stars and rolls them into a ball and flings them at the Buddha."

John stands his ground. "But the Buddha turns himself into a ghost and it goes right through him," he said.

"Nice move," Peter said.

"Go for him, Jesus," Vincent shouted.

I bent down and made motions of gathering something up around my feet. "Jesus collects a thousand truck loads of ghost sucking leeches, and flings them at the Buddha," I say.

"The Buddha is disgusted," John admitted. "But he gathers together a million maggots and throws them back at Jesus."

I was laughing almost too hard to continue now and John was too. Most of the boys were screaming and laughing as well. "But Jesus..." I said. I had to stop to catch my breath.

"Come on, come on," John said. "What does Jesus do?"

"He gathers up ten million tape worms and stuffs them into the Buddha's mouth I said."

"Foul, foul," John mumbled, pretending that his mouth was full.

"It is foul," I said, and we both fell to the ground laughing.

The boys clapped and cheered. "Who won?" asked Zack.

"Tune in next week and find out," I said.

After we all settle down a bit I noticed that the French-toast was burning. I leaped up and ran over to rescue it.

Melvin shrugged his shoulders and shook his head. He looked first at me, and then at John. "You guys're going to hell," he said.

*****

I am in my room. It's 3:52. I told you about my room. I told you about it because I want you to know where I am. I still doubt that you have a very clear idea of my room. The images that words carry back and forth between us are always a little on the blurry side. But I didn't even tell you everything that was obvious about my room – the kind of information that words could handle. Over to my right, below the Gauguin print, I have a small white cabinet containing a couple of shelves. It's one of those simple particle board creations that you can buy at the K Mart and put together yourself with a screwdriver. I have coffee, cups, filters, spoons, and things of that sort on one shelf. On a second shelf I keep my dictionary and thesaurus and a collection of office things – paper clips, a stapler, scissors, tacks, extra pens and the like. On the top there is a small coffee pot – the sort that uses a filter, and a clock. I dwell on my room not because I think it is in of any intrinsic interest. In fact I have omitted much – the smudges on the walls, the names of the books I have, the nature of the wood work around the window, etcetera, out of fear of boring you. Yet by virtue of this room being where I am, it is a part of me – of my now. If I want to touch you – have you touch me – must I not include it?

Another memory comes to me – a memory of Stephan and me. I see myself and Stephan at the YMCA. He is coming into the shower room... I will get to that. First, though, there is something that confuses me.

I am in my room. Yet in your "now" – in the moment in which you are reading this, I am not in my room. The one reaching out to you from this particular place is no longer where I say I am. I am, perhaps, in another room. I want you to see Stephan through the eyes of the person I am now in this room I am telling you about – it is this fallible memory I want to pass on to you. This is far too convoluted. We are back into philosophy again. Yet somehow this is important. My encapsulation against you is a layered thing. The frailty of memory. The disturbing fact that the self, my own self, that I try to contact in memory comes to me in much the same way as my knowledge of another person. Lies. Yes, lies. We haven't even talked about lies yet. Let me just say that they too are a factor. The clumsiness of words. The ambivalence of all attempts at communication. The alchemy of my transformation from a subject to myself into an object for you, and then into an object for myself too. The shifting sands of past and future. Still though, I write. Something may get through from my room now to you, whoever you are, wherever you are, whenever you are.

But, look! It's Stephan. His image is as vivid as the first bird to sing in the morning.

He walks across the shower room toward me. I have told you about his whiteness. And his gray eyes. I see his penis now for the first time. We have come to the Y several times, but up until now he has been shy. His penis is circumcised – wounded – like mine.

He turns the water on for the shower head next to me. In this Y they do not insist that we hide away from each other in little stalls. In the Y where I learned to swim we were naked even in the pool. They encapsulate us in progressively narrow confines. Soon there will be no room at all in which to live.

We are the only ones in the shower room. I wash myself a second and a third time in order to be able to stand beside him.

"Wash my back," he says, and edges in under my shower head.

I wash him and include his white buns — whiter even than the rest of him which has received at least a little sun this summer.

He turns part way around and smiles at me. I see he has an erection. I am beginning to be aroused myself. Suddenly, like a burglar alarm going off, I hear the creak of the door that opens out into the pool. I shove Stephan back under his own shower head as I hear footsteps coming down the short hallway between the pool and the door of the shower room. I turn my back to the room just as a man in blue swimming trunks enters. I notice that Stephan still has an erection. It is soon gone, but I wonder whether the man has noticed, and if he did, whether he would draw any unwarranted or even warranted conclusions from this. My heart is trying to pound its way out of my chest. I gather up my things and hurry to the dressing room with Stephan not far behind me. I notice that the man keeps his blue swimming trunks on as he showers.

*****

What was I doing all at once in the shower room of the

YMCA with my beautiful Stephan? How did this come to be, you might ask? And I wouldn't blame you.

More than a year has passed since the canoe trip I told you about earlier – the one in which we enacted the now famous struggle between Jesus and the Buddha. I never saw Ackroyd after that. I heard that his uncle did indeed find a place to live, and that Ackroyd went to live with him. I am happy for them both. I was, on the other hand, able to reestablish contact with Stephan. He lives in Colesville with his mother, Anna Niles. His father has been in prison – something to do with drugs – ever since Stephan can remember.

It seems that Stephan liked me a lot and talked with his mother about me. She had been trying to get a Big Brother for Stephan for some time and was on a waiting list that was about two years long. So she called me and asked whether I might be willing to be his "big brother" – unofficially. I jumped at the chance. I began doing things with Stephan twice a month. Usually we went to a movie once, and to the Y once.

The YMCA and the good movie theaters are in a small city about 50 miles from here. Some of the best times Stephan and I had were in the car driving there and back. It was a perfect time for conversation. We talked about everything – his dad, his dreams, school, what he liked to do, his mom, how he was getting along with his friends, and of course from time to time we picked up the theme of God and the Buddha again. I tried to be a gentle but persuasive evangelist for my liberal views. I tried to persuade him that all the different religions were human efforts to establish a relationship with the same God, that God is loving and creative – not autocratic, vengeful, and repressive, that our bodies and their feelings are part of a good creation, that the idea of a literal hell is a beastly and sacrilegious human creation, and so on. After six months of this he was a virtual new age boy, or so it seemed. I had saved him from the Colesville Full Gospel Baptist Church, an institution he and his mother attended faithfully up until about six months before last summer's canoe trip, at which time Anna had a falling out with the pastor about whether it was permissible for women to wear pants.

Another memory. It was a couple of weeks after I washed Stephan's back in the Y. I was driving back with him from a movie. He was wearing his white shorts – which had survived the canoe trip – and a blue and white striped T-shirt. His mother must have used a fair bit of bleach on the shorts. They fit him a little better now. He looked over at me. We had not been talking at all for about ten minutes.

"Do gay people ever marry?" he asked.

"Sometimes they might," I said.

"Do they ever have kids?"

"Sure."

"How come?"

"Well, I think that people aren't just one way or another," I said. "I think most people might feel lots of different things."

"You mean they might like both men and women?"

"Well, yes. Some do."

"That's bisexual, right?"

"Yeah. But maybe it's even more complicated than that. See, if there are boys and girls and men and woman, that's four different kinds of people a person might have feelings about. I think most everybody has some feelings about all of them – even if its only a little bit."

We discussed this at some length until I felt he had the general idea. I told him that each person has his or her own particular pattern and that we could call that a "love map." By the time we were a little better than half way home we fell silent again. For the next twenty miles nothing was said. Then just as we were coming into Colesville he turned to me.

"Are you gay?" he asked.

"In my love map both women and boys seem to be especially important," I said. My heart was beating wildly.

He looked down and said nothing.

"Does that bother you?" I asked.

"No. I understand that," he said. He looked up and smiled.

*****

I am sitting up here in my room looking out at the darkness. It's 4:06. I'm wondering how you might be taking everything I'm telling you. Probably you're assuming that it's leading up to a big climax in which Stephan and I do something overtly sexual together, right out there in the world, something prosecutable. In all honesty now, I can say to you... I can say... well, yes. Maybe a little something along that line did happen. Not a lot, really, but, yes. It might have been about a week or so after our conversation about love maps in the car.

*****

I was in my room with Stephan. It's the same room I've been telling you about. My wife was working night shift and my daughter was at a sleep-over with some girl friends. I had invited Stephan in to watch a movie with me. I ordered "Lord of the Flies," the older version by Brooks, just for this occasion. I have a set for showing videos that I keep on a little table over by the book case, and close to the door. Stephen and I were sitting together on the couch. It had been a very hot day. The sun was just setting. Stephan was sitting cross ways on the couch with his feet and part of his calves in my lap. He was wearing his white shorts again, and white socks. I pulled one of his socks off and massaged his foot. A naked foot is a beautiful thing.

Stephan purred. I liked his foot being rubbed.

In the movie, Simon had just been murdered by the boys. We watched children walking up a beach. Some of them appeared to be naked. "It's good to be naked," I said.

Stephan nodded in agreement.

"Sometimes I like to be naked when I watch videos," I said.

He didn't answer. We watched as the boys came into a little clearing. You could see them close up now. Three of them were naked.

"OK," Stephan said.

"OK, what?"

"Lets get naked."

I was not hard to persuade.

We slipped out of the few things we are still wearing, and rearranged ourselves on the couch. I leaned against the arm and spread my legs out. He slid, rear-end first, between my legs and leaned back against me. I put my arms around him. We watched Piggy being killed with the big boulder.

I massaged his chest and belly and legs as we watched the rest of the movie. When the movie finished I begin to play with his penis. He spreads his legs ever so slightly to allow me to reach him more easily. He made a little noise between a sigh and a groan as he reached a climax.

Before he left we worked on our plans for our overnight camping trip. I had expressed an interest in taking him camping to celebrate his thirteenth birthday. His mother agreed.

I drove him home. As he prepared to get out of the car he turned to me and said, "I'm going to the youth revival with Melvin next Saturday."

"Oh?"

"You remember Melvin, from the camping trip?"

"Sure."

"He invited me."

"I see. What's this revival about?"

"It's a youth revival. An evangelist from Indiana is leading it. I guess it's about Jesus and all that sort of thing."

I nodded.

"Well, see ya," he said and jumped out of the car.

*****

I'm thinking about something that never happened.

I am on a camping trip with both Ackroyd and Stephan. Just

those two. We are camping on an island that we have all to ourselves. We don't bother to wear any clothes. When we go swimming I can watch them through my goggles, and see the shimmering patterns of light that the sun casts on their bodies. We wrestle in the water. I watch the two of them wrestle. Then as night comes on we all get into the tent together. I give them both back rubs. They turn over and want me to do the front too. I begin with Stephen. I rub his chest and belly, gentiles, and legs. He likes this. Then I turn to Ackroyd and first play with his foreskin to see just how it works. Then I massage his chest and thighs and belly. Then Stephan begins to massage him with me. He lies down beside him and they wrap their arms around each other and kiss. They reach down and begin to feel each other's penises and buttocks. Heaven begins to flow into my being and... and...

But that never happened. It's important to keep these things clear. There are things that happened and things that never happened.

I'm sleepy.

Finally I'm sleepy. It's 4:22 AM.

*****

I dozed off. It's 5:16. I didn't even sleep an hour. I see a little lightness in the sky. It was the dread that wakened me. That thing that never happened, you can forget about that. It doesn't count. I suppose I had been thinking about those boys too much.

The dread is about the really bad memories. I have to tell you about them. They are very much on my mind. But I'll try to get them out of the way as quickly as possible. The dread is also about my having told you too much – and maybe about the future too. As you read this, some of it will already have happened, the future I mean, but I don't know what that will be. What woke me up was mainly the memories.

*****

I was driving home from seeing a movie with Stephan. The conversation in the car had not been very spirited, but I chalked that up to the movie. Neither of us liked it much. Finally he turned to me and said, "I've decided to accept the Lord as my personal savior."

"Oh?" I said. I couldn't think of anything to add.

I remembered then that he had told me about the youth revival he was going to with Melvin. So this was the outcome. I glanced at him, and sort of smiled.

"Well," I said with false cheerfulness. I shrugged. "Hm."

"Aren't you glad?" he asked.

"Well, yes, I suppose so. If that's what will make you happy."

"I didn't think you'd like it," he said, and turned away from me to look out the window.

"It's just so sudden," I said.

A lot of these quick conversions go as suddenly as they come I thought, trying to give myself hope.

"I told you I was going to the revival," he said.

"Yes," I said. "You did. How was it?"

"It was all right."

"What did you learn?"

For some time we are both silent again. Finally he answered my question. "The preacher said that being gay was a bomination."

"It's a bomination, eh?"

"Yeah." He scrutinized my face.

"What's a bomination?" I asked.

"Something really bad."

"I see."

He looked away again.

"Are you afraid that the things we did in my room will make you gay?" I asked.

"I'm not gay," he said.

"A person might have a lot of different feelings," I said.

"Remember, we talked about that."

"I'm not a fagot."

It took me a moment to absorb this word, and the emotion surrounding it. Finally I turned to face him. "Look," I said. " It's not as though I ever forced anything on you."

I saw the scowl on his face before he turned his head away. He didn't answer.

"I'd never pushed anything on you that you didn't want," I said, trying to soften my tone.

He shrugged, then after a pause said, "I know that."

He stared out the window again and fell silent. This time the silence lasted until we pulled into his driveway.

"So is the camping trip still on?" I asked.

"Sure," he said.

"Next Thursday, then," I said.

*****

That's the memory that woke me up. It was the beginning of the dread. These bad memories are like those super greasy White Castle Hamburgers I used to eat when I was a kid. There are only so many of them a person can digest at a sitting. Bear with me though. There are only a few more.

*****

It was the following Thursday, that is the Thursday after Stephen told me he had accepted the Jesus as his savior. It was early in the morning. I was out in front of the house, fastening the canoe on the car. I was feeling a little uneasy because Stephan hadn't called me. For some reason I didn't feel like calling him. But the plans were clear. He would be waiting for me. Then I saw a cop car pull up in front of my house and stop. Two officers got out. Colesville is not such a big place. I recognize them both as they approach..

"Mr. Foster?" Chief Michauld said.

"Yes?"

"I'm afraid I have to ask you to come with us."

"Am I under arrest?"

He nodded.

"What's this all about?"

"There has been an allegation of sexual abuse."

I looked around at the windows of my neighbors. I hoped none of them were staring out.

*****

I won't bore you with the details about my few hours in jail, about getting out on a personal recognizance, and so on. They asked me a few questions but they didn't rip off any of my fingernails, nor even grill me under the blaze of unforgiving lights. I didn't tell them anything. It was all very business like.

Was there any loose talk down at the police station after I left? Did anyone see the arrest being made? If so, how did they interpret it? I don't know. But each time I leave the house to buy some toothpaste, or to mail a letter, it's a struggle. I am always looking around to see who might be staring at me. I scrutinize the faces of anyone I am doing business with.

"Do you have any coupons with you, Mr. Foster?"

"No." Does she know?

"Do you have your Rite Aid card with you?"

"No." Does she think I'm staring at that kid over there?

"That will be a dollar and 68 cents then."

"OK." Does she think I'm a scum ball?

"I'm sorry, but I'm out of quarters. I'll be right back."

Christ. Leave me standing here like some freak for everybody to stare at, will you?

I want more than anything not to be left standing where people will stare.

And so it goes. For the most part, I haven't any idea really who knows anything and who doesn't, or what they think if they do know anything. As of today, of course that will change. I will be able to assume that everybody knows.

I knew as soon as I saw the police car stop in front of my house that Stephan had told his mother. I think I knew he was going to from the time he told me he had decided to accept Jesus as his savior. Ah, lovely child, how can I think of you as my betrayer? How can I believe that of your own free will you took the gift of joy I offered to you, repackaged it in new words, and delivered it over to the authorities as evidence of my depravity and my deservedness to be punished? You were not yourself. You were, as they say "out of your mind" – infected with the insanity of the evangelizers. I cannot believe that while you were in your right mind you betrayed yourself, as well as me, by abandoning the true configuration of your love in favor of the approved model as seen on TV? Surely you are aware that this acclaim, this moment of glory, that you have undoubtedly enjoyed in the eyes of the approved doorkeepers of society is a thin and quickly consumed stew for which to sell the full and rich birthright of your love.

Is it you that I should denounce from the bitter podium of my private thoughts? Or is it Jesus who has betrayed us both? Not the Jesus who caroused with sinners, scandalized the respectable, provoked the authorities, and preached love. He would never have done such a thing. But what of the Jesus preached from the pulpits of narrow little men evangelizing their hatred of freedom and love as it actually bubbles up within our souls — before it is twisted, beaten, punished, hammered, medicated, stamped, tortured, threatened, electrocuted, bribed and crammed into the approved shape — is he the betrayer? This Jesus who speaks of human beings as though they were scum and would prepare a place for any who did not believe in him in an eternal pit of torture? This sadist who in his capacity for cruelty is a throwback to pre-human states of evolution? This slug? It is easier to believe it of him than of you, my love.

There is still one more bad memory I must tell you about. Otherwise you will never understand my conversion. I am thinking of Anna Niles – tall, blond, handsome Anna with the big hands and the piercing blue eyes. She of course, knew. More than anyone, I dreaded running into her. It happened in the Bank parking lot. I am trying to keep these bad memories brief. But this one you need to know about. The parking lot is in front of the Bank.

*****

I was on foot, on my way to make a deposit. Suddenly there she was, standing beside her red Subaru, parked three cars down from the Bank. She had already seen me – was staring at me. How hard, yet vacant, her eyes were! I did not blame her. She was bewitched by the incantations of media priests and priestesses – by all those thousands, perhaps millions, of word bites she has unconsciously absorbed into her being all these past twenty years. She sees things that are not there and cannot see other things that are as obvious as the sidewalk under her feet. She's under a spell. I did not blame her, but I did not want to be trapped.

I looked down and veered off to the right, where I was able to partially conceal myself behind a blue van. I walked slowly to give her time to get into her car and leave. But when I emerged from the protection of the van, she was guarding the same spot like a sentinel, and she continued to stare at me. I had not eluded her for a microsecond. I averted my gaze again and made a dash for the bank door. For the next four or five minutes I attended to my business there.

I was sure she would be gone by the time I came out. But I was wrong. I saw the red Subaru and then, sitting in the driver's seat, I saw her with the same lowered brows. She had been lying in wait. I pivoted in the direction opposite her Subaru, walked rapidly across the parking lot and started up the side walk. Surely she would drive off in the other direction and leave me in peace. But again I was mistaken. She drove up the street, opposite me at a snail's pace, still trying to penetrate my armor with her fierce laser gaze.

I was at a loss. Then a ford pickup with a gun rack in his window pulled up behind her and beeped. The first beep was a polite reminder that others shared the road with her. Intent on keeping me pinned like some loathsome insect to the store front at my side, she ignored the beep. The man in the pickup beeped again, with greater determination, this time.

Bless you, I thought, for your impatience, for your absurd belief that getting wherever you are wanting to go a minute earlier will make you happier – for you intolerance – for your capacity for rudeness – for your gun rack and your flannel shirt – for all the lonely trucker cowboys who are your ego ideals – for everything that goes to make you up. Bless you, for today you are my savior, the one who delivers me out of the jaws of the Tigress.

She slapped the steering wheel. Make a note of that. She slapped the steering wheel. She slapped it impatiently with her large beefy hand. Her hard eyes were still burning holes in my armor. And she then sped up. Ah, sweet deliverance.

There is an empty lot behind the Rite Aide that nobody seemed to assume any responsibility for. Having escaped from Anna Niles, I followed a path that wound through the weeds, flowers and tall grass growing in this lot. I was aware of the intensity of all the colors of the flowers – yellow, blue, purple, red. I don't know the names of these flowers. They are weeds really. I remembered hunting for lizards in the hot sun in fields at the edge of town when I was a boy. Those fields were full of weeds and flowers like these, and full of the same intensity. I remembered the taste of ice scavenged from the milk truck on a day like this.

*****

I think you should know that I have achieved Buddhahood. Samadhi. Nirvana. I am the Bodhisattva. Enlightenment came to in the moment that Stephan's mother slapped the steering wheel. The steering wheel was, of course, a substitute for my face. It was the closest she could come to doing as she wished without herself coming into conflict with the law. And in the humiliation and shame of receiving that slap, the scales, as they say, "fell from my eyes."

Let me tell you how that slap brought me to enlightenment. I was reading the words in the hard looks that Stephan's mother directed at me. "Pervert." "Creep." "Bastard." It was not hard to read her mind. And what was the reality? I had loved her son and had caressed his genitals along with the rest of him, and he had loved it as much as I did, until he became frightened off by a word. Fagot. If he liked this, might he be a fagot? And through the open door of this word, the adults in his life poured the poison of all their other words into his being – "victim," "perp," "purity," "manliness," "the 'word' of the lord," "abomination." And by these words he was trained to retroactively reinterpret his own experience, and find it vile. It was thus that they prepared him for his betrayal of me.

I was mulling these thoughts over in my mind in a somewhat confused fashion when she slapped the steering wheel, and I suddenly understood the essence of my whole life history in a flash. I understood that for some years after being born I had been awake in this world. It was not entirely a pleasant experience but it was vivid – intense. My nostalgia for childhood, I now understood, was neither more nor less than my desire for this wakefulness. But I was lulled back into sleep again by words – words by which I learned to systematically falsify my inner life, mislabel my feelings, camouflage my real crimes against others, throw mud on my true needs, transform the earth which gave birth to me into my enemy, and create barriers of hatred between myself and my fellow creatures. Words are the poison that adults pour into their children. It is a slow acting but relentless and totally effective poison from which few recover.

I saw that Anna Niles was asleep in words. Stephan also had now had fallen asleep. I had been asleep, but I had wakened from the tyranny of words, and could now be their master. In this way Anna Niles inadvertently served as my Zen master as she slapped me into wakefulness.

There is not so much self inflation in this as you might think. It's not quite the same as crazy people in this country claiming to be Jesus or God. There is room for many of us to be the Bodhisattva. Still, you might ask, if I am the Bodhisattva what am I doing up at 1:27 in the morning (or 5:42 now), chased from my bed by a terror that makes me fear that I might (as they say) "shit in my pants."

I mention in passing that I am not actually wearing any pants. I'm wearing only a T-shirt. Nothing more. If I am to have you know where I am – what my room looks like and so forth – then you should also know what I look like sitting in that room. I don't want to arouse you if you are the sort who might be arousable by such things – by a middle aged man sitting in his study in only a T-shirt. But I thought you should know. The T-shirt has a picture of a sea turtle on it – bright green – almost chartreuse – in a Technicolor ocean.

But to return to the issue of my Buddahood, how is it that someone who has achieved Samadhi is in a state, metaphorically speaking, of being about to shit in his pants? This requires a description of my inner space. I told you some time ago about my room and the yard, etc.– my outer space. But I have not yet told you about my inner space. If I do not tell you everything, how shall I be able to attach any hope to these words – words that I send out much in the same spirit as an astronomer beeps out signals, hoping to encounter a fellow insomniac somewhere in the vast sleep of space, a consciousness with which to overcome the loneliness?

My inner space then. Picture a vast landscape of war and tribulation. Ben Hur streaks around an oval track in a deadly chariot race. Creatures from Jurassic Park roam the countryside popping citizens into their bloody maws, relishing them one by one, as casually as you might help yourself to a bunch of chocolate covered cherries. The star ship Enterprise hovers overhead threateningly and is threatened in its turn by an approaching armada of ships under the diabolical command of Darth Vader. Pterodactyls imported from the Lost Continent share the skies with space ships while subterraneously "IT" lurks in the sewers ready to ooze its way up throughout the nasty-stuff pipes to grab the ass of any Mama, Daddy or kiddy who might be trying to take a dump. IT shares its dark world with Them – huge ants transformed by an atomic accident into creatures that threaten all human life on this earth. The creature from the black Lagoon hovers in the swampy depths while Jaws patrols the clear waters of the Oceans. All of this is not to mention Frankenstein's monster, Gollum or the

Terminator. The surface of the earth, the sky, and the subterranean domains, both watery and dry, are ubiquitously occupied by horrors – some that have been named, others that slip the mind, and still others yet to be discovered. One has collected a good many creepy crawlies, technologies gone awry, and things that go bump in the night by the time one is middle aged. Meanwhile, Charlten Heston trudges up Mt. Sinai to seek salvation from such a world, or at least a better deal, but down in the valley his constituency is already addressing itself to the performance of some serious debauchery. It does not look hopeful. One is tempted to cast one's lot with Carlton Heston's faithless constituency.

But look. There is something that might easily escape your notice in this inner landscape. In the very center sits a little brown Buddha. "The center?" you might ask. "What center? The center from what point of view?" Good questions. "The center," I say," from all points of view. That's the magic of the little Buddha." And as you look at him, he grows larger and larger. Bigger that It. Faster than a star ship. More powerful than the Terminator. His peace and compassion becomes the light by which the entire panorama is illumined and by which this chaos becomes bearable. And because this is the Bodhisattva, He/She does not retreat into the heavens, but remains here at the center of this bedlam, this struggle to the death between the natural world and civilization – the Bodhisattva remains at the center – at all centers – untouched. Yea though Ben Hur run over me with his chariot, Darth Vader zap me with his ray, a tyrannosaurus grinds me in its teeth, or It" grabs my ass, I will fear no harm. There are fountains within, and a quiet place which remains untouched. The terrorist who has captured me may place my left testicle in the vise and begin to tighten the screws... Ah. But I have gone too far here. I overstep myself. I don't recall that the terrorist was a part of my inner landscape in the first place, so lets just leave him out of this. At the center is the Bodhisattva. That's the main point to keep in mind.

*****

I am thinking of Ackroyd.
I am thinking about him on the beach.

When I am on a canoe trip I often get up early and have an hour or so by myself before all the hectic activity begins. It's quiet then. If the weather permits, I wash off and take a little swim. On the third morning of the canoe trip last summer, I was down by the lake, getting into my private time.

You can look. The self, my own self, that I try to contact in memory comes to me in much the same way as does my knowledge of another person. This could be your memory. So let's both position ourselves off to one side – among the trees at the edge of the beach, and watch together.

The sun has not yet lifted itself above the horizon. Mist is rising from the water, like steam. How still it is! The frogs are no longer croaking and the birds have not yet begun. I have my shaving kit with me. I take off all my clothes and wade into the water. Then I remember that I need the biodegradable soap from the shaving kit. As I turn to go back to shore I see that Ackroyd has followed me.

He is standing by the edge of the beach, looking at me.

"Hi," I say. "You the only one up?"

He nods. "What're you doing?"

"Taking a bath and then a swim. Want to join me?"

"Sure, he says." It's warm so he is wearing only an oversize a T-shirt which he uses as a night gown. He slips out of this and wades into the water with me. We stand side by side, knee deep in the water, soaping ourselves and rinsing off. I notice that he is uncircumcised, and compare his penis to my own wounded member. His genitals, like the rest of him, are perfectly proportioned. We soap and rinse each others backs, but still do not speak. The sky slowly lightens. The birds begin to sing. Then we swim a little – quietly. Finally we come out of the water. He is ahead of me. The sun is just rising. I admire his perfectly rounded buttocks as he walks to the shore. He doesn't seem naked. His skin, with the first sun of the day just now shining on it, is dark waffle brown. After I have looked at the parts that are usually not seen, they don't seem so special any more. All of him is beautiful – he is a seamless garment.

We stand together drying off.

"You said the day before yesterday that the Buddha tries to save us from this hell we live in," I say. "How does he go about that?"

"My uncle says he saves us from the "gottas.""

"The 'gottas?' I say. What are those?"

He laughs. "You know. Gotta have this and gotta have that. My uncle says it's the gottas that make us sick."

I laugh. "So that's how the Buddha saves us from hell?"

"I suppose so," Ackroyd says. "It's what my Uncle says."

"What do you think?" I ask.

"I don't know. Maybe he just loves us."

I am aware of the birds. They are calling to each other – saying whatever it is they say every morning.

We are dressed now, and we start back up the path.

*****

It's 5:53 AM.

I see the sunlight touching the tops of the elm trees, painting their leaves in a mottled pattern – dark and lighter green – olive and chartreuse – the colors of the turtle on my T-shirt. Bright yellow branches fork though the green like inverted photographs of lighting. The line of the sunlight descends and captures the smoke stacks of the mill. Lovely clouds of rose and pink float into the air, conveying to the sense of sight no knowledge of the sulfuric acid they contain. Then the steeple of the Full Gospel Baptist Church that Stephan now attends with Melvin is illuminated. I have to wait a little while before the green and red shingles of my neighbors roofs are washed and brightened in the light. Finally the light descends to the grass. As improbable as it seems, I think I see a ring a mushrooms growing in my lawn – a fairly ring this is called. But of course, improbable things are to be expected.

My indictment will appear in the newspaper today.